THE C

"It would seem as though you ... ...ete control of the beast, then," Charles shouted over the noise of the train. "I had wondered how you could handle such a large and inherently wild creature."

No sooner had he finished speaking than the engineer gave a shout of alarm and began to pull and push at the levers and buttons on his control panel. The iron dragon's speed had been gradually increasing, and now suddenly they were racing along so quickly the walls of the cavern were a blur. King Charles and the other passengers clung to the handrails as the dragon shot through the cavern workshop like a bolt from a crossbow and then hurtled out into the cold clear air of the mountain peaks.

Gangs of dwarves who were working on the rails with picks and sledgehammers leaped aside as the dragon came barreling out of the mouth of the cavern, their shouts of anger whipped away on the wind of the dragon's passage. Up ahead, an elf threw a switch and then waved at them as they steamed rapidly past him.

They were being jolted violently from side to side now as they careened down the mountain. Princess Tianna began to wonder if the wheels would hold their grip on the rails. At that moment, as if in answer to her unspoken question, the dragon flung back its massive head and trumpeted long and loud in its own voice, as well as with the steam whistle, into the frigid air, the primitive call of his kind, exultant and challenging. . . .

MOUNTAINS & MADNESS

ROSE ESTES

BAEN

IRON DRAGONS: MOUNTAINS AND MADNESS

A Baen Books Original

Baen Publishing Enterprises
P.O. Box 1403
Riverdale, N.Y. 10471

ISBN: 0-671-72190-9

Cover art by Larry Elmore

First printing, October 1993

Distributed by
SIMON & SCHUSTER
1230 Avenue of the Americas
New York, N.Y. 10020

Printed in the United States of America

CHAPTER ONE

Disaster

The first hint of trouble came while the ships were still within sight of port. The City of Blue-Feld and the ramparts of the castle were still clearly visible. The wind had been against them, a constant stiff breeze out of the northeast, the water exhibiting row after row of slight dips stretching all the way to the horizon, which made it necessary to tack back and forth to gain any headway at all. The captain of the quadrene, the *Eastern Star*, a four masted, deep bodied cargo ship had argued against leaving port until the wind died, but the tide was with them and Prince Tyndal had been anxious to be gone. Autumn's storms would not be long in coming and any clear day was an invitation not to be ignored. And so the convoy of six ships, heavily loaded with valuable cargo as well as crews capable of shouldering arms, sailed out of the sheltering bay, carrying with them the mercantile hopes of the king and his kingdom.

Prince Tyndal was at first bemused by the conflicting current which appeared out of the southwest, causing the converging waves to jump and spurt in little crests as they clashed.

He frowned down at the water, trying to remember if he had ever seen such an unusual occurrence. One saw such movement at the mouths of rivers when they entered the ocean, but they were well out to sea and the wind was blowing north northeast, so the crosscurrent could not be blamed on the effect of the wind. The ship was too heavy to be affected by the resulting chop which presented no danger to them, but still, it was odd and Tyndal was no fool. With the Bright Kingdom's shipping routes besieged as they were by political enemies, pirates and sea dragons, who had proved often enough that they would stop at nothing to gain control of the ships and their rich cargoes, nothing, not the slightest oddity, was to be taken lightly.

Tyndal frowned and beckoned the captain to his side as the wind buffeted him, plastering his heavy fur cloak tight to his long, lean form. The captain, who was nominally in command of the vessel, knew better than to keep the crown prince of the Bright Kingdom waiting. He hurried forward clutching his broad brimmed dress hat tightly to prevent it from being blown away. In the short time it took him to cross the quarterdeck, the wind from the southwest had increased to such a degree that he was staggering to keep his balance.

"What do you make of this wind?" Tyndal shouted, his words all but whipped away by the cold wind. The captain shook his head and as he did so, the wind curled under his prized sheared beaver hat, the symbol of his rank, and sent it sailing aloft where it tumbled across the sky like a skipped stone and was quickly lost in the vast panorama of clouds.

Cursing bitterly, the captain stared after his hat for a moment, then gripping the railing tightly, he shouted, "Never have I seen such a wind, to spring up out of nowhere against the prevailing wind . . . certainly not in clear weather." Even as they spoke the wind from the north which had been blowing strong and steady for the last hour increased in force as though to combat the wind from the opposing quarter. The two men clung to the rail to keep their balance as the ship began to pitch violently from side to side. Alarmed voices filled the air, and turning, they saw two able-bodied seamen lose their balance and plummet over the side into the dark waters below. Their shipmates and comrades were clinging to whatever object they had been able to grab hold of and although one seaman threw a knotted rope overboard, Tyndal knew that it was a hopeless gesture.

"There's no way we can go back for them!" the captain shouted as he watched the men disappear behind them.

"Hold your course!" Tyndal grimly confirmed his captain's decision. The thought of rescue was impossible in this sea. A sharp cry of alarm rang out across the waters accompanied by a loud brittle crack. Tyndal watched in helpless dismay as the main mast of the following ship, the *Mother Bren*, broke in half like a felled tree and collapsed into the rigging of the mast behind it, stripping it of sails and sailors. The wind belled

in the broad sails of the two remaining masts.
That, in combination with the mast, rigging and
sails now dragging in the water and acting as a
sea anchor, turned the *Bren* sideways into the
trough of the waves. It rolled violently from side
to side in wild sea. Tyndal could hear the voice of
the *Bren*'s captain bellowing orders to his crew,
who were swarming around the wreckage trying
desperately to cut it loose. But the force of the
wind coupled with the angle of the ship and its
violent gyrations made it all but impossible for
them to obey his demands. A few brave souls
attempted to scramble up the rigging, but were
plucked away by the demonic winds and flung
screaming to their deaths.

Tyndal watched in stunned silence as the
Mother Bren rocked hopelessly in the seas.
Great waves came crashing over her sides as
though some giant invisible child was playing
roughly and carelessly with an unloved toy which
could be cast aside without a moment's thought.

"Break, damn you, break!" shouted Tyndal,
commanding the remaining masts to fall for only
that would stop the imminent destruction of the
ship. But the masts did not break, nor did the
sails split or rip away from their rigging. In
horror, the prince and the captain watched as
the *Bren*'s stern dipped below the surface of the
waves. The decks were awash now and waves
crashed across the deck and poured into an open
hatch sending tons of water into the hold. A
deep groan escaped the captain's lips for it was
obvious, even to the most unlearned observer,
that the ship was doomed. It was gone in a blink

of an eye, a fully loaded four hundred ton cargo ship and its crew of ten score brave sailors, erased as though it had never existed. Even as the *Bren* went under, the captain was bellowing orders to save his own ship.

"All hands to the braces!" boomed the captain through his speaking trumpet. The order was repeated across the deck, now lined with sailors who had been watching the disaster. Most of the tars had relatives or friends serving aboard the doomed ship. Like ants, the crew leaped for the rigging, realizing their own peril. The thin piping of bosun's whistles could be heard above the howling winds and Tyndal knew without looking that the captains of the other four remaining vessels had also reacted to the loss. The following minutes were an agonizing struggle of man against nature as the sailors struggled to survive the maelstrom. The winds increased in magnitude, blowing at forces Tyndal had never experienced in all his years at sea, still beating them from opposing directions, sometimes sucking the very breath from their lungs, then bludgeoning them with the force of a hammer. It was dizzying, confusing, and impossible to find a rhythm, a way out of the madness. Tyndal was an accomplished seaman, priding himself on possessing almost a psychic bond with the sea, but never had he seen such a storm. And overhead, the sun still shone brightly and small fluffy clouds drifted lazily across the calm sky. It was like being inside one of those glass balls with a tiny scene filled with water and snow. Shake the ball and the water was filled with a flurry of flakes, an instant storm created by artificial means.

"Magic!" Tyndal gasped in sudden realization. No wonder the winds and waves went contrary to nature! No wonder they were unable to fight their way out of the seething maelstrom! He looked skyward, searching the heavens for what he knew he must find. They were almost directly above him, riding the thermals, two large hawks, surveying the scene below, serving as the eyes of those who were behind the destruction and with a sinking heart Tyndal knew that they were doomed. Still, the prince was no coward, he would not face death without a fight.

He reached beneath his cloak and drew forth his bow. Bracing himself against the rail he ratcheted the tensor back to its greatest trajectory. He chose his arrow carefully, knowing he would get but the one chance. He picked the heaviest shaft, one taken from the heart of an ancient ironwood tree, tipped with a large keen metal point and fletched with the feathers of an eagle. It lay heavy and deadly in his hand, the finely honed head shining in the sun. Tyndal slipped the arrow into the waiting haft at the angle of the tensor, rested the shaft in the notch of the curved bow and angled it upward, drawing bead on the larger of the two ominous birds. The tensor was against his cheek, the strong flexible metal wire humming with tension and, he thought, the joy of the kill. The arrow was in line with his vision, focused on the target.

"Fly true, my beauty," he whispered, adding the words of a simple spell to guide it on its way, praying for it to find its mark, knowing that it was their only chance. Other eyes watched the flight of the arrow as it cut cleanly through the violent winds, the weight of its shaft and the force of the release cleaving the air before it. One of the sea hawks saw the approaching missive of death, squawked loudly, tilted his wings slightly, picked up an updraft and drifted out of range at just the last moment.

The other bird was less fortunate. Tyndal's arrow struck true, smashing into the bird's heart, killing it instantly. The limp form fell erratically in an odd spiral down into the sea. The force of the wind from the north immediately abated, cutting the fury of the storm nearly in half.

The silvery eyes that peered into the stone basin of black water using the hawks for sight as well as the transmission of his deadly mischief winced in pain. The man lurched back holding thin trembling fingers over one eye.

"Carry on!" commanded a shrill voice. "You still have enough vision to carry this off! Do not lose your concentration.

The man with the silvery eyes took a deep breath and leaned back over the bowl of black water. It was time for the next step in the deadly game.

Tyndal slipped another arrow into the haft of the tensor, but in his heart he knew that it was useless, for the remaining hawk climbed quickly out of range. He had had his chance and failed. Almost immediately, the fury of the freak storm

came back with renewed vigor. A groan slipped
from Tyndal's lips and a sickness gripped his
heart. All around him men shouted to one
another as they tried valiantly to save their ship
and their lives. Now it was but a matter of time.
His thoughts turned to his father and how he
would react to this failure. And there was
Tianna, his twin sister. Suddenly a ray of hope
shone in his breast. Tianna, well trained in the
magic arts . . . was she watching from the castle
ramparts? Could she? Would she be able to
help?

Even as Tyndal thought of her, the princess
Tianna stood on the ramparts of the castle,
which towered above the seaport and witnessed
the horrible drama that was being played out on
the distant sea. She had sensed her twin
brother's peril at the first hint of trouble, and
come rushing to the castle walls. Early in her
life, it was discovered that she was adept at
magic arts, and for years the princess trained
under the best mages in the land, but there were
no wizards here to aid her now.

She began assuming the mental state necessary to weave the spells, and watched in horror
as the first of the ships was dragged beneath the
waves. Soon the whole fleet was being driven
back towards the city, apparently to be dashed to
splinters on the docks and the sea wall.

Tyndal's ship was suddenly thrown across the
water, propelled forward with no attempt at
concealing the destruction under the guise of a
sudden, unfortunate early autumn storm. No
natural force was moving the ship, this was vile

magic at its worst. The *Eastern Star* hurtled across the water and rammed into the last ship of the line, the *Golden Sprite*, catching it broadside and splitting it in half before coming to an abrupt halt while the vessel it had rammed sank beneath the waves with a loss of all hands.

Tianna cried out in spite of herself as she worked frantically to summon a spell of her own that would serve to halt the destruction of the fleet and save her beloved brother. She summoned everything she knew and began with Calm Upon the Waters, muttering the incantation and letting the power flow from her body. The waters in the bay, indeed, went calm. But the ships were still blowing wildly toward the shore.

Tianna cursed and threw the spell from her consciousness. She began a Cease Wind, and when she had spoken the words, the air around her and on the sea went dead calm. The silence was alarming, especially so to the hapless souls aboard the doomed ships. But much to everyone's dismay, despite the cessation of the wind the ships were still being driven inexorably closer to land and destruction. Tianna knew she was up against a powerful force, one that did not fear revealing itself. Yet there was a strange sense of familiarity to the evil magic she was attempting to oppose.

Frantically she threw off the Cease Wind spell and struggled to cast a Feather Fall spell, not sure just what effect the spell would have. She was flustered; the gale winds returned and her spell served only to bring all the drowned corpses to the surface where they bobbed about the remaining ships, a ghastly vision which terrified those who still lived. Tianna changed her tactics. Now desperate, she attempted to draw together the four ships which had so far managed to stay afloat, binding them with invisible bonds so that they would float in a solid square, side to side, prow to stern, unsinkable, unassailable. For a moment it seemed as though the ploy might work, for the ships ceased their landward movement and began to drift together.

Then the worst happened. Inexplicably, the *Hyperion* and the *Royal Sovereign* slammed against each other shattering their planking from gunwales to the waterline. Tianna staggered back, breathless, her thoughts a roil of fear and worry. Feather Fall had already been used, it could not be cast a second time so soon after the first invocation. Nor would it serve those now in need, only those who had been in the water at the time it was cast. The casting of three spells one after the other had drained Tianna severely, but this was no time to give in to exhaustion; the life of her brother and hundreds of brave sailors depended on what she did next. What, what could she use to protect them?

Ideas for spells raced through her mind, but most of them were inappropriate or took too long to cast. The *Eastern Star*, Tyndal's ship, and the *Black Belle* were the last two ships afloat and even as Tianna worked to save them, the *Black Belle* was lifted out of the water by the stern until it balanced on the water at the point of its prow. It was only a few hundred yards from

shore now and Tianna shuddered as she watched
officers and men dropping out of the rigging and
falling into the sea like ripe fruits shaken from a
tree. Then, the ship seemed to quiver for a
moment before it plunged straight down into the
deep. The wind brought the terrible cries to her
ears. Tears blinded her eyes and she began to
cast her final spell, the only spell she could think
of that had any possible chance of saving her
beloved brother.

Summoning every bit of mental strength that
remained to her, Tianna muttered the incantation, raising her hand into the air with great
difficulty. The *Eastern Star* rose slowly up out of
the boiling waves. Rivulets of water streamed
from its exposed keel. Slowly she drew it toward
land, praying that she would have the strength to
bring it the distance. It was just high enough to
clear the sea wall and she hoped to place it
gently down on a city street. Tianna could feel
herself weakening with the incredible strain;
another force was working against her, she could
feel it resisting her, but she was prevailing. The
great ship crept slowly toward her, floating eerily
above the chaotic sea, masts and spars standing
like trees against the blue sky, water still pouring
in sheets from the hull.

Now the princess could even hear the cheers
of the men and make out her brother's form
standing at the prow with arm upraised, fist
clenched in a sign of victory. It was an effort to
hold herself erect, she gripped the stone rampart
with her fingers, feeling her nails crack and
break. Her body began to shake, trembling like

one stricken with ague. Her vision clouded, but
still she hung on, focused, channeling all her
energy on the ship, drawing it closer, closer to
safety. It was so near now, it was possible to see
Tyndal's eyes locked upon her own, as though
sending his own strength to her. She almost
dared allow herself to believe that she had
succeeded, that the *Eastern Star* and its crew
were saved.

An alarmed shout from Tyndal, a frantic grab
for his bow, and horrified hands pointing
toward the sky broke her concentration. Despite herself she looked upward and saw a lone
sea hawk plunging toward her with talons outstretched. Too late she wrenched her eyes away
from her own danger and back to the ship. Too
late she tried to reattach the raveled ends of the
broken spell, too late to do anything but watch
in despair as a giant wave reached up out of the
sea and snatched the *Eastern Star* with its
foaming crest and drew it down, down beneath
the dark waters in a massive explosion of sea
and spray.

A darkness seized her then, whether a darkness of devastation or the unprecedented stress
of casting so many spells in a row, she was never
to know. The result was the same, Tianna fell
unconscious upon the shallow ledge, spared the
awful sight of the waters, now calm and still with
only broken planks and a few casks to mark the
grave of the *Eastern Star*. Nor did she hear the
victorious screech of the hawk as it braked its
flight and then soared into the bright sky,
winging its way back toward its master.

Hidden from sight and mind, a man with silvery eyes sank back in exhaustion from the bowl of black water and collapsed into his chair. The figure next to him smiled, more than a little pleased with the day's work.

CHAPTER TWO

Kroner

The Bright Kingdom was thrown into a state of shock and total chaos with the death of Prince Tyndal and the maritime disaster. Losses at sea were not uncommon, in fact they were expected, but it was clear to everyone, even the most ignorant serf, that there had been forces at play other than natural events. Magic had destroyed the heir to the kingdom, and the cream of its merchant fleet. The word was whispered everywhere, on every tongue and filled the minds of the populace: magic! But how, and most of all . . . why?

The Bright Kingdom, named for the beauty of the land and the hopes of its first settlers, was located at the very easternmost tip of the continent. Its rich loamy soil produced bumper crops of wheat year after bounteous year. Its forests produced fine hardwoods, treasured throughout the world, and the newly built smelters at Bremmner churned out the best steel available on the continent. The cattle, lovingly raised by the ranchers of Bulatz were said to be the fattest in the world. All in all, the Bright Kingdom's farmers, workers, and artisans were numerous and gifted and turned out goods for which their customers were willing and able to pay vast sums.

But now, thanks to the freak magical storm destroying their fleet, the kingdom lay all but isolated from the rest of the continent. High, treacherous mountain ranges protected as well as isolated the lush valleys that were their home. And beyond the mountains, assuming one could find a way through the passes, lay dangerous forests, bare, open plains known as the Orc Wastes, desolate deserts and vast, uncharted inland seas. All of these lands were inhabited by various races of humans, non-humans and beasts of all descriptions, inimical to the civilized denizens of Bright.

Yet beyond them the New World was growing. Without interaction and trade, those inland cities, as well as those of the Bright Kingdom would die . . . And perhaps that was the point; it appeared that someone or something wished for them to cease to exist.

King Charles Edouard, beside himself with grief, worried and fretted over his two remaining children. Tianna, who had depleted herself attempting to save Tyndal, lay abed for a week, and young Kroner, always a sickly boy, had fallen ill at the same time. After a time of anxious vigils, the royal children recovered, and the king called his councils.

The disaster, and the idea that someone was out to destroy the kingdom, as well as many other theories, were discussed, argued *ad infinitum* in the Council Chambers. At the king's side, his children, young prince Kroner on one hand, and on the other, Tianna, both sat quietly and listened as one after the other of the king's advisors offered up their sage opinions.

At length, when all had spoken, the king retired and thought on their words, pondering the counsel. He paced back and forth for many hours, admitting no one, not even his children.

Tianna was afraid. Though she had recovered from the physical effects of her attempt to save Tyndal, she was still weak and pale, and now felt more alone than ever in her life. Tyndal had been her best friend and trusted confidant as well as her twin brother. She needed his strength and his love, needed the bond that had sustained her in life even more now that he was dead. With her father locked up in himself, there was no one for her.

Her thoughts turned to Kroner and a wave of shame pulsed through her body. Her seventeen-year-old younger brother had scarcely entered her thoughts. The grief and shock of Tyndal's death had shrouded her mind leaving no room for thoughts of others, save her father. She and the king had clung to each other like survivors of a disaster in the days that followed Tyndal's death, depending upon each other, allowing no one else to comfort them, and paying little attention to Kroner.

As though she had summoned him with her thoughts, there was a soft knock on the door, and Kroner slipped in quietly. "There you are, sister. Still feeling bad?" He walked over and placed his hand on her shoulder. She was not comforted and perhaps unfairly, resented his attempt at closeness.

Kroner was two years younger than Tianna and Tyndal and had been born to a different mother, a foreign princess whom Charles Edouard had wed following the death of his first queen during an outbreak of plague that swept through BlueFeld. Charles had remarried hastily, upon the advice of his council who argued that if anything were to happen to the twins, the kingdom would be left without an heir.

Kroner's mother had been a fragile beauty from the Old World, used to more temperate climes. When she learned that she was with child, she sealed herself in her room with fireplaces roaring and maids streaming in and out to humor her every whim. But all their efforts were for naught; she had a difficult labor and she gave up long before the child was born, lying in a morose, pain-wracked lethargy, refusing to answer when spoken to.

The young queen drew her last breath just as Kroner was drawing his first: a long, bleak, anguished wail.

That cry had set the note for the rest of his life; Kroner seemed to be a child who was swathed in an aura of darkness. His wet nurses spoke of a strangeness in the child, an air that was both cold and hostile, sucking out all that they could give, leaving them empty and dispirited. They did not feel a sense of nurturing or the desire to comfort the poor little motherless child. In fact it was difficult to keep a wet nurse or a nanny for longer than a day or two and as the whispers spread among the womenfolk, it became impossible. No amount of gold would sway them from their decision.

In the end, the tiny scrap of a prince was raised on goats' milk and the rough, unpracticed hands of man servants who liked him not one whit more than their women. They were, however, more easily swayed by the king's commands and the sight of gold.

Charles Edouard had made an effort to care for the boy, had told himself a thousand times that the child was the seed of his loins, brother to his beloved twins, but nothing worked. He would hold the child and feel the warmth of his body drain out of him and flow into the child who seemed to absorb all of his energy, lying silent and dour in his arms, staring at him with huge black eyes that seemed to confer blame as well as hatred.

Charles was not alone, the twins tried to love their new brother as well, but they were stricken even more severely by contact with the infant. Tianna broke out in blistering welts the first time she took the child in her small arms. Tyndal, rushing to help on hearing her cry, was struck temporarily blind and fell to the floor, cutting his forehead open on the rough slate floor. There were other attempts after that, but more from duty than from love. As Kroner grew into a small, dark, secretive wraith of a child, so grew their antagonism, never spoken, never intimated by any wayward word or glance but as thick and insurmountable as the mountains that surrounded their land.

Tianna did not want to be with Kroner now, even though she no longer broke out at his touch. "Please." She pushed his hand from her shoulder. "I would like to by myself for awhile."

A twisted smile crossed his face. "As you will, Tianna, I just came to let you know that I'll be holding the royal levee today." He fretted with impatience. "You know it's about time I was accorded the respect due an heir apparent! It's high time father confided in me and included me in his plans!"

Tianna went cold with shock at the words and looked at Kroner as though seeing him for the first time. She saw a thin, nervous young man, his face narrow and triangular, the chin ending in a sharp point. His hair and brows were ebony black, as were his eyes, but all were dull and lackluster without the sheen of health. A wispy mustache and goatee sprouted from his sallow skin. His frame was painfully thin, appearing almost undernourished . . . collarbones, ribs, elbows and knees poking the fine fabrics that clothed him. His fingernails were chewed ragged below the quick and his features and various body parts twitched nervously, never still, never ever at rest. He turned and walked toward the door.

"After all, I am the crown prince now."

Tianna felt like slapping him, but he was gone. She frowned and shook her head. She had drawn a wall between herself and the rest of the world following Tyndal's death. Despite her father's words, she felt personally responsible for the death of her brother. She thought back on recent events, playing them over and over in her mind, examining each happening like a link in a chain, trying to think of what she could have done differently, what action she might have taken that would have changed the final outcome. Nothing was revealed, no answer presented itself yet she was not exonerated, her grief demanded an answer, someone who could be blamed, held responsible for Tyndal's death. Since she could find no one else at fault, she bore the burden alone. Her father's sorrow was nearly as great as her own, yet he was spared that terrible open wound that bound her still to Tyndal. The bond that had always existed between them in life, an invisible connection that linked them, allowing them to touch each other's hearts and minds with every breath had not been severed with death but existed still, an invisible stigmata that ached and bled with every beat of her heart.

Now Kroner insinuated himself at her side at every opportunity, and much as she would have liked to banish him entirely, she could not always do so; it would have been unseemly and Tyndal had been his brother too. Even though she and Kroner had never been close, their differences paled under the circumstances, she thought, healing was needed, not further wounding. And so Tianna had sometimes allowed her dark, silent brother to remain at her side and tried to accept his comforting words. Yet, despite the words of kindness that dripped smoothly from his tongue, Tianna felt a sense of cold arrogance, an aloof smugness beneath the bland exterior.

There was no hint of such on the surface, no overt action that bore out her suspicions, but she could not deny what her senses told her. She wondered briefly if there was some way that Kroner could have caused the destruction of the ships and Tyndal's death, but immediately rejected the thought. Kroner might be unpleasant and unloving, but the destruction of the fleet had been the work of a master wizard, more than likely several master wizards working in concert; one young prince could never have mastered such a feat. Not even if he had wanted to.

She suddenly retraced her thoughts. A group of wizards! Such a group existed in Bright: the three dour magic users that had been sent from the old world by Kroner's grandfather to school Kroner in the magic arts. But no. She knew each of them, especially Threlgar the Unwise, who could be quite amusing at times. They were harmless enough; they had been unable to add anything to her own extensive training, and the most she had ever seen Kroner do with his magic was to summon a raincloud and spoil a perfectly good picnic. She could not trouble her father with such baseless suspicions, and there was no one else to turn to.

Tianna rose to her feet and wandered through the narrow hall that led to the balcony. The sun was out and the sky and sea were blue. A fresh breeze brushed her hair. She would ordinarily have enjoyed the view, but the disaster was still fresh in her mind and dark thoughts of Kroner were still heavy on her mind. She could do nothing more than attempt to erase her unkind thoughts. Kroner had never been close to Tyndal and could not be expected to feel his loss as deeply as she did. But more than his lack of grief troubled Tiana, Kroner had stated several times that with Tyndal's death, he, Kroner, had become the sole heir to the throne. Tianna told herself that Kroner was young and inexperienced at concealing his inner thoughts. But Kroner had continued to raise the subject of his inheritance and Tianna had grown increasingly silent. Her initial suspicions returned full blown.

Kroner was wrong in his suppositions, he was not the sole heir to the kingdom; Charles had made it quite clear to her that she would become queen if he were to die. However, it was not her position to tell Kroner. He would learn when it was appropriate. Until that time came, she would watch him closely, try her best to establish a bond between them and learn what she could about this troubled young man who was, after all, her only remaining brother.

CHAPTER THREE

Strange Visitors

In an attempt to assuage the grief that pervaded the city there was an elaborate funeral for all those who had lost their lives, and a brief official period of mourning. Emerging from his solitude, Charles Edouard then summoned his advisors and opened the executive sessions to all who cared to attend, the matter under discussion being the future of the kingdom, and the means of their survival. Merchants and artisans from all over the kingdom attended, and the arguments were many and loud.

"It appears that we have two routes open to us, my Lord," droned the lord high chancellor. "We can once more attempt sea passage to reestablish our trade routes to Iron Holm and Eusarch, or we can isolate ourselves and become a kingdom unto ourselves, dependent upon no others for our needs."

"That is a choice?" asked Charles. "And how are our merchants to survive? What markets will buy our goods? It may be true that we produce most of what we need to exist, but to sever ourselves from the rest of the world is unthinkable!"

A loud outcry followed his words as the

factions who would be affected by an isolationist maneuver expressed their displeasure.

"Your majesty, let the rest of the world find its way to us," the high chancellor replied airily. "Then if losses occur, they will befall others, not ourselves."

There was more disgruntled noise from the crowd.

"Spoken like a true politician," the king replied dryly.

Privately, Charles and his daughter conferred, and she was placed in charge of the Royal Mages in an effort to locate the source of the magic that had destroyed the fleet.

Days passed and the council argued back and forth. However, no satisfactory solution emerged. It was now autumn, and while the chancellors and important merchants had made a good deal of noise, no ships left BlueFeld, or any other port in the Bright Kingdom. Equally distrubing was the fact that no ships arrived either, for word had spread like wildfire around the harbors of the world of what happened to ships that came near the Bright Kingdom.

The harvests continued, produce piled up in heaps, grains filled all the existing granaries and rose in mountains on the ground. Everywhere prices fell with the overabundance and goods were all but given away to those few who needed to buy. It was, indeed, a buyer's market, but with no customers.

Discontent had risen to all time proportions in the kingdom, and Charles Edouard was at his wit's end when the strangers arrived at the city gates. They were an elf and a dwarf, both neatly dressed and mounted astride large black horses. Each was bearing a long cylinder made of thin strips of cedar and bound with leather. At the gate, they surrendered their arms.

Since elves were seldom seen and had little commerce with humans, and dwarves were only to be found near the forges of Bremmner, this arrival was as unusual as it was mysterious.

"We seek an audience with His Most Royal Majesty Charles Edouard," the elf stated as he bowed politely to the bemused guards at the city gate. Messengers ran back and forth, and the unusual pair were admitted to the city and ceremoniously escorted to the castle by a troop of palace cavalry clad in polished steel armor.

Court had been dismissed for the day, once more ending in a hopeless babble of argument and disagreements between merchants, farmers, and various branches of the bureaucracy. The unusual visitors, however, were swiftly escorted to the king's personal chambers.

"Welcome to the Bright Kingdom." The king turned to a servant. "Bring wine and refreshments for our guests."

Charles was seated at the end of a massive wooden table, and his visitors stood across from him. It was obvious at first glance that the elf was no ordinary traveler, his rich clothing was fashioned from the finest tanned leather, and soft, tightly woven linen. A wealth of precious metals and gemstones adorned his tall, slender body. A haughty, regal bearing confirmed his accoutrements. This was no ordinary wood elf. The dwarf, however, was dressed in a more austere fashion and did not have the air of a diplomat about him.

"I am called Gaelwyth Grae, Envoy for His Majesty, King Ninius of Glyth Gamel." The elf bowed low. "My companion is the famous Orrik IronFist, from our neighboring kingdom, Rakhatz." Charles raised his eyebrows at this statement. Glyth Gamel was the ancient enclave of elves located on the Bright Kingdom's far western border hard against the flanks of the Iron Mountains, and Rakhatz shared a common border with both the Bright Kingdom and Glyth Gamel, being itself situated atop the Iron Mountains.

The two visitors allowed themselves to be seated and accepted goblets of the king's finest wine. The dwarf was silent and the elf was pleasant but reserved; they waited patiently until Tianna arrived, seeming to know without being told that nothing would transpire without her presence.

Kind words were offered and accepted on the grievous loss to the Bright Kingdom. The words were ordinary and to be expected, but they were spoken by the elf with an oily, unctuous smoothness that somehow belied and negated their sincerity. It was his very smoothness, almost a sense of smugness, that surrounded him like an aura that instantly repelled Tianna when she arrived. A glance at her father showed her that he did not seem to sense this note of falseness in the elf and appeared to be accepting his words at face value, accepting him as a highly respected envoy from a foreign court. The princess carefully concealed her unease and had a servant move a cumbersome wooden chair closer to her father's side where she could watch the elf more closely and listen to his words. But what he had to say was so astonishing, so totally revolutionary, that nothing could have prepared her for his message.

"We bring a proposal of great importance to our three mighty kingdoms that have lived together in harmony for so long. Our worlds are separate, our people seldom in touch, yet we have much in common," said the elf. He took a long, appreciative sip of the amber colored wine before continuing. "For as long as we can remember, we have fought to protect our forests from invasion by man and all other races with destructive urges. And while it is true that we draw most of our needs out of the forest, there are goods which we do not produce to which our people have become accustomed. Then too, there has long been an established trade with humans in the fruits of our forests and our wines, and in our spells of protection, which are eagerly sought after. There are also our medicines and potions which are sorely needed by all in these troubled times."

Gaelwyth seemed to have momentarily lost his train of thought, for he stammered at this point. Tianna began to think he was more sincere than she had first believed.

"There are many elves who assume — indeed, who have always believed — that elves must remain sequestered from the rest of the world, live and die in total isolation, untainted by the ways of the world. But there are others among us, myself included, who believe just as strongly that we are a part of this world. If we do not make every attempt to join it on our own, on favorable terms, then we will be swallowed up whole and destroyed."

Tianna sat forward, her interest piqued by the elf's strange words. Gaelwyth continued: "We have been following your troubles and share your concerns that the sea routes are now effectively closed to you. It is equally obvious that you have few options. Even if the mountains did not hem you in on all sides, the elflands, our vast forests which shade the far slopes and continue on for many leagues would be too dangerous to penetrate without our cooperation."

The king nodded his agreement. Gaelwyth's words were unrefutable.

"What we propose is an alliance, an alliance between the kingdoms of Glyth Gamel, the Bright Kingdom, and Rakhatz. Thereby creating, a manner of taking goods to market, trading with the rest of the known world in relative safety."

"What you propose is of great interest," said Charles, tenting his fingertips and peering over them at the elf, examining him with sharp eyes. "But what is this talk of taking goods to market? The mountains and the forests are but a portion of the problem, as you undoubtedly realize. To get to where we can sell our goods we would have to cross swamp lands, the Orc Wastes, the deserts and the treacherous badlands, all of which are filled with dangerous races that will honor no treaty and make travel all but impossible save for the most swift and heavily armed. Large, heavily loaded caravans have proved impossible to defend. And even if such a caravan did cross the continent, it would travel slowly, and the expenditure in time and man power would all but negate any profits that might be made."

Charles Edouard leaned back in his chair with a frown. "While I welcome the thought of our three peoples working together, I fear what you propose is not a viable plan."

The elf did not seem the least disturbed by Charles' words. Draining the last drops from his goblet, he set the beautiful piece of crystal down on the table and drew forth a long, curious cedar container, its fragrant wood filling the room with its rich essence. At the same instant, the dwarf at his side did likewise. They unscrewed the rounded end pieces and drew out sheaves of tightly rolled papers, spreading them on the table and weighting them down at all four corners. The drawings that were thus exposed were even more astonishing than anything the elf had said.

They were drawings of machines, the like of which Charles and Tianna had never seen before. All had large spoked wheels like magnificent carriages, but they were different. Most impressive, however, was a drawing that the dwarf unrolled. Superficially, it looked like a dragon. Although Tianna's eyes were seeing the image, her mind found it all but impossible to comprehend what she was viewing. The fore and aft of the dragon were as expected; a head and neck at one end, and a long powerful tail at the other. But there all semblance of normalcy ended. Where the dragon's midsection should have been, there appeared a strange, boxy affair, like carriage coachworks, complete with windows and doors and fitted out with numerous pipes and smoke stacks and a variety of other objects that Tianna could not interpret. Further, where the dragon's feet should have been, there were large metal wheels, huge wheels attached at the end of powerful legs that rose halfway up the dragon's body! These immense wheels were fitted onto two horizontal lengths of metal that extended off the edge of the drawing. A series of long-bedded wheeled carts stretched behind the dragon's tail.

The elf noticed that their eyes were fixed on the one drawing, and gestured with a grand flourish, "Behold, the iron dragon!"

"The iron dragon?" said Charles.

"It consumes iron," said the elf, speaking to the astonished humans, "thus its name. Any iron will do, even the crudest sort. It will even accept old rusty implements, anything, so long as it is made of iron or steel, which it converts into pure energy."

"It . . . it looks so very odd," Tianna stammered.

"You have heard of fire dragons, no doubt," the elf asked. Tianna and her father nodded.

"This creature is very similar. Just as there are fire dragons made of flames and ice dragons made of ice, so this dragon is made of iron. Molten metal flows in its veins; it has the strength, power and stamina to cross the continent from sea to sea, through the plains, over the mountains and the Orc Wastes. No enemy can overcome its power, penetrate its iron scales, nor cease its relentless progress. Here, sir, madam, is the answer to your . . . our problems."

Charles rubbed a hand over his chin and then walked around the table to get a closer look at the unrolled parchments, studying the drawings from all directions. "Powerful as it might be, I don't see how it could possibly help us transport goods to Eaglehawk and Izyndyl. How does it move?" He asked at length.

"Along these, ah . . . rails, sire — that is what they are called, aren't they, Orrik?" Gaelwyth replied promptly. The dwarf nodded with a rather bored look on his face. The elf continued, "The rails are laid parallel across wooden boards . . ."

"Ties!" Orrik corrected him. When the dwarf finally spoke, his voice was low and raspy.

"Oh, yes, the rails are laid across ties to form what they call track. The wheels you see here," his finger touched the drawing, "move along the rails, or track, forming what they call a rail road. The beauty of a rail road is that it may be used in all weather, for the wheels never sink into muddy ruts when it rains."

"And how is it that the power is gotten from the creature to the wheels?" Tianna asked, more than a little confused as to how the thing could even exist.

"A good question, your highness, but I'm afraid that I can only give you the basics. The details are quite complicated and I'm not certain that I truly understand them myself. As I have been told, the dragon consumes iron. As you can see," Gaelwyth explained, moving aside the picture of the dragon to reveal further drawings, "this cart directly behind the dragon is loaded with raw iron. The dragon is fed at regular intervals. Now this is where it gets a bit hazy for me . . ."

"The raw iron is converted into energy by the dragon," interrupted the dwarf, who seemed to know a lot more about the inner workings of the strange beast. "The dragon converts water into steam. The steam is transferred through pipes to the cylinders here," Orrik pointed at the drawings with his stubby fingers, "where it forces this rod to turn the wheels. The force generated is hard to describe, but it propels the wheels, the dragon itself and the carts trailing behind along the track. It can do the work of a thousand horses."

The elf wiped his brow and sat down as though suddenly exhausted. Orrik stood, hands spread on the table, smiling lovingly at the picture of the iron dragon.

"Amazing," Charles muttered softly.

The dwarf pulled out other drawings, "As you can see, here, earlier versions of the rail road engine were not all powered by dragons. This one burned wooden faggots to produce the steam."

"It looks like a teapot with wheels," giggled Tianna.

"Indeed, that was the name of this particular engine. But now we have perfected the iron dragon, the time is right for the grand undertaking.

"How do you make the iron dragon go where you want it to go?" asked Tianna. "What's to prevent it from just flying away or going backward rather than forward or just sitting still and going nowhere? Dragons are very fractious creatures. I cannot picture them demurely following directions."

"Well," the elf said vaguely, patting his brow again with a silk kerchief, "It just follows the rails wherever they go . . ." He seemed unable to answer her questions.

Orrik intervened again. "We did experience some . . . difficulties in the early stages of the project, but most of those problems have since been, ahem, 'ironed' out. For one thing, the dragons are too heavy to fly and are dependent upon their handlers for their rations. Each of them has been tended since birth by the dwarf chosen to be their handler, thus they have bonded closely and obey them as they would their mother. Driving the dragon is the full responsibility of the handlers. Finally, they are bonded to the undercarriage, this frame and these wheels by a powerful magic spell. Dragon and machine are as one."

"And there are no problems with the creatures now? None at all?" Charles asked pointedly, demanding a more specific answer.

"Well, in the very beginning, as I have said, there were some problems, a matter of design really. Several years ago we began using salamanders and other dragons . . ."

"Several years ago?" interrupted Tianna. "Why have we not learned of these, 'rail roads' until now? And just where are they?"

The dwarf shrugged. "We have kept them a secret until recently. Most of the existing rail roads are underground in the Iron Mountains. At first we dwarves used them as a means of moving ore out of our mines, but the commercial possibilities soon became obvious and a track was built between the dwarven city of Railla and a mine. The development of dragons as motive power was the idea of the elves who have worked with us from the beginning."

Tianna seemed satisfied.

"Now back to our early problems. Early on, the dragons were bred with two heads, one at either end to facilitate changes in direction, make them doubly effective, so to speak."

"Yes, sounds logical," mused the king. "What went wrong?"

"Well, the two heads never could seem to agree on which of them was in control. There were some nasty incidents with both heads tugging in different directions and fighting with each other. It was quite unpleasant," the dwarf said with a shudder. "As you know, once a dragon sinks its fangs, it will never let go until its opponent is dead."

Gaelwyth seemed anxious about all the adverse information the dwarf was supplying and mopped his brow more vigorously and pressed the kerchief firmly to his mouth. He cleared his throat noisily.

The dwarf ignored him and continued. "It was quite dreadful, one head ripped the other off at the neck. Of course that was that, all it succeeded in doing was killing itself. Obviously, that was a model that we eliminated from the breeding program."

"Obviously," echoed Tianna, feeling more than a little ill herself at the picture Orrik had painted.

"But, there have been no problems since that time," blurted the elf nervously, "And, ahem, the project now appears to be advancing full steam ahead!"

"Well then, if it's going so well, why do you need us?" asked Tianna.

"It's a matter of basic economics," Gaelwyth replied with a large show of pearly teeth. "We ourselves, despite our proficiency, cannot hope to fully load the transport, owing to the great length of time needed to produce our superlative goods. Thus an iron dragon expedition would be somewhat less than cost effective."

"Ah, the moneylenders," sighed the king. "Do I take this to mean that even your 'superlative' nation is plagued by the accountants and so would thus lower yourselves to deal with a less than superior people and their ordinary goods in order to underwrite the cost of this unusual venture?"

"Your words, sire, not mine," the elf said with an elaborate show of dismay. "Never would I have . . ."

"Let me see if I understand this," Tianna said with a frown, cutting through the elf's hypocritical words. "You need us to throw in with you to help offset the cost of the project. This I can understand. But what costs are we speaking of? The dragon appears to be yours for the using and if it requires iron for fuel, well, the Iron Mountains are sitting right in your own backyard; scratch the surface and there's all the iron in the world for the taking. So where's the expense?"

"What you say is true," the elf admitted. The dwarf snorted. There was more to mining than scratching the surface of a mountain, no matter how rich the lode. The elf continued on over the dwarf's grumbles. "But there have been large developmental and shall we say, start up costs that have been borne by the dwarves alone. We have struck an agreement with the Basalt Clan dwarves but they do not come cheaply. Also, we have a need for work parties to advance the rails whereby the creature travels."

"Let me guess," Charles said wryly. "Elves do not enjoy work parties and have no liking for heavy labor."

The elf drew himself up stiffly. "Elves do not shirk from honest work but we are uncomfortable away from our native lands and much of the route will traverse unfamiliar territory. There is no reason for insults, sire. You will find the Glyth Gamel to be stalwart and true, more than willing to bear their fair share of the burden. It is simply a matter of logic. Humans seem to toil willingly under adverse conditions. So you see, it's really quite logical. You need a safe reliable means of moving your goods to market and we need a dependable partner to share the burden of expenses and labor. It is the ideal partnership!"

A black thought took root in Tianna's mind. How desperate were the elves to establish ties with the rest of the world? Despite what the elf had said about opening trade routes, the proposal sounded very odd to her. Elves were among the most elusive and secretive of all the races, especially the Glyth Gamel, who were the original inhabitants of the land. They were notoriously resentful of the humans of the Bright Kingdom who had colonized the land which had once been theirs. It seemed unlikely that they would actively seek out contact with the outer world much less go to such great effort to develop this iron dragon. Yet, if what Gaelwyth had said was indeed true, what lengths would they go to in order to assure themselves of the Bright Kingdom's cooperation? Was it possible that the elves had had something to do with Tyndal's death? Try as she might, she could not rid herself of this painful thought.

There was a moment of silence, broken by the dwarf. "Show them the map," he said gruffly. The elf pulled another parchment out of his cedar container and unrolled it on the table. It was a chart of the New World, with all known cities, mountains, forests, and rivers drawn upon it. In the center, was a tiny red line, drawn from Railla, capital of Rakhatz, the dwarven kingdom, to a point nearly touching Glyween, the southernmost city in Glyth Gamel, the elven kingdom.

"That thin red line is the extent of the rail road to date," said the dwarf.

A dotted red line on the map ran from Railla, across the map eastward to BlueFeld, connecting all the cites in between. Another dotted red line ran south to Silvarre, the southern kingdom. Yet another dotted line crossed the map entirely, reaching west across the Orc Wastes to Eusarch and Iron Holm, the two large kingdoms on the far western edge of the New World.

"For the project to be a success, we must lay iron rails across the whole of the land." The dwarf's eyes glowed with excitement as his hand swept across the map. "Bridges must be built across rivers, tunnels cut through mountains, and hills must be leveled. The number of workmen will be staggering, and costs will be so great, that we will have to sell shares of the great rail road to finance its construction."

"You see," said Gaelwyth, "we need your money and assistance. But likewise, you need our money and assistance as well. Imagine selling a hundred carriage loads of cattle to a merchant in Elsmworth, or a similar load of steel carried to Izyndyl. And the trip would take only a few days."

"A few days!" the king said in astonishment.

"Four days at most," stated the dwarf confidently.

"What you say is of great interest," Charles said at length. He smiled graciously. "I'm sure that you will understand when I say that you have given us a great deal to think about. My daughter and I will need to talk, to discuss the idea with our advisers. We would ask you to give us a period of time to consider your proposition."

The elf seemed less than happy with Charles' words, deep lines appeared between his eyes and etched into his cheeks. His eyes grew dark and lost their cheerful twinkle. Suddenly, he was no longer the pleasant, smiling envoy. "I shall leave Orrik here to answer any questions you might have, and I will return for your answer in one week's time," he said after a heavily weighted moment. And without further comment or even a polite bow of leave-taking, he turned and walked out of the room leaving a thoughtful silence behind him.

CHAPTER FOUR

Sper Andros

Much to the disgust of Kroner, whose only assignment was to handle the royal levees, Tianna and her father spent the next week closeted in lengthy conferences. They turned the meeting with Gaelwyth inside out, taking it apart and examining it from all sides, analyzing every word the elf had spoken. They studied the odd drawings closely and summoned those who would had a greater understanding of dragons and machines. They also spent a great deal of time with one Sper Andros, also called Steffan, the resident expert on all things elvish.

The king, Tianna, Orrik, and Sper Andros were seated around a table, in a small room high in the great tower that they had designated their "dragon" room. A gentle breeze drifted through the room and sunlight shone cheer through the windows, making the use of lamps unnecessary. Steffan was convinced the elves would only agree to rail roads in their lands for military reasons.

"The alliance Gaelwyth mentioned between Glyth Gamel and Silvarre is the key to the elves' participation in this whole scheme," Sper Andros stated flatly. "It is my opinion that the only reason the elves would agree to this unnatural meddling with nature is for military reasons."

Orrik nodded and grunted in agreement. "I'm certain of that, myself. Only after the orc raids became more numerous and the elfin death toll rose did Ninius send emissaries to Rakhatz."

Tianna sat silently at the table, staring openly at Sper Andros. She thought back over what little she knew of his unusual story. He had been part of a wagon train, a small group of tinkers traveling through the Gamelian Forest with only their wits and their own strong arms to protect them. It had not been enough. Everyone and everything in their band had been ravaged by a pack of dire wolves. Sper Andros was the only survivor. He had been found buried beneath a mound of heavy grain sacks which had created an effective barrier against the hideous beasts. Even that bastion would have failed had the elves not arrived in time and dispatched the vicious creatures with well placed arrows.

Sper Andros had been reared among the elves only returning to the world of humans after he reached adulthood. Many believed him to be half-elf, for he was not completely at ease in either world and spent his time equally between both. His human name was Steffan. He was a quiet thoughtful man, one who could be counted on to do whatever he promised.

But despite his honesty and his impeccable ethics, humans were often uncomfortable in Steffan's presence. He had the disconcerting habit, common to elves, of unblinking concentration. He listened when spoken to without interruption, never taking his eyes off the speaker. It was polite, but most unnerving. He was also silent, seldom speaking unless he had something of value to relate; small talk with Steffan was unthinkable. Still, he understood elves as no other human did, and in the past he had served as an envoy of the Bright Kingdom, working out treaties between the humans and the Glyth Gamel as smoothly as such things could be done, for he enjoyed the complete trust of the elves.

Tianna found herself oddly attracted to Steffan despite his unusual traits. Or perhaps because of them. He was a tall, slender man with a thick shock of chestnut brown hair, highlighted with red, slightly curled and worn long in the elvish manner. Despite his human bulk, he carried himself with the unconscious grace of an elf. His features were finely chiseled, his cheekbones high and sharply defined. His eyes were a dark sea green and fringed with long eyelashes that would have been the envy of any woman. His lips were slender and curved, his mouth wide, often quirked up at one side as though in amusement. His jaw-line was smooth and un-bearded, cleft in the middle. It was an altogether pleasing face.

"Well, Tianna, what do you make of this?" her father asked suddenly, breaking into Tianna's reverie. With a shock of embarrassment, Tianna realized that she had not heard one word that either man had said and now both were looking at her, expecting a reply.

"Uh, I'm sorry, father, I seem to have been

thinking my own thoughts. Forgive me for my inattentiveness." Steffan's green eyes rested upon her, his solemn, level gaze, coupled with the quirk of his lips unsettling her further. Did he know that she had been watching him . . . watching the way his lips moved, wondering what it would be like to kiss him? She turned a bright crimson and began to stammer, wrenching her eyes away from Steffan and smoothing her already smooth skirts. Whatever had come over her? She was acting like those frivolous ladies in waiting, she so detested. Soon she would begin to blither and flutter her eyelashes when she spoke. She could feel the heat of her embarrassment as it worked its way down her neck.

"No matter, my daughter," her father said with a look of puzzlement. "I have found it difficult to concentrate myself these days. Steffan was just telling us what might lie behind the elves' actions."

Instantly, all thoughts of flirtation fell away, Tianna leaned forward across the table interested in what Steffan might have to say.

"I was just telling your father that in recent years the elves have been beset with more than the usual dangers when crossing the mountains. It has always been a dangerous journey but the numbers of dire wolves, wandering orcs and mountain giants has been steadily increasing."

"We have noticed much the same thing," Tianna replied, glad to have something relevant to add. "We have lost numerous miners returning to the city, and shepherds in the far west of our land have reported increased mortalities among their flocks. We have added to the numbers of patrols along the elven border."

Steffan nodded solemnly, his eyes never leaving Tianna's face. Once again she flushed and fought for control.

"To what do you ascribe these increased dangers?" her father asked. Thankfully, Steffan transferred his attention away from her.

"The Glyth Gamel do not know the answer, sire. It could be a cyclical surge in the predator population; such things do occur from time to time, but that would not explain the number of orcs and other such abominations who are invading the forest in force. The Glyth Gamel have always enjoyed total sovereignty within the confines of the forest, but that is true no longer. Women and children are guarded at all times and even fully armed bands of male elves have been assaulted."

"The same thing is occurring in Rakhatz," added Orrik. "We spend much more time hunting down orcs and wolves these days, though our cities inside the mountains are more secure than the forest homes of the elves."

Steffan nodded agreement. "Contact with Silvarre, our sister clan on the far side of the Iron Mountains, has all but ended. It is my understanding that they have been besieged by armies of orcs from the Wastes. The orcs send hordes that are uncharacteristically well-armed and whose numbers do not seem to be diminished by the Silvarrean defenses. The Glyth Gamel may not be willing to share their concerns with you for they have little trust in humans, but I believe that they fear for the Silvarreans as well as themselves. It is possible that if a safe passage is not found, a way to reinforce the Silvarreans, the elven way of life will disappear." The words were said calmly but it was apparent that they were spoken with deep concern.

"Why have the Glyth Gamel not come to us before matters reached such a critical level?" asked Charles. "Why did Gaelwyth not speak of this matter instead of proposing this preposterous trade scheme? The elves are scarcely known for their desire to fraternize with humans. Surely they would know that we would view their wish for expansion of trade with suspicion!"

A silence fell after Charles spoke. Steffan appeared to be considering his words carefully before replying. He sighed deeply. "Sire, you must try to understand the Glyth Gamel. They are a proud people, steeped in ancient traditions based upon complete self-sufficiency. That they have survived with their traditions and ethos intact surrounded on all sides by outsiders who desired their forests and viewed them as an irritating obstacle to be overcome, is a wonder in itself. Is it any wonder that they are less than completely forthcoming especially when to do so would reveal their vulnerability?"

Stung by Steffan's references to unscrupulous outsiders, Tianna protested. "But we of the Bright Kingdom have always treated the Glyth Gamel fairly! We have coexisted peacefully for many, many years!"

Steffan lowered his head, nodding in agreement.

"For many years," he echoed. "This is true, Princess. But in the past such was not the case. The Glyth Gamel have lived upon the face of this land for time out of mind, long before your ancestors even dreamed of leaving the Old World and settling on this continent. When humans first landed on these shores, they found the Glyth Gamel open, friendly and willing to ease the hardships of establishing a new colony. Their friendship was turned against them; they were slaughtered and their womenfolk seized and cruelly used, their lands stripped of their forests and cleared by fire. All of the Bright Kingdom was once virgin forest from the sea to the mountains. Now the Glyth Gamel hold to the narrow strip that has been left to them and watch as you plow and plunder their ancestral lands. They have long memories. They do not forget. Do you blame them for being somewhat reticent?"

"You speak as though you are one of them, elven rather than human, Sper Andros," Charles observed. "Your sympathies clearly rest with the Glyth Gamel. Tell me honestly, where do your loyalties lie?"

Now it was Steffan's turn to flush, his cheeks burning with a bright spot of color high in the center of each cheekbone. "You have the right to question me. You are my king, and I have accepted you as my sovereign liege. While it is true that I was reared by the elves who treated me no differently than one of their own children, there were always differences. The Glyth Gamel never sought to influence my thinking, allowing me to pick my own course. As I grew to manhood, it became obvious, even to me, that I was human and that their world could never truly be mine. While I will always be welcome in the forest and the Glyth Gamel will always command my heart, I have made my choice. I am human. I am here." He stood proudly and was silent.

"We will speak on it no more," said Charles, clearly impressed by the man's bearing and obvious sincerity. "Now, let us talk some more about this wonder, this iron dragon. Orrik, explain again to an old man how such a thing could be."

CHAPTER FIVE

A Request

The drawings and the maps had been examined from every angle, pondered and discussed till there was nothing left to say. But there were still many unanswered questions for it seemed that the more they studied the drawings, the more they talked among themselves, the more questions arose. Merchants were brought to the castle and the question of raising large quantities of gold was raised. Charles, however, had not yet made up his mind. So it was that when Gaelwyth appeared to receive the king's decision, after the allotted period of time, what he heard was not what he had expected.

"You want to do what?" he asked in astonishment staring at the trio of humans, his gaze resting longest on Steffan.

"We wish to visit this iron dragon, see it for ourselves before we make our final decision," the king replied calmly. "It seems a reasonable request. Is that a problem?"

Gaelwyth fretted and spluttered, trying to find a reason to refuse their request. While it might have been reasonable under other circumstances, humans did not enter the elven forest uninvited and invitations were never given. The occasional trader might choose to take the forest paths as Steffan's parents had done, and miners made their way to and from the mountains on clearly established routes, but it was always a risk, for the elves were quick to loose their arrows and ask questions later. The problem was that there was never anyone left to question once the arrows found their mark. No human other than Steffan — and Gaelwyth was sure Sper Andros was part elf anyway — had entered the forest with impunity for several centuries.

But, since the elves had approached the humans and proposed the unprecedented alliance, there was little that Gaelwyth could do to refuse the request. Trying to fix his face into an agreeable mask, the ambassador smiled stiffly.

"I know your majesty must be a very busy man. Such a visit might well be a lengthy one. The needs of your country must be considered."

"Oh, come now, I do not think that will be a problem," Charles responded with a bland smile. "You yourself pointed out that this great enterprise was to be for the mutual benefit of both our kingdoms. It is a matter of top priority. Do not forget that I have lost a son and scores of brave sailors, and that the financial viability of the Bright Kingdom is at stake. If such a thing is indeed possible I will do whatever is necessary to establish a safe overland route so that no man, elf or dwarf sacrifices his life needlessly. No amount of time is too much. Fix the date, Gaelwyth, the sooner the better."

There was no denying the king's intent. No

way of wiggling out of the meeting. Gaelwyth bowed low and withdrew from the king's chambers. That very day, the elf, and Orrik, rode off at a hard gallop.

Seven days later a flat wooden box, cleverly carved out of a single piece of cherry wood, self-hinged and adorned with intricate carvings, was presented at the gates by a trio of elves. The box was immediately delivered to the king as directed and he freed the peg, a small carved acorn fitted into a twisted branch, which allowed the box to open. The interior of the box was lined with shimmering silver silk and on it rested a single sheet of ivory vellum made from the gossamer fibers of a milkweed pod. Written in gracefully turned script were the words: "Safe Passage. An invitation to view the iron dragon is extended to King Charles, Princess Tianna and Sper Andros." Using the common calendar which counted from the date of the humans' arrival in the New World, rather than the countless eons that the elves had made it their home, the visit was fixed for two days hence. It was further stated that a "guide" would present himself at the gates for their convenience.

The time passed slowly. Tianna found herself thinking about Steffan often. She was glad that he was to accompany them into the forest. On the other hand, she could not help but wonder, despite his words of assurance, whose side he was really on. Why was he and no other included in the invitation? What role did he play in this unfolding mystery? Despite her unease, she did not share her concerns with her father, nor could she have said why.

The event had, however, precipitated yet another crisis. At the supper table that evening, Kroner took the news that he was not included in the upcoming visit, very poorly.

"Father, it is cruel enough that you excluded me from those mysterious meetings you held with Gaelwyth Grae, Steffan, and that dwarf." Kroner banged his cup hard on the table.

"You are only seventeen, Kroner. Do well with the royal levee and as you grow older, I shall give you more responsibility." Charles spoke in a kindly manner attempting to soothe the young prince. "Responsibility is earned by effort and merit, not merely by birthright."

Kroner reacted like a scalded cat all but hissing and spitting as he screamed at his father, demanding inclusion in all things that concerned his future kingdom. He cast scorn upon Tianna's participation in the meetings, daring to rebuke his father for including a mere woman, instead of "a man and the heir to the throne."

Charles' features settled in cold stony lines as Kroner railed hysterically. Slowly, the hot spate of words died on the young man's lips as his father's heavy silence penetrated his consciousness. Tianna watched in awe as Charles plucked the young man up by the nape of the neck and hurried him away, toes barely touching the floor. The chamber door banged solidly shut behind them.

Charles never said what words had been exchanged with his son, and Tianna could not bring herself to inquire. But things changed drastically from that moment on. Charles made no further attempts to speak kindly to the young prince; in fact he did not speak to him at all unless it was absolutely necessary, and then only in terse, clipped tones.

Kroner, for his part, appeared to simmer with a barely controlled rage. At times, when his hot eyes fell upon Tianna, it seemed that flames would shoot from the black orbs. His words were dipped in acid, cutting and burning whomever they touched. He avoided Tianna, for which she was grateful, and she found much to her dismay that she was somewhat fearful of this young man who was her brother. But faced with his burning disdain and obvious hatred, she found that she could gather up no feelings of filial concern. Kroner had finally become what he had always been, a stranger, who by a peculiar quirk of fate, shared the same name and the same father.

She was relieved when the day of the journey finally arrived, and she sensed that her father shared her relief. The very air inside the castle seemed heavy and oppressive, crackling with tension which emanated from Kroner's quarters. Of the young man himself, there was no sign. A steady stream of servants had been kept on the run, emerging from his chambers with frightened, downcast eyes. This circumstance had prompted yet another conflict between father and son. The lord high chamberlain would rule in the king's absence. After that, there was nothing but the brooding silence.

The guide arrived that evening, at the appointed hour. Tianna, Charles and Steffan set out on sturdy horses and trotted out of the city gates. Tianna turned in her saddle and looked back at the castle. A tiny figure stood alone on the parapet. Even at that distance, she could feel the weight and heat of Kroner's hatred fixed squarely between her shoulder blades. At her urging, they passed through the massive gates and allowed them to swing shut behind them. Only then did the feeling ease.

CHAPTER SIX

Across the Bright Kingdom

No sooner had the gates closed behind them than the rest of their "guide" appeared on the broad stone causeway that led to the city. A heavily armed elven patrol, more than twenty strong, emerged from the mists so silently that it seemed as though they had been blown there by the damp, foggy air. The elves were alert and watchful as though expecting to be attacked at any moment. They would not relax their guard until they reentered the forest.

Following Steffan's suggestion, both Tianna and Charles had packed plenty of sturdy outdoor clothing and several layers of warm woolens to wear under their leather outer garments. The leaves on the trees were beginning to fall, and the chill of winter would not be long in coming. They wore tall leather boots that rose to the knee and long leather gloves, and heavy capes with deep hoods protected their heads and faces from thorns and low branches. They left their hoods down for the time being, since it was a three day ride across the Bright Kingdom and its cleared roads before they reached the border with Glyth Gamel.

The elf patrol split in two, ten elves leading the procession and ten elves following. At a word from Charles, the whole group started down the road. A small crowd of people who had gathered along the causeway cheered as their king rode off into the mist. Although they had no mounts, the elves easily kept pace with the horses. After a time some of them broke into a song. The words were in a language that Tianna did not understand, but it was pleasant to the ears and somehow made her feel more secure. Steffan, who was riding behind her, joined in with a clear baritone, and she turned and gazed at him in amazement. Another talent was revealed in this mysterious man she was coming to admire so much.

The first night was spent in pleasant company in Bremmner Castle, where the local lord was beside himself to have the unexpected pleasure of entertaining the King and the Princess. After a small reception and modest feast, Tianna found herself standing on the castle wall beside Steffan, staring out into the starry night at the surrounding city. Great clouds of smoke rose from bright glowing fires in the distance.

"The dwarven foundries," said Steffan quietly.

"I thought as much," she answered, hoping for once to catch his eyes. But he was deep in thought and his gaze was fixed on the lights in the distance.

"I have a feeling those fires will soon be making the rails upon which we shall cross this continent and the weapons that will be needed in the battles to prove our sovereignty."

Tianna nodded silently. A cold wind came up, and she pulled her cloak tight around her. Romantic thoughts faded from her mind with these ominous words, and she retired quietly to her chambers.

Soon after dawn, they were on the march again, traveling the coast road, with the deep blue waters of Boras Bay to the right and a dense forest to the left. They passed through a small fishing village, where the king was greeted with happy huzzas from the populace.

"If things don't change soon," Charles remarked sourly, "my presence will no longer be so gladly welcomed."

"That will never be the case, father; we shall turn things around," Tianna replied loyally. "We're going to build the great rail road."

They rode on, and the forest to their left gave way to low hills, that were soon replaced by steep cliffs. The road became narrow and treacherous in places, winding up and down, precariously balanced between mountains and sea. Sometime after noon, they turned south, away from the coast and headed down the center of a vast glacial valley. On either flank rose green, tree-covered mountains, while the valley floor itself was dotted with small farms. Here much of the wheat in the Bright Kingdom was grown.

The second night was spent at an inn in a small farm village. The innkeeper was beside himself, what with having the royal party as his guests for the night, and apologized constantly for the poor state of accommodations, the meager fare, and lack of fanfare. Charles and Tianna reassured the poor man as best they could and were both relieved when at last it was time for bed and the apologies came to a temporary halt.

They set out the next day in a gentle but steady rain. Very soon Tianna felt sorry for their elven escort, who slogged along through the muddy ruts of the road, uncomplaining. They began to sing again, and the tone was different. She turned and looked at Steffan, who had not yet joined the others in harmony.

"It's a song about the rain," he answered, without her having asked the question. "The rain and the life it gives." He smiled pleasantly and then began to sing with the others.

The procession mucked along as best it could for a time and then the valley veered to the west and grew narrower. There were fewer farms, and the land took on a wilder look. Tianna assumed they were nearing the border with Glyth Gamel. The wagon road had disappeared and was now only a narrow muddy trail. Every now and then she could see mountains looming on either side, and they were making their way into a forest that grew increasingly dense. Late in the afternoon, they came to a small village which was filled with a rather large garrison of the king's men-at-arms. The soldiers, who had been alerted that their king was coming, were arrayed in two long rows on either side of the muddy track, and they saluted smartly as the royal procession rode past.

Charles stopped and spoke with the local commander. They had reached the border with Glyth Gamel.

The officer in charge was a thick short man, with a dark beard and black eyes. "You should have no trouble, your majesty, especially considering your elven guards." He knew full well that the twenty elves accompanying his king were worth more than a hundred of his own men in the woods.

"I take it, then, that the border has been peaceful of late?" asked the king. And indeed, there had been no sign of dire wolves or orc raiders in the area for more than a fortnight.

The rain had stopped and Tianna took the opportunity to change into dry clothes. The brief conference was soon over, and the march continued.

They pressed on into the woods until nearly dark, and made camp near a loud rushing stream. They slept under the trees that night, and when morning came, Tianna was surprised to see that they had been joined by even more elves.

"We can go no further on these horses," said Steffan, after conversing with the newcomers for a moment.

"Do we walk then?" Tianna asked in secret dismay, wondering if she could keep pace with the elfen guard.

Steffan stepped forward to reassure her. "Horses will not do in the forest; their scent attracts predators and while we could most certainly win out against them, it would be unnecessarily costly in terms of both time and energy."

"So we go afoot," Charles said with a sigh, for it had been many years since he had been called upon for any amount of strenuous physical effort and even three easy days on horseback had tired him.

"No, sire," Steffan replied with a smile, "the elves have arranged for . . . different mounts." There was considerable noise in the woods around them. Over the noise of the rushing stream there could be heard a good deal of grunting and odd snorts and muffled roars. Even as Steffan spoke, he gently escorted the princess and the king forward through the watchful ranks of the elven guard.

Their elven escort, which now had almost doubled in number, were now mounted, but not on horses. Each one sat upon the shaggy back of an immense brown or black bear tacked out with silver and leather bridles and small carved wood saddles! Apparently Ninius was taking no chances with the safety of Charles Edouard. Tianna was too astonished to speak. The bears were evidently excited by the diversity of scents wafted from the newcomers by the constant easterly breeze. The animals rocked back and forth, shuffling from side to side, moaning and grunting deep in their chests, as they raised their muzzles to draw in the enticing aromas.

Tianna pressed a hand to her chest. She did not think of herself as a weak, fluttery female, but the thought of riding a bear made her very nervous. She could see that her father was no less happy at the thought. Then, a sudden lowing filled the air, an odd moaning sound that ended

in a series of short, choppy grunts. The bears
became agitated and moved aside reluctantly,
their meaty brown haunches skittering sideways,
jerking the elves who held their bridles about
like feathers. As the bears moved aside, Tianna
saw an even more peculiar sight.

Great velvet deer, those immense beasts used
for their meat, milk, leather, and transport by the
inhabitants of Koland, the most remote of the
frozen north lands, shoved their way through the
bears. Their racks of velvet-covered spatulate
horns were festooned with a multitude of tiny
silver bells that pierced the tines at each level,
and tinkled and chimed with every step of the
broad, saucerlike hooves. Each animal's bells
were of a different tone, which Tianna assumed
would allow her, and the elves, to identify them
when they were out of sight. The deer were
quite a bit taller than the bears, taller even than
the horses they were about to leave behind. Had
the eyes of the deer not been so gentle, shining
with a deep brown luminosity and fringed with
long, thick, curving lashes, Tianna might have
been more afraid of them than the bears. The
deer, too, were bridled and reined, with supple
leather covered with fancifully worked embroi-
dery. Brightly colored tassels dangled from chin,
brows, ears and reins. Their saddles were fashioned from wood with high back pieces and a
comfortable curl to the front portion where an
inexperienced rider might grab hold. The saddles themselves were amply padded with
cushions to protect the rider from the discom-
forts of a rough trail. Snorting in protest, urged

along by elves who prodded them with shaved
withes, the great beasts knelt down before
Tianna, Charles and Steffan.

Steffan's eyes twinkled as he watched Tianna's
expression turn from fear to astonishment and
then finally to relieved acceptance. He helped
settle the princess into her saddle and showed
her how to hold the reins as well as how to use
the willow branch to prod the beast when the
urge took it to browse, rather than travel. When
Steffan went to help the king mount, Charles
waved him aside and seated himself, his expression less easily read than his daughter's; but the
king swung into his saddle as though riding
velvet deer were a daily occurrence.

Once the royal party was settled, Steffan
mounted his own beast and the elves leaped
atop their bears. Amid a great cacophony of
groans, bleats, roars, and grunts, the odd caval-
cade set off into the depths of forest. After the
first few anxious moments, Tianna allowed herself to relax. It was strange being up so high, and
the lurching, swaying gait of the velvet deer was
quite unlike anything she had ever experienced.
But by the time the tall dense, towering walls of
the forest that were so typical of Glyth Gamel
drew near, she had mastered the technique
necessary to ride the great beast. One simply
relaxed and allowed the body to move and flow
with the motion. Once she learned this, Tianna
was amazed to discover that the gait of the giant
deer was far smoother than that of a horse.
There was no jolting up and down movement,
no constant impact to jerk and shake one's neck

back and forth, but a smooth gliding motion similar to canoeing on a still pond.

The deer, however, tested its new rider frequently at first, ducking its head down to nibble tasty bits of grass or pulling from one side of the trail or the other to snatch a mouthful of greenery. Tianna learned to apply the willow stick, under Steffan's watchful eye, softly and ineffectively at first, and then more vigorously. The deer rolled its eyes back at her after a particularly sharp thump and groaned pathetically as though to say, "why are you being so mean to me." She ignored the protestations and from that point on, her steed was relatively well-behaved.

They had donned their leather outerwear for the ride, and it wasn't long before the heavy garments grew uncomfortably warm. After a short time Tianna threw back her hood, freeing her long auburn tresses, to enjoy the occasional breath of the cool autumn breeze that slipped between the tall trees and ferns that lined their path. She took in every detail, enjoying the beauty that surrounded her.

The trees were so tall that their uppermost branches were lost to sight in a swaying criss-cross of limbs and leaves. Fragrant red cedar and majestic mahogany grew alongside shaggy evergreens, their boles massive and marked by the years. It would have taken a dozen humans to encircle any given trunk. There was little new growth; the venerable giant trees absorbed all of the sunlight. Only occasionally were there gaps in the canopy where some giant had fallen, the victim of storm or the ravages of great age, and here the sunlight streamed down in broad beams that seemed overly bright after the dim, pearly gloom. In these spots, tiny seedlings seized the opportunity to reach for the sky and fought each other for dominance. Only one could be the victor; the others would die, closed off from the life-giving golden orb, and all too soon the shaft of sunlight would vanish and the forest would once again be dim and cool. Ferns, most taller than her head, even atop her unusual steed, arched over the trail, sprinkling icy cold crystalline drops of dew on all who passed. Soon, it became necessary to cover her head and shoulders with the hooded cloak and she was grateful for the warm garments that enveloped her.

Once they were moving there was little sound other than the soft tread of deer hooves on the dense mat of leaves and needles that covered the ground. She heard the sweet trills of unseen birds and the drone of insects but no sound of voices. The party's silence was easily understood; the forest seemed to impose the weight and majesty of its great age upon all those who entered its environs. They traveled in this pristine beauty for long hours, all the while climbing higher and higher up the shoulders of mountains that could not be seen for the trees.

CHAPTER SEVEN

Glyth Gamel

The shadows of night were darkening the dense undergrowth when suddenly, without any advance warning, they arrived at the elven camp. One moment they were surrounded by the forest, the next, they had stepped into a wonderland of beauty, a joining of nature and everyday life in a unique and harmonious manner.

The great trees still stood but now there were large spaces between them. Ferns and flowers, green and blooming in spite of the lateness of the season, had been arranged in graceful lines that delineated avenues that led from one tree to the next. Elves peered down at them from the trees above, their high-pitched voices twittering like bird calls. Circular platforms of woven leafy limbs ringed the trees like shelf fungus, and these were draped with vines and climbing flowers. Small enclosures nested on the platforms, providing shelter. Lianas, intertwined with branches, connected the trees and platforms and on these were elven children who shrieked with excitement and pointed out various features of the strangers who had entered their world. Many of the smaller children swarmed down from the trees with the ease and unthinking grace of squirrels and flung themselves on Steffan, calling him by his elvish name.

"Sper Andros!" they shrieked over and over again. Their joy at seeing him and the way in which their tiny hands infiltrated his many pockets indicated great familiarity and obvious affection. Finding what they sought, brightly colored paper wrapped gobbets of pulled taffy, they danced and frolicked at his side, besieging him with laughing, teasing voices.

A small girl child, so fragile and ephemeral as to appear like a sprite or some other fey creature, separated herself from the pack and wandered over toward Tianna who was still perched atop her gentle steed. The child had a small, delicately featured face with large, luminous silver eyes and a tiny pointed chin. Her cheeks were deeply dimpled and her hair cascaded round her face in a torrent of frothy white-blond curls. She was clad in a silken tunic and tights woven of a nubbly homespun material, pale green in color. Shyly, she held out her hand and offered Tianna the prize that rested there, a handful of thick red blossoms.

Tianna dismounted and gravely accepted the sweet smelling offering. Reaching into her own pocket, she could find nothing that would appeal to a child and without thought of worth or value, she quickly removed a gold heart amulet that she wore and arranged the delicate chain around the child's slender neck. The child looked down at the glittering present and then up at Tianna with a wide smile and gripping her hand with tiny fingers, proudly walked back to her friends drawing Tianna along like some hard won prize.

"Well," Tianna said with a laugh, "it appears that I have been captured."

"I'd say that it was you who has won the greater victory," Steffan replied with an indulgent smile. "Llanni is the daughter of Ninius and he loves her more than life itself. Winning Llanni's friendship can mean a great deal, for her instincts are true, she has the gift of intuition. Had you unkind thoughts or wickedness in your heart, Llanni would know."

Tianna stared at the child with interest, thinking that such a gift would be very useful indeed.

Charles Edouard had just dismounted when a delegation of elves approached from the far side of the clearing. A tall, burly elf wearing a silver tunic with a large faceted silver stone at the shoulder was in the lead, a troubled expression on his bearded face. "My sincerest apologies, good friends," he said in a deep voice, advancing with outstretched hands. "I am Ninius, King of the Glyth Gamel. A bit of unexpected excitement delayed us even though we had been told of your imminent arrival. Please forgive our unintentional rudeness. Welcome to Glyth Gamel. And welcome to Woodsong, my home."

As he spoke Tianna could not help but notice the scorched edges of his tunic and the fact that a large portion of his beard was charred. The unmistakable scent of burned hair clung to the king and those who surrounded him. More than a few of his party appeared nervous and agitated, although they did their best to conceal their distress.

"Your journey will have tired you; please accept our hospitality and the opportunity to rest. We will speak further when you have refreshed yourselves," said the king. He held out his hand to Llanni who allowed herself to be wooed away from Tianna, wrapping her lissome arms around her father's neck and settling in his arms. As they took their leave and were led away, Tianna wondered which of them needed the rest and refreshments more than the other. It appeared that things were not as peaceful in this neck of the woods as she had been led to believe.

Her suspicions were borne out when they were summoned to join the elf king shortly after nightfall. He had donned more formal attire and his beard had been neatly trimmed, now cropped close to his chin rather than flowing onto his chest as before. His deputies had similarly removed all signs of their earlier disarray. A warm, fragrant herbal tea was offered as well as a sparkling white wine. Delicately spiced appetizers and then platters of steaming roots, mushrooms, and vegetables were placed before them, and all talk, other than light, casual pleasantries, was suspended for the course of the meal. Only after they had cleansed their palates with an icy cold wild strawberry sherbet did they settle themselves for serious conversation. Llanni had remained beside her father during the meal but now placed herself between Tianna and her father as the talks began.

Long minutes were filled with assurances of mutual esteem and fond regards as the two leaders satisfied the customary protocol required at the meetings of two such prominent Heads of State. Tianna found it tedious. She and Tyndal had accompanied her father on many such meetings and while Tyndal had shown a flair for such flowery, complimentary exchanges, Tianna hated the boring rhetoric and found it the cause of many a lingering headache. Why were such things necessary? Why could people not just say what they wanted to say without all the extraneous blathering?

Her father caught her eye and frowned slightly, silently admonishing her to do her part. She tried to think of something to say, but all that she could think of was to compliment the elven king, Ninius, on his beautiful daughter.

"She is as intelligent and precious as she is lovely," Ninius replied, his features softening as they gazed fondly on his child who snuggled closer to Tianna. "She seems to have taken a particular fancy to you. Be certain that the little minx does not annoy you. Give her a swat and send her away!" Yet one could easily judge that never had he raised a finger to the child and woe unto the unwitting person who did. She could also see that it was as Steffan had said, a clear advantage that the child did seem to have taken a liking to her.

After a long, circuitous, conversational route, the talk touched on the troubles with the invaders of the forest and finally settled on the reason they had come, the iron dragon, and the

building of the great rail road which would join
their worlds and span the continent. But barely
had the subject been broached when Ninius,
stifling a yawn, announced that it had been a
long and difficult day for all and suggested
reconvening in the morning.

Tianna was upset, all of this travel and time
spent on worthless pleasantries when all she
wanted to do was to go see this iron dragon and
now the fellow wanted to go to bed! She opened
her mouth to speak but a sharp elbow in the ribs
took the words out of her mouth. She cast an
indignant glance at Steffan who pretended not
to notice. The elven child, Llanni, squeezed
Tianna's fingers and gave her a warm, reassuring
smile, which in some way eased the band of
anger that had closed around her heart. She
sighed deeply, resigning herself to the elvish
plan of events.

She was rewarded for her patience when the
child crept into her shelter at first light and
slithered beneath the blanket, wakening her
with tiny kisses and soft pattering fingers
smoothing and twining through her long,
unbraided hair. Llanni danced around the small
woven twig room, examining Tianna's wardrobe,
pulling out leather riding breeches and tall
leather boots as well as a heavy leather jacket
that buttoned from neck to waist as Tianna rose
and made her toilet. Tianna had planned to wear
a lightweight flowered dress, a warm russet color
that brought out the red in her hair, but she gave
in to the child's selection, reasoning that Llanni
knew better than she what to expect.

Although she would not have thought herself hungry after the previous night's festivities, she found the meal provided — warm, fragrant buns, rich wheels of cheese and bowls of fruit stewed with nuts and topped with thick, buttery cream — impossible to resist. The entire elven community joined in as they broke the night's fast and there was much curious conversation and many speculative glances cast their way during the course of the meal. Tall cups of bitter, sharply flavored acorn tea closed the meal as well as a benediction bestowed by Ninius. It had been so the previous night as well. Tianna thought it odd that the benediction should be given at the end of the meal rather than the beginning but, she reminded herself, it was their world, not hers.

Steffan had been seated elsewhere and now that the populace was dispersing, he came toward her with a heavyset matronly woman clinging to his arm and an elderly man in tow. The woman scarcely reached Steffan's chest but the beam of pride that lit her face lent her the bearing of a queen. The elf who brought up the rear was grinning broadly but could not look at Tianna without blushing a deep beet red.

"Princess Tianna, I'd like to introduce you to my parents," Steffan said with great and obvious affection. "This beautiful lady is my mother, Mistress Wren, and this handsome fellow is my father, Master Woodsong. Those delicious biscuits, the ones that kept floating off your plate and then melted on your tongue, were made by my mother."

Tianna picked up the cue and complimented the plump motherly figure on her biscuits, declaring them to be the best she had ever placed in her mouth and to be honest, there was not much exaggeration in her words. Before long, the two women were deep in conversation, discussing cooking, of which Tianna knew little, and Steffan's merits, which interested her far more. Steffan and his father interjected comments of their own from time to time and Tianna lost all track of time in the pleasant company.

She was startled when a call came to mount. Looking around she saw that a full elvish party stood at the ready, and only she and Steffan were still afoot. Disentangling themselves from the proud parents was only accomplished after promises were extracted, whereby Tianna agreed to join them after her return, for "a bit of something to eat."

CHAPTER EIGHT
The Mountain Pass

Their mounts were led forward and Steffan and Tianna quickly joined the party. They trotted out of the clearing and down a narrow trail. The path soon opened into a stony gully and the bears and deer were forced to pick their way carefully across the slippery scree. The gulch led downward at a steep angle and Tianna made good use of the carved pommel to avoid being thrown over her mount's neck at each lurching step. Finally, the stony corridor leveled off, the sides opening and giving way to thorn encrusted brambles and vines growing sparsely in the rocky soil. Tall spires of rock rose upward, piercing the land sharply, forcing them to wend their way between the outcrops, and Tianna could see massive snow capped mountain peaks in the distance.

The elves had been especially alert ever since leaving Woodsong and Tianna began to see signs of past trouble along the way. Suddenly, she understood why many of their group, including Steffan, were now carrying shields in addition to their bows. Scattered among the stony litter at the side of the path were broken bones and bits

of torn clothing. Beside a great boulder was a
heavy wooden shield with crude orcish symbols
burned into its surface. And there, lying beneath
a bramble bush, was a leather boot with grayish,
rotting flesh and gnawed bones protruding. As
she passed, a watchful blackbird perched on the
toe of the worn leather and wrenched a grisly bit
of stinking flesh free, observing the riders with
bright obsidian eyes. Tianna's stomach turned.

The elves had become ever more watchful;
many of them had their arrows nocked and
bowstrings pulled half taut. Their large silver
eyes scanned the landscape ceaselessly, roaming
back and forth over every object large enough to
conceal an enemy. They rode without the use of
their reins, controlling their shaggy steeds with
their knees. The bears appeared closely attuned
to their wishes and often seemed to anticipate
what would be required of them, behaving far
more tractably than Tianna would ever have
imagined possible of such wild natured beasts.
Tianna urged her mount closer to Steffan.

"What is happening?" she asked. "What danger lurks in this place?"

Steffan appeared to choose his words carefully. "There has been some concern over orcs of
late. They have been rather bold about appearing openly and have challenged the elves'
ownership of this place. As you see, they have
not won their claim."

Tianna shuddered as they passed yet another
orc corpse, its features pecked into a horrific
pitted landscape by the carrion birds. "Why do
you leave the bodies strewn about?" she asked.

"Why are they not buried or burned? The sight is unpleasant and the stench appalling."

"It serves as a deterrent to their former comrades," Steffan replied. "A reminder of what could happen to them if they are so unwise as to attack again. Orcs are not overly intelligent and need frequent and vivid reminders. As for burial, the carrion birds will see to their disposal."

Although they traveled for some time without incident, the elves did not relax their watchful attentiveness. As they passed inside the shadows of a narrow passage between two mountainous slopes, a hoarse shout came from above, and their vigilance was rewarded. Orcs suddenly rose up on either side of them and loosed volleys of arrows into the ravine. The elves were at a temporary disadvantage as the orcs commanded the higher ground and were firing down directly upon them. But the defenders were not without resources; they reacted quickly, raising their shields and placing them over their heads, and held them firmly in place by chin straps! These shields were as tall as the elves themselves and shaped like long oval leaves, thus protecting both elf and bear from most of the missiles that rained down upon them. While the shields absorbed the brunt of the attack, quickly taking on the appearance of spiny porcupines, the elves were free to bring their own weapons into play. Being much better shots than their opponents, their well-placed arrows soon began to make an impact on the larger, clumsier orcs.

At the first shout, Steffan had pulled Charles and Tianna off their mounts and pressed them up against a tall granite boulder, shielding them with his own body. His own great shield, twice as large as any of the elves', was driven into the ground point first. From this narrow bit of shelter he guarded the royal party, firing off one deadly shaft after another. Charles drew his sword and beat off the one orc who was foolish enough to hurl itself down the slope to attack their tiny fortress. The hideous creature died with a gruesome screech. His heart's blood dripped down on them from the wound in his chest, but his stinking corpse provided them with an effective rooflike barrier between shield and rock.

Tianna began softly chanting the words to a spell of protection, but before she could bring it into action the conflict came to an end. The orcs were falling to the elven arrows in great numbers, and they quickly realized that they could not win the encounter despite their seeming advantage. There was no signal, no planned form of retreat, only a ragged rout as one after another of the snarling creatures abandoned the fight and scrambled away over the rocks, while others, who had not yet realized that they were being left to carry on the fight, covered their cowardly backsides. Soon, even those few who were braver — or perhaps more stupid than their companions — realized what was happening and they too gave up the battle and fled. Tianna dropped the threads of her spell, unfinished.

The elves had been waiting for the orc's retreat. Dismounting swiftly, they pulled the bits

out of their mounts' snarling jaws and gave the
bears their freedom, allowing the fierce beasts
who had lost all sign of gentle domesticity, to
follow their true nature. The rocks rang with
hideous screams and an awful crunching as the
fleeing orcs, unable to escape their bloodthirsty
foes, fell beneath the sharp claws and ravening
teeth. They had gone from victor to vanquished
in the blink of an eye. And now they had become
prey.

Even as the narrow gorge echoed with the
awful cries, the elves clambered up over the
rocks finishing off any orcs who showed signs of
life, relieving them of their weapons and retriev-
ing their own expended arrows.

Tianna and Charles stepped out of their
defensive position while Steffan retrieved the
velvet deer who were grazing nearby, uncon-
cerned by either battle or bloodshed. Tianna
took in the ghastly scene; orcish blood turned
the rocks from gray to black. Bears fed upon
the corpses, their powerful jaws and long white
teeth grinding and pulverizing flesh, bone, and
even armor into bloody bits wrenched off the
unprotesting bodies and swallowed whole.
Never had she seen such a terrible sight. The
sky turned dark with the sudden arrival of
hordes of blackbirds which descended like
plummeting rocks and strode in to snatch gobs
of flesh from the very jaws of the blood-crazed
bears. Tianna steeled herself to watch,
commanding her stomach to behave, knowing
that if it were not for the elves' valor and the
natural instincts of the bears, she and her father

could well be lying dead on the stony earth.

Charles did not stay to comfort his daughter but joined the elves in dispatching the remaining orcs.

Ninius came hurrying over toward Tianna, a worried look, on his face. "Good, you're safe." He glanced around anxiously, "And your father?"

"He's fine, just over there, dispatching orcs," she replied, forcing her voice to remain steady as she pointed out her father's figure.

"This never should have happened." The elf king shook his head sadly. "The vile creatures ambushed our scouts and we fell right into their trap."

"Still, they had the worst of it, I'd say." remarked Steffan, who stood nearby wiping orc blood off his shield with a rag. "Did we lose any of our own?"

"Only the two scouts. We found their bodies atop that rock." Ninius gestured behind him. "But that is two too many; they were good elves and true."

Finally all was done; the bears were drawn away from the last of their victims, although not without a good deal of growling protest. Had the bears' bloodthirsty nature as well as their stomachs not been sated, it might have been a more difficult deed. They made a funeral pyre for their own dead out of dead trees and branches. Ninius led the elves in a sad song and the fire was set alight.

At length, the party remounted and left the grisly scene behind them before the sun had traveled another notch in its daily journey across the heavens.

They were climbing steadily now through rocky draws and across thinly treed slopes. The air was clear and bright and exceedingly cold, biting into the lungs with each and every breath. The bears and velvet deer seemed unaffected by the cold as did the elves who did not even bother to draw their hoods over their heads. Clouds of steaming vapor rose from the animals' muzzles and tiny icicles bearded up beneath the deer's chins. Tianna shivered inside her warm clothing and drew the cloak across her nose, moderating the temperature.

Night found the expedition camped inside a small cave at the base of a forbidding rock face. A large fire at the entrance made the place nearly comfortable, in spite of the high mountain chill of night. It was clearly a well-used way station, for the cave was filled with provisions and the walls were lined with austere, but comfortable beds, complete with straw mattresses. As Charles and Tianna sat round a small wooden table with Ninius and Steffan in the warm glow of the fire, the discussion turned again to their mission.

"Tomorrow we shall reach the tracks of the line that is being constructed between Railla and Glyween," said Ninius. "And you shall at last see what it is we intend to build."

"Will we see the iron dragon?" Tianna asked, excitedly.

"No, not just yet. None of them are yet in service, but perhaps you will see something of interest on the morrow, just the same."

"It would seem to me," said Charles, apparently

deep in thought, "that this rail road of iron and steel, cutting its way through your forests, would be the last thing elves would want in their lands."

"All too true." Ninius nodded sadly. "There are many of my people who oppose this scheme. But I bear the responsibility for the well-being of all my subjects, and to some extent, an obligation to our brothers in Silvarre. There is a growing class of merchants among us and trade is becoming ever more important. Moreover, the increasing number of orc invasions requires us to be able to move large numbers of warriors over great distances, and to do so quickly."

"You have done this?" Charles leaned forward with interest. "Moved large bodies of troops on the rail road?"

"I have seen it done. The frontier post at Ritla was besieged by a band of orcs only a month ago. A train with seven carriages filled with dwarven soldiers was brought up from Railla in less than two hours, and the orcs overwhelmed."

"Is it not unusual," asked Tianna, "for elves who have ever enjoyed a reputation for maintaining a steadfast isolation, to form alliances with other races?"

"Unusual indeed," said Ninius. "But these are unusual times. Far better to draw on those resources that are available and survive, even if it means change, than stand fast clinging to the old ways and die in the process. We have chosen life over death. It is that simple."

The discussion went on long into the night, and covered the military significance of the rail road, its impact on the forest, the huge amounts of money that must be raised, clearing the necessary land, and more. By the time they adjourned to sleep, the deal was as good as done. Charles and Tianna were convinced, and they still hadn't even seen the iron dragon that they had come so far to view.

CHAPTER NINE

The Rail Road

The wake-up call came before dawn, and after a brief breakfast of bread and hot tea, the party mounted and set out once more. There were heavy clouds overhead and light snowflakes drifted in lazy circles around the silent riders. Tianna stretched uncomfortably; she was saddle-sore in spite of all the padding. The morning sun climbed above a distant mountain peak and its golden rays shone on their backs, cheering one and all.

The elves started a song, and the path grew easier as it descended from the high mountain pass. They were following a roaring mountain stream down a broad u-shaped valley and the trail was beginning to take on the appearance of a well-traveled road. On the way, they passed a party of elves leading a string of velvet deer loaded with supplies. They were the caretakers of the cave where the party had spent the previous night, and were bringing up fresh provisions for future travelers.

By noon they had left the stream and crossed onto a flat plain, surrounded by mountains on all sides. After a short time, they came across two peculiar metal lines fastened to the ground with great spikes and a ladderwork of pine slabs.

"This is it!" Ninius remarked cheerfully as he wheeled his mount around alongside Charles and Tianna. Charles dismounted and knelt on the ground studying the construction. Tianna was a little disappointed at first. She had expected more. She stared down the track in both directions and took note of its form. This strange pathway did not bow to the vagaries of the land, paid no heed to deep ravines or standing trees, but forged on, straight as an arrow, in a way quite contrary to nature. She could see several bridges that had been built over low places and trees chopped level to accommodate the unrelenting path of the metal road.

Near the rails there were several sturdily fenced areas, and Ninius bade them all bring their mounts inside. Soon the animals, bears and deer alike, were tethered securely inside the compound. Tianna could not help but wonder why such precautions were being taken. The answer was not long in coming.

In the distance she heard a long, low, musical sound, much like the tones made by the long trumpets used on special occasions at the castle. Everyone was pointing excitedly to the south and the animals grunted, snorted, and stomped restlessly. In the distance, down the track, she could make out black smoke billowing into the air, as though some giant blacksmith was stoking his forge. A thrill ran up her spine and she ran to her father's side.

Ninius and Steffan stood nearby. All eyes were fixed on the approaching cloud of smoke.

"That was its whistle," Ninius commented calmly. "An operator can signal his arrival from great distances, and it is also useful for clearing animals from the tracks."

"I should say so!" Tianna exclaimed excitedly. "Is that an iron dragon?"

Ninius squinted into the distance. "I think not. As I have said, the iron dragon is not yet in regular service. This train appears to be pulled by what the dwarves call a 'Sardar,' named after the pompous village rulers of Janoshal. It burns wood or coal and has no dragon to power it."

Now Tianna could see the source of the smoke, a huge iron machine, and it was pulling a string of strange looking carriages behind it. Her heart was in her throat, and she trembled with excitement, holding her father's hand tightly. The ground beneath her feet began to rumble and shake as the monstrous metal thing came closer and closer, belching great black clouds of smoke and hissing white clouds of steam out its sides. She jumped as the Sardar's whistle sounded once again, much louder than before.

The massive device chuffed, clanked, thundered, and wheezed to a majestic stop in front of the royal party. Tianna was astonished to see a familiar bearded face smiling at her from inside the machine. It was Orrik IronFist! The dwarf climbed through a door and slid easily down a ladder attached to the side of the immense smoking, hissing machine. He strode quickly forward and greeted the royal personages. While

greetings were being exchanged, Tianna noticed
the carriages that had been pulled along behind
this "Sardar" thing. In each one stood two
dwarves in chainmail, armed with a battleaxe
and shield. Tianna was amazed. It was one thing
to talk about the rail road and see pictures of it
on paper. It was quite another to actually see,
and feel, and experience its power. Now she
understood the need for those sturdy steel rails
fixed to the ground. Steffan shook her from her
thoughts.

"Come, it's time to climb aboard." He took her
by the arm and led her to the carriage farthest
from the Sardar. Two elves brought along her
bags and tossed them up to the dwarves inside.
Charles and Ninius had preceded them and
were already seated on low, wooden benches at
the end of the carriage. She watched as the other
carriages were filled with most of the elves who
had accompanied them. Others would remain at
the compound with the animals.

"Well, you're about to take your first train
ride," Ninius said with a smile. "I hope you shall
enjoy it."

"I already am," Tianna answered, her eyes
shining with childlike anticipation.

"Better hold on to the side," he warned. She
took his advice and clutched the wooden arm
rest tightly. Tianna jumped again as the whistle
sounded two short blasts. The noise was disconcerting. The whistle that had sounded so
melodious from a distance was overpowering up
close. The Sardar made several loud clanking
noises; she heard a series of short crashing

sounds, then the carriage jerked suddenly forward. Soon, they were rolling down the track at what seemed to be an alarming rate of speed!

Tianna thrilled to the feeling of power and smooth motion as they rolled along at a speed three times that of a horse's gallop and far, far more comfortable. It was the most thrilling means of travel she had ever experienced. Her eyes met those of Steffan's and in his eyes, she read the same excitement that she was feeling. Their shared exhilaration was as intimate as a lover's kiss.

Tianna broke from Steffan's gaze and turned to Ninius. She yelled above the roar of the train. "How far do we have to go? How long will it take?"

The elf king laughed and leaned toward her. "A very long time at this rate. At the moment we're going the wrong way!" he confided.

"What?" Tianna exclaimed.

"Don't worry," he replied cheerfully. Even as he spoke, the tone of the Sardar changed and they began to slow down. "We're about to turn around." He pointed ahead, and Tianna saw the track separate and branch mysteriously off in two directions. "It's called a wye," Ninius continued. "It is a means for turning a train completely around. It is best that the engine always be at the front."

"Like keeping the cart behind the horse?" commented Charles, who was taking everything in with great interest.

"Exactly."

The train came to a stop and a dense cloud of

smoke drifted over them. Tianna blinked and coughed.

"The dwarves have also made closed carriages, with glass panes over the windows to keep out the smoke," Ninius said, anticipating the complaints. "Passengers will not always have to endure smoke and rain. This, however, is but a construction train, not really meant to convey passengers. It is all the dwarves had available to receive you on such short notice."

"Even so, it is quite a remarkable system of transportation," said Charles.

A dwarf had jumped out of the Sardar, walked ahead of it, and was pulling on an iron lever beside the track.

"That man is throwing the switch that will put us on the side track," explained the elf king.

The royal party from the Bright Kingdom watched with interest and the train traveled up one leg of the wye, stopped, backed down the other, and then resumed travel in the opposite direction from which they had come.

"Quite remarkable," yelled Charles above the din.

"Many things you are about to see will amaze you. You will soon understand why elves have embraced the rail road as a means of transportation."

"I think I already know."

The train rolled back across the valley, over the bridges and through the groves of trees, then slowed as it began to climb steadily around the flank of a tree-covered mountain. It passed through a short tunnel, carved laboriously out of a steep rock face, and the track leveled off once more. The whistle sounded and they slowed. They had come to a clearing beside a small river, which was traversed by a sturdy wooden trestle. They passed the gruesome remains of orc bodies, mostly skeletons and skulls, impaled on poles and then they were in the midst of a collection of small stone buildings with steep sloping timber roofs. The train stopped in front of a building that had a cobblestone platform in front of it that extended up to the track.

"This is Ritla," explained Ninius, "the place I mentioned last night. We passed out of Glyth Gamel in that tunnel, and are now in the dwarven kingdom of Rakhatz."

Several elves disembarked and two dwarves rolled a wheeled cart piled high with burlap bags, alongside. In a moment the bags were loaded, the whistle sounded, and once more they were on their way. Soon the train was climbing ever higher, and cutting its way through a series of low hills.

Tianna was a little perplexed and turned to Ninius. "Why has this workshop for the iron dragon been placed at such a great distance from Elven Home? Would it not have been more convenient to have it closer?"

"More convenient, yes. Safer, no," Ninius replied.

"Is there danger then?" Tianna asked, wondering why they had not been advised of the fact and wondering, despite her liking for Steffan and the elves, whether or not this might be a trap. After all, with Tyndal gone, she and her father *were* the Bright Kingdom, save Kroner. Her thoughts skittered away at the very thought of the boy. She had assumed a short visit of state would be safe, since her father had proposed it himself, but now she was not so sure. How would their deaths benefit the elves? Her musings were somewhat eased by Ninius' reply.

"There is little danger now," said the elf king. "But there was much difficulty in the early days of the project. We would not have risked your royal personages then and only do so now that the threat of an unexpected incident is greatly reduced. It took us some time to learn how to deal with the dragons' temperament; how to appease them, how to train them."

"I know that the elves are able to work miracles with animals; I have seen this with my own eyes with the bears and the deer, but I do not understand how it is that you have tamed dragons and bent them to your will, much less magicked them to create this new wonder."

"We cannot take all the credit for ourselves," said Ninius. "Initially, it was our rapport with the dragons that enabled us to work with them, but it was an alliance with the dwarves that allowed us to create the machine itself. As you know, dwarves are wizards with metal and all things mechanical. Give a dwarf a gear and a pulley and he can invent a machine to solve any problem! They invented the rail road engine. We just added the dragon as a source of power."

Anything more that he might have explained was cut short by what happened next. The train had slowed to a crawl, and was passing through a narrow canyon between two towering hills that were the shoulders of even greater mountains. There was a loud hallooing and dwarves, fully armed and wearing chainmail, appeared on all sides. A full contingent of elvish archers and dwarven pikemen appeared where an instant before there had only been bushes, rocks and trees. More cries of welcome rang out from all directions and raising her eyes, Tianna saw archers high above her in the branches of those fir trees still capable of growing at such great altitudes. Other cries came from still higher up the mountain where cleverly camouflaged elves detached themselves from the rocks and raised their spears and bows in salutation. Seconds later they had disappeared, once more indistinguishable from their surroundings.

"Needless to say, this place is well defended." Ninius swept his hand up and around at the guardians of the mountain enclave.

The twin rails circled around the side of the mountain on a narrow ledge with a sheer drop to the valley below on the far side. What lay beyond was completely hidden by the flank of the mountain. As the train moved effortlessly along at the slower pace, Tianna gulped as she looked down over the side. Her heart began to pound in her chest and her throat was clogged with fear. She tried to avert her gaze from the valley below, but it was impossible. She leaned to the left, away from the chilly emptiness. The wind was icy cold and plucked at her cloak with frigid fingers. As they rounded the curve, the wind filled her cloak and belled it full of air like a child's kite, tugging at her, urging her to loosen her heavy grip on the earth and fly free. And then they were past the curve and once more solid, stony earth surrounded them on both sides.

Steffan sensed her fright but he made no mention of it as he placed his arm around her shoulders to reassure her. She looked up into his handsome face, suddenly forgetting the terrifying chasm. Their eyes locked once again and she met his gaze frankly in a manner most unbecoming a princess and a commoner. For a moment, they were alone, despite the thundering of the Sardar, the clatter of the rails beneath them, and the others in the carriage. The whistle sounded, but she didn't hear it, and then the moment was gone. She felt herself being led away, but it was as in a dream, unreal, some how, in some unspoken way, they were still connected. And then Steffan turned, drawn away himself, as the carriage jerked to a halt and the link between them was severed completely.

Tianna looked about her in amazement. Before them, higher than ten humans standing one atop the other, was a great opening in the face of a mountain. Naturally formed by some feat of nature, the hollow plunged deep into the stony heart of the massive rock face. The surrounding area was filled with feverish activity as elves and dwarves rushed back and forth carrying slabs of rock and loaded them upon flat-bedded carts which stood upon other tracks of the rail roadway.

CHAPTER TEN
RedCliffe

The whistle sounded once again. The Sardar lurched and then inched its way into the mountain. Numerous fires roared nearby and great metal kettles hung above the flames, stirred by heavily muscled dwarves, their fire-darkened skin dripping with sweat as they swung long metal paddles in great sweeping circles. The entire chamber was filled with a haze of sulfurous smoke and wisps of steam trailed from the dwarves' heavily callused hands; the sweat of their brows dripping into the kettles and sizzling on contact.

The train stopped once more, very gently. Outside their windows, dwarves pounded metal with great mallets, beating upon the glowing red forms held by huge tongs over white-hot flames. Elves struggled with enormous bellows to keep the fires burning at the correct intensity, while still others fed lengths of pine to the ravenous flames, satisfying their voracious hunger. The vast cavern was a beehive of activity with all the workers rushing about at full speed, as though driven by some invisible, demonic master. Tianna understood little of what she saw. Her father, too, looked on with great interest as the elves and dwarves went about their chores.

"Amazing, isn't it?" Ninius said as he stood up in front of them. Tianna saw with displeasure that the unctuous Gaelwyth was climbing aboard their carriage. He greeted his king and the others present, rubbing his hands together in an unappealing manner, his mouth fixed in a fatuous smile; but his eyes were cold and hard.

"Welcome to RedCliffe. So glad you could come," he said smoothly, his lips remaining in their fixed smirk even while he spoke. Tianna wanted to take her kerchief and scrub the smile from his face. Her dislike surged within her although she could not have said why he caused such a reaction. He was insincere and smarmy, but so were the majority of foreign envoys. Still, there was something about Gaelwyth that set her teeth on edge and her nerves jangling. Tianna trusted her instincts; the most serious mistakes she had made in her young life had occurred on occasions when she ignored her intuition. This time she would not ignore the warning. There was something wrong about the elf and she intended to watch him closely.

"And where is this iron dragon I've heard so much about?" her father inquired.

"Further on, sire," Gaelwyth replied. "I thought first you might want to settle into your chambers and freshen up after your journeys. Tomorrow we can show you all around."

Charles glanced at Tianna, and the answer was apparent on her face. "It's not that late, and we're not that tired. Why don't you show us now."

Gaelwyth looked dubious, and conferred hurriedly with a servant who had been standing respectfully behind him. In a moment the servant scurried off and the ambassador bowed. "As you wish, majesty. A tour of the workshop, first, however, to get a larger view of the entire process, before we visit the creatures."

"Most certainly," said Charles. "Although I can't say that I can make much sense of what I'm seeing right now," echoing Tianna's own thoughts. Orrik IronFist came walking back from the front of the train, summoned by Gaelwyth's servant. He climbed aboard the royal carriage and bowed. He was to be their tour guide.

Taking their leave of Ninius, they followed the dwarf as he headed for the wall of the cavern. "First you must understand why the we placed the workshop in such an isolated position. The first step was, of course, decided by the maternal dragon herself; her nest was not far from this place. That in itself was quite unusual, for dragons of any sort are rarely found this far south. Only later did it appear that the site was suited to our own needs as well. Surface deposits of ore enable us to feed the dragonlings with a minimum of effort. We dwarves already had a small iron mine here, and were soon asked by the elves for assistance. The presence of large deposits of ore made it possible for all that came afterward. Here, we will have an unlimited amount of iron to satisfy the creatures' appetites for many years to come. This will be what you might call . . . their home base. Here they will eat their fill, stoke themselves for outgoing journeys. The carts will be loaded with enough ore to refuel them along the way and supply them as they travel the continent."

They had arrived at the face of the wall and Tianna watched as long lines of begrimed dwarves hammered and chiseled their way into the stone. They were following an obvious reddish brown layer of rock, prizing it from the surrounding stone in layered slabs which a never-ending line of elves loaded into wicker baskets slung over the backs of sturdy mules. Once loaded, the large-eyed, gentle beasts were led away toward the flat-bed carts. These in turn rolled down the rails with a rumbling clatter when filled to capacity, disappearing into the flame-lit interior of the cavern.

"And what of the smithies and stirrers," Tianna asked, far more curious about their tasks than the self-explanatory actions of the miners.

IronFist led them away from the miners who scarcely bothered to lift their eyes from the rock and notice the visitors, totally absorbed with their own enterprise. The party approached one of the dwarves who, metal paddle gripped firmly in his horny, thickly callused hands, stared into the pot, watching the smooth, incandescent flow of the contents. Smoky-gray in color, the fiery mixture circled the pot like a whirlpool, slipping around the sides of the kettle in a silky circle, hissing as it lapped the higher, cooler edges. A filmy froth bubbled atop the mixture, all the colors of the rainbow reflected in the fragile domes as they emerged from the molten mixture, grew larger, popped and were reabsorbed again.

Orrik greeted the dwarf politely, but so intent was the worker on his task, that he barely grunted in reply. He barked out an order to his elven assistant who pumped the bellows ever more strenuously, the strain of the exertion obvious upon his delicate features. The dwarf leaned into his paddle, stirring faster and faster and as the coals burned a bright, white-gold, the pot hissed and seethed as the mixture rose higher and higher, bubbling and foaming furiously. Suddenly, the mixture turned from gray to a pure, silvery white.

The dwarf gave a sharp cry and the elf leaped back, his arms hanging from his shoulders like deadweights, his chest heaving with great, sobbing breaths. The dwarf pulled his paddle from the pot and dropped it without a second glance. It fell to the ground with a clanging rattle and bright droplets of liquid metal showered down, sizzling as they struck the cooler earth. A single drop landed on the edge of Tianna's boot, and thick and tough as the leather was, she could feel the extreme heat as the tiny droplet ate its way through the gathered layers and passed through to the ground without touching flesh.

Her eyes lifted from the little singed hole and met those of Gaelwyth; for an instant, before he began to mouth his concerns for her safety, she read disappointment. She brushed him aside curtly and turned back to watch as the dwarf seized the lip of the pot with a pair of outsized tongs and tipped it sideways to allow the boiling metal to flow out into a waiting mold. Four molds were filled and the pot emptied before the dwarf ceased his efforts and then he too allowed his weary arms, the enlarged veins raised up in prominent pathways atop the corded muscles, to rest. The dwarf's large hands and thick fingers appeared misshapen as they twitched and flexed unconsciously at his sides. Finally, his massive barrel of a chest slowed its anguished intake of breath, and he wiped a hardened palm across his face and smoothed his grizzled beard. Finally, he looked around, as though he had only just become aware of their presence.

"Well done, master dwarf," Gaelwyth said, leaping into the breach. He seized the dwarf's hand and began to pump it enthusiastically. The dwarf removed his hand from the elf's grip, and for a moment, Tianna thought that he would wipe it on his pants, but he merely looked at the elf coldly, and said nothing.

"If you please, sir, can you tell us what it is that you have labored at so diligently?" Charles asked, breaking the awkward pause. With a final stony look, the dwarf allowed his attention to be drawn from elf to human king. He spoke in a gravely voice that rumbled from deep in his chest. He seemed unaccustomed to the common tongue and the words were oddly formed and wooden sounding, as he slowly shaped his reply.

" 'Tis wheels for using by the Great One, surr. Iron wheels that I have maken." He gestured toward the huge circular molds with one of his immense hands. His fingers stroked the molds which still glowed with the heat of the molten metal with all the delicacy and love that a mother might bestow upon a newborn infant. They roved gently over the surface of the great circle and the delicate yet sturdy arches that spanned the space between the central hub and the outer circumference. Each wheel was a good four feet in diameter.

"When they be cool, I will be cracken the molds and taken them free. They being the feets of the Great One, they go fast and true." The dwarf spoke with pride as he viewed his work, and then, seeming to forget his guests as though they had never really existed, he barked another order to the exhausted elf and together they turned the great pot on its side and began scraping the inner surfaces free of the clinging residue before it could harden.

They visited with other, equally taciturn dwarves as they went about their various efforts, and found that in comparison, the first dwarf had been almost talkative. But no words were really necessary; they could understand much of what they saw without interpretation. Everywhere they intruded upon the feverish activity, keeping a respectful distance from the heat of the fires and the exertions of the workers. Everywhere they looked, they saw evidence of the workers' efforts. Gleaming blue steel rails, in criss-crossed layers, towered above them on either side like walls of some strange avenue. Huge silver wheels leaned against the stone walls in descending order from great to small in countless scores. Spikes, gear wheels, nails, and a multitude of other objects whose applications were less apparent, filled cart after wheeled cart, lined up on offshoots of the main rail line. Finally, they came to the end of the tour and all eyes turned to their guide, Orrik IronFist.

"All very interesting and informative," said Charles, "but I am anxious to see this creature you dwarves call the Great One. It is time to view the iron dragon. If it is as exceptional as the miracles we have seen so far, I know we will not be disappointed."

Ninius had rejoined them and now his eyes caught those of Gaelwyth and the two looked as though they were reaching some silent decision. "All right," said Orrik, having made his own independent decision, "but I must beg you to keep your distance and speak softly."

The dwarf turned and led the way following a set of rails as they entered a slightly narrower corridor cut through the rock. "Say no disparaging word, nor make any outcry. The mechanics of the thing are settled, but there are still kinks, shall we say, in the fine tuning of the temperament. We are still discovering things that disturb the creature and we would have you safe and unharmed." They came to a huge iron gate that blocked their path. At a signal from the elf king, two burly dwarf guards saluted, put down their arms and began slowly pushing the gate to one side. It disappeared into the side of the stone wall with screeches and clanks. IronFist, who walked at the side of the elf king, took a torch from the wall and led on. The passage was dimly lit and although they met the occasional elf or dwarf traveling from the opposite direction, the corridor lacked the frenetic activity that marked the larger cavern.

The underground complex had been filled with the smell of rock dust, the resinous scent of wood smoke, and the hot stink of molten metal. The air had been filled with sharp guttural dwarven curses and the ringing blows of metal upon both rock and metal. But now, as they worked their way deeper into the dark passage, the sounds and smells changed. The air became noticeably warmer, and as Tianna sniffed curiously, it seemed to her that the air smelled like a piece of clothing left too long under a red-hot iron. It was more than that, but all that she could really liken it to. There were new sounds as well, but soft and murmuring, with none of the raucous clatter of the outer cavern.

The darkened interior brightened, flickering shadows lighted the walls like shapes in a child's shadow show. And then the corridor widened once again, and the full scene imploded on their startled senses.

CHAPTER ELEVEN

The Iron Dragon

Tianna was no coward, in her young life, she had dealt with the death of her mother, an attempted kidnapping by a rival kingdom, the attack of a rabid boar, the dreadful struggle to try to save Tyndal, and the recent onslaught of the orcs, but none of her past experiences had prepared her for the sight that now confronted her.

To give her her due, Tianna was not the only one whose heart shrank. The elf, Gaelwyth, slipped back and flattened himself against the wall of the corridor. His skin blanched whiter than a corpse and the rapid pulse of his heart visible to the naked eye. Even Charles had taken a step back, one hand pressed against his chest, the other gripping the hilt of his sword. Only the dwarf and Steffan seemed untouched by the sight of the monstrosity that stood before them, glaring at the group with baleful eyes.

"It's a magnificent sight, is it not?" IronFist asked as he led the others reluctantly forward. He spoke in calm, gentle tones, a conversational everyday voice as though he were merely discussing a handsome specimen of horseflesh. But the creature, no, the *thing* that stood before them a mere twenty feet away was anything but an everyday vision. Tianna shuddered and tried to respond to the confidence that the dwarf exhibited. She wanted to have Steffan's arms around her once more.

Surely Orrik would not be walking so close if there were any danger. Once again her thoughts leaped to treachery. What if Steffan was in with the others and this was all an elaborate plot to kill her and her father and render the Bright Kingdom rulerless? They could die here and none would be the wiser. As though sensing her thoughts, feeling her fear, Steffan moved beside her, squeezed her hand gently, and looked down at her with a warm smile. The tension and suspicion drained out of her. No. This man was no plotter, somehow she knew that he would never harm her. She raised her chin and bravely stared at the monster before her.

It was a dragon, yes, but not like any she had ever seen before. It was alive, but yet it was not. It was a machine, but it was also not a machine. Not even the drawing, detailed though it had been, had prepared her for the reality of the thing.

The head towered some twenty feet above her with jaws agape, wisps of steam escaping with every exhalation. Glimmers of light like a banked fire could be seen glowing at the back of its throat. Its eyes burned an eerie coppery orange; slotted by the narrow vertical ebony slits of the pupils. Fleshy tendrils trailed from the bottom of its jaw, waggling about like hungry feelers, testing the air for the scent of prey. These same gruesome extrusions cascaded down the crest of the spine acting as a grotesque mane. Each tendril writhed and twisted, independent of the others. Several of the hideous things twined about each other, strangling and flailing at each other with pointy tips.

The scales themselves were unlike any Tianna had ever seen. She had not seen many live dragons in her life, but she had been taught much about them, and seen pieces of dragon-skin. Most dragon scales, from the smallest fern dragons to the largest sea dragons, had scales that appeared delicate and filmy, shimmering with luminescent colors despite the fact that they were often stronger than the finest human armor. But these scales made no pretense of beauty. They were thick and heavy looking as though hewn out of rock. They overlapped each other in rows like slate shingles on a roof and were every bit as thick. No arrow, no spear, no projectile of any sort would penetrate that living armor.

Slate shingles split from a block of stone shared a likeness of color, either blue or black, but always the same color. These scales appeared to have been excavated from a number of different sites for some were ochre in color, while others were stained a malevolent rusty orange, as though they had been brushed by acid. Still others were blackish red, like old, dried blood, and some were a sickly sulfurous yellow. Scales were like fingernails or claws and were formed by living tissue, but it was hard to

imagine that these vilely colored slabs had ever
been alive; far more likely that they had been
mined from some evil pit far below the surface
of the earth.

The head and neck were covered by a broad,
circular, flanged plate which in turn merged with
a powerful chest, but, as she dared to examine
the creature more closely, Tianna could see that
here the resemblance to any other living creature ceased abruptly. Where one would normally
expect to see wings there were huge iron wheels
like the very largest that she had watched the
dwarf pour from the boiling pot. Great thighs
extended from the body of the monster and
where the lower limbs should have been, there
was a connection with the immense wheels.
There were no screws, no nuts, no bolts, no
mechanical couplings but a seamless fusing
between living creature and the axle.

Emerging from the nostrils were two great
flexible pipes that wound back under its body.
On top of its head were two smoking chimneys,
much like the one at the front of the Sardar, but
these chimneys seemed to be part dragon and
part machine. Monster and machine had indeed
been merged.

While she was still staring in amazement, her
father moved toward the dragon. "It's true! Just
like you said!" he exclaimed, wonder and excitement in his voice. "Never would I have dreamed
to see such a thing!" He reached out to touch the
side of the monstrosity.

"Please, sire!" Steffan leaped forward in alarm
and gripped the king's arm, normally a forbidden

action, and drew Charles back a number of paces. Suddenly aware of the visitors, the thing stirred, its great head swung in their direction and stared down at them with evil burning eyes. The firelight within the throat fanned higher and the scales on neck and head flushed a deep, dark red.

Orrik interposed himself between the party and the dragon. "If you please, sire, do not place yourself in harm's way. The creature has been modified to meet our needs but it is still a wild thing and we cannot always control its actions!" The dwarf spoke calmly and quietly while Steffan escorted the king to safety, but it was obvious that he was alarmed. As the king was removed from its reach, the dragon began to huff and chuff deep in its chest, a glottal growl that reverberated throughout the cavern sending a vibration up through the soles of the feet. A number of elves and dwarves came running, alerted by the sound of voices and the dragon's ominous rumblings.

Instantly, the new arrivals set about calming the great creature, shoveling huge scoops of raw ore directly into its open hissing mouth as fast as arms and hands could work. Mounds of pure iron ingots were placed on the ground in front of the monster and these it deigned to nibble as though they were tasty tidbits. At last the dragon was appeased, and it seemed to forget that it had been cheated of a royal treat. A satisfied, contented rumbling emanated from the monster machine and it closed its eyes and rested its hideous head upon its breast, seemingly in slumber. Only then did the small party dare to relax.

A dwarf hurried over to them, eyes sparking behind thick smudged glasses; hands aflap in displeasure. "What on earth were you thinking of!" he demanded, not noticing or not caring that three of those who stood before him were of royal status. "IronFist, you should know better. Do you not have a liking for your lives? If you wish to take leave of this good earth, please do so elsewhere, I do not care to have your blood on my hands!" He muttered as he turned and strode off without allowing them a word in their own defense. "Fools! Dunderheads! Imbeciles!"

"The Master of the Dragons," Orrik said somewhat sheepishly. "This has been his baby from the beginning. The elves provided him with the raw materials, a clutch of young hatchlings, and he has overseen the entire program from that point on. He does not like anything that disturbs his charges. I should have sent word that we were here and asked him to give us a tour. Let us see if he will so honor us or if he will choose to remain angered. It is his domain and we will have to abide by his wishes."

Keeping close to the walls and remaining out of the dragon's view, they made their way toward the dwarf who was now seated in a large chair behind a table angrily sifting through a mountain of papers by lantern light. His face was set in a fierce scowl. Tianna did not think much of their chances. The dwarf appeared to be an unpleasant, cantankerous old grump and she could not imagine that Orrik IronFist would succeed in talking him out of his mood. But in this she was wrong. Within a short period of time, and with the passing of a generous plug of tobac, the dwarf was all atwinkle, his face wreathed in a gracious smile.

Orrik and the Dragon Master, his hand extended in welcome, came walking back to the group.

"Ragnor RockJaw, your obedient servant, your majesties. Old IronFist had ought to tell me when he brings important visitors." Introductions were made and the dwarf, unskilled as were all of his kind in conversational pleasantries or subtleties, did his best to express his pleasure at their visit and managed to stumble through an apology for his earlier harsh words.

"No apologies needed, good sir," said Charles, as he shook the dwarf's extended hand. "It was my ignorance that caused the incident and if you will be so good as to share your knowledge and expertise and educate us as to the ways of these marvelous creatures we will do our best to mend *our* ways."

The dwarf blossomed under the king's extravagant praises; his chest expanded and his ruddy face glowed with pleasure. " 'Twill be my honor, sire," he responded with a deep, sweeping bow. And taking Charles' words to heart he immediately set off at a brisk pace, tossing out a bewildering torrent of facts and figures that they did their best to absorb.

"The big one back there, him who tried to take a bite out of you . . . name's Fire King, our oldest model. Powerful but tetchy, can't always know what he'll do, if you get my meaning. Don't always take to ore, him seems to want a bit of red meat now and then. 'Twon't do of course, can't have him nibbling on the work crew, it's hard to replace them."

"I would imagine that it's not good for morale either." The king chuckled, smiling.

"You could say that, majesty."

An understatement if Tianna had ever heard one.

Ragnor RockJaw led the tour group farther down the cavernous room and continued, "So we worked at it a bit longer, refined our design. The newer models be a bit more obedient like. These here, they be our newest hatching." He waved toward a large box some ten feet by ten feet square filled with a mixture of gravel and iron nuggets. "Grow fast they do, we'll be starting to work with them in a fortnight."

Snuggled down into numerous depressions were nine small dragonlings. Tianna had had limited experience with dragons and had never, until that day had the opportunity to study one close up. It was general knowledge that, if a dragon got close enough for you to examine, it was unlikely that you would be around to relate the tale. Dragons were feared and respected throughout the New World, and fortunately, they lived mostly in the Northern Wastes, far from the Bright Kingdom.

To her utter amazement, Tianna found herself smiling indulgently at the tiny creatures. Her fingers actually twitched with the desire to pick one up. What was wrong with her! And yet, she snuck a quick look at her father and noticed that a fatherly grin had crossed his face. One had to admit that they were enchanting. Each of the dragonlings was round and roly poly, so very chubby that they could only wallow about in their nests. It appeared that their eyes had only just opened; these were a pale opaque shade of blue, completely devoid of the sinister evilness of their older relative. Of peculiar note was a large square indentation at the very top of their backs.

Three of the infants were sleeping but the remainder were awake and occupied with clumsy, uncoordinated activities. One, a mottled red and brown, was practically turning somersaults attempting to catch its own tail. Another, a solid black with russet overtones, was gumming a large chunk of ore which it could not quite fit inside its mouth. Nudged just a bit too hard, the choice tidbit rolled down the slope, out of the reach of the dragonling who stared after it with saddened eyes. Surprising everyone, the tiny creature opened its mouth wide and uttered a heartbroken wail of despair. Instantly, an elf clambered up over the edge of the nest box and hurried over to comfort the little creature.

"There, there, little one. I'm back with your bottle, don't you be crying dragon tears, you'll set your scales to rusting!" Crooning soft words he settled himself crosslegged beside the little dragon and offered a large bottle filled with an unpleasant-looking rusty brown fluid. The dragonling immediately left off its wailing and fastened onto the bottle uttering soft little squeals of pleasure around the nipple. Sensing food, the other dragonlings, even those who seconds before had been sound asleep, set up a great screeching, tiny heads flung back, crying as though they were all starving to death.

Another dwarf trundled up, huffing and puffing with exertion, pushing an awkward cart over the rough stone floor, causing the contents to rattle and clank against one another.

"Step aside, folks! Coming, coming!" he cried, frantically looking about him in all directions. "Where be they?" he shouted in despair. "I can't feed them all myself! Where be they?"

"Here!" his gaze fell upon the visitors. "Ragnor, you'n yer people will be havin' to help! I just can't do it all myself!" The dwarf thrust bottles at them and when they stood looking at him with wide, puzzled eyes, he waved them toward the nest with cries of impatience. "Hurry up now, get to it or they'll set the big one's off and we don't want that!"

There was nothing to do other than follow his urgings and climb into the nest box. Tianna had not even taken a step before one of the little dragons reached out and seized hold of her boot with a grip that stopped her in her tracks.

Just as good a spot as any, she thought and sat down roughly between two of the dragonlings. She thrust a bottle at the jaws which were holding her boot fast, sucking hard on the leather. She could feel a trickle of heat coursing down her leg. The dragon let go of the boot and snapped fast on the heavy leather nipple.

The other dragonling left off its squalling, its

long, snaky neck coursing the air, sniffing out its own bottle. Not wanting any other portion of her body or clothes to be grabbed, Tianna jammed the second bottle into its mouth. Instantly it began to suckle. Only then did she notice that a large circle of leather was totally gone from her boot! The dragon had either eaten it or dissolved it with its saliva. A chilling thought. It could just as easily have been her leg. She cursed silently, now both of her fine leather boots were ruined. This place was certainly hard on her footwear . . . she was lucky she still had both feet!

All around her the others were settling themselves on the gravel and extending bottles to the wailing infants. A great calm settled over the area and soon all that could be heard was the slurping, gulping, sloshing, as the large bottles were drained of their contents.

No sooner were the bottles emptied than the infants sunk down into their individual depressions and began a sonorous murmuring with eyelids drooping.

"Look, you," the elven attendant called softly. "Stroke their necks and throats thusly until they expel the air they swallowed, else they'll get tummic aches." He demonstrated the technique, stroking the short neck of his dragonling with a firm yet delicate stroke upward from the very base of the neck to the end of the long jaws. After a dozen or so such strokes, the dragon emitted a great, deep, belly belch and a puff of reddish vapor emerged from the tiny mouth. The elf patted the infant on its scaly head. It sighed and curling itself in a ball, fell into an even deeper slumber.

They were amazingly warm to the touch, and the skin, even on these infants, actually felt as hard as a piece of iron. One of Tianna's charges was annoyed at being disturbed and snapped irritably, but knowing what human infants with colic were like, she persisted until a large, moist, red bubble burst from the dragon's mouth showering her with a gritty residue. Startled, she found herself laughing along with the others as she wiped her face clean with an oversized kerchief offered by the elven dragon keeper. The kerchief was stained in numerous places, leading her to conclude that the spraying was a normal occurrence.

One by one as quietly as possible, they removed themselves from the nesting box. "They shouldn't wake up, leastways I don't think so, but 'tis best to be careful rather than sorry. Can be a miserable affair onc't they wake up before their nap be done, all cranky-like and snappy and screechin' like all get out. I thank ye for your kind assistance," the keeper said looking down at his sleeping charges. He was as puffed with pride as any mother surveying her children, all fed, neatly scrubbed and bedded down for the night.

"It was a pleasure," Tianna replied, and she found to her surprise that she meant it. She turned to Ragnor. "What was it we were feeding them? What was in those bottles?"

"Crushed iron ore, high content, diluted with water and a dose a minerals for good measure," the dwarf replied. "The young'ns are in a high growth stage now. It comes on 'em now and then and we have to feed 'em often. Soon, they'll be too big to fit in one box and Arf and me, we'll have to separate 'em. But for now, they like being together. They're all from the same clutch."

Arf, the assistant dragon keeper thanked them once again for their help and then loaded the empty bottles with the shredded ruins of their nipples clinging to them and trundled away with the cart.

"I do not understand what it is that I have been seeing," the king said in a more serious tone. "I've been told that iron dragons are a combination of animal and machine but I see no machine, only an oddly shaped dragon. Part of its body appears to be missing." He turned cursious eyes to the dwarf dragon master.

" 'Tis not really missing, sire, although I do admit that it appears so. The alterations that have been made to the creature's design cannot be seen. The parts are still there, it's just that they aren't as big as they used to be."

He pointed at the peculiar square indentation in the center of the dragon's back. "That is where the driver's cab and all external fittings will go, but as those parts of the machine are made of wood and metal there is no way that they can be attached at this young age, for the creature will soon outgrow the fittings and they would have to be replaced. Instead, we wait until the beasts have put on some size before we fit them, and even then, only with a light framework."

"But what about their poor little feet," Tianna asked, referring to the fact that the limbs only extended so far as the knee joint before ending abruptly in a sharp tapered point. "How do they get around? It seems so cruel!"

"They cannot miss what they have never had," Ragnor answered brusquely. "They get along just fine without them at this age and by the time they are ready to leave the nest, we fit them with a sort of . . . training wheels." To illustrate, he walked over to a set of wooden cabinets by the wall and opened the door. With a grunt, he pulled out what looked like a miniature version of the underside of Fire King, complete with wheels, cylinders, pipes and other gear she did not understand. It rolled easily across the floor. On it she could clearly see where a young dragon would be fitted.

"We change their wheels, or undercarriage, often as they grow. Fire King over there went through seven sets before reaching his full size, and the old fellow is still fattening up in the middle. We're manufacturing a new underside for him, even now."

A whistle sounded from somewhere deep within the cavern. Ragnor smiled, "Ah, that's the dinner whistle. Will your royal personages be dining amongst us workers this evening?"

"Actually I've had a special table prepared for our guests, Ragnor," said Gaelwyth, who appeared suddenly out of the shadows where he had been ensconced. "I'm sure you all must be tired after the events of the day."

Tianna realized she hadn't eaten since breakfast, back in the cave in the mountains. All this excitement had made her forget her stomach which was rumbling in a manner similar to that of the dragonlings!

CHAPTER TWELVE

Three Kings

They were led partway back down a grimy corridor filled with assorted machinery, and spare undercarriages, till they came to a small door carved out of the rock face.

"This whole place, of course, was built by the dwarves; their mining abilities are practically beyond belief," said Gaelwyth as he held the oaken door open. Ninius went through first, followed by Charles, then Tianna and Steffan. IronFist had been called away to attend to some urgent business. The elven ambassador continued his tour as they made their way along a narrow, but well lit, passageway. It soon opened up into a larger room, obviously carved at great labor out of solid rock.

Tianna could see the red/brown tinge to the stone for which RedCliffe was named. The dwarves had tunneled deep into the heart of the mountain, and a small city was concealed beneath the lofty peaks above. The royal party was split up and shown to individual quarters, "quite luxurious," Tianna thought, "for a city carved out of the bowels of the very earth."

Her room was small, but colorful and homey;

the solid stone walls were lined with elaborate tapestries of the kind made only in the Old World. She spent a few moments admiring them and the other appointments of the room before readying herself for dinner. She was still wearing her multi-layered traveling garb . . . and her ruined leather boots, of course. She went to her bags, piled on her bed by dwarven stewards, and pulled out what she hoped was an appropriate outfit for Gaelwyth's dinner.

Only minutes later as she combed her hair in the small mirror set into the wall there came a knock at the door.

It was Steffan. "I was hoping to escort you to the main hall," he said, flushing deeply. "The others are waiting." Gladly she took his arm and they made their way through a maze of narrow tunnels. He seemed to know where he was going, and after following several torch-lit passageways a great, well-lit hall, with high, vaulted ceilings opened before them. There were torches everywhere, but unlike Castle BlueFeld, to which she was accustomed, the room was not filled with smoke. She looked up and noticed the greasy clouds disappearing through numerous holes, and fresh air from the surrounding mountainsides played pleasantly upon her nostrils.

Her escort led her across the great hall, filled with heavy stone tables and benches. Hundreds of dwarves and elves, sat elbow to elbow, chattering merrily. Her spirits rose at the sight of the obvious camaraderie between the two races. With such close-knit sodality the rail road project could not help but be a success.

At the royal table, Charles and Tianna were introduced to the mayor of RedCliffe, Hammner IronFist, Orrik's brother, and another personage Charles had very much been wanting to see, the king of Rakhatz, Bagor StoneHeart the Third. An immense round dwarf, with a dense red beard that covered his chest, Bagor rose and extended his hand to Charles.

"So pleased I am to meet you and your lovely daughter, at last." His voice was deep and his broad smile warmed Tianna to him immediately. "When word came that you had arrived, I boarded a train in Railla and came immediately. In fact, we only just arrived, didn't we, Harod?" He elbowed the well-dressed dwarf who sat next to him.

"With ten minutes to spare, sire," the other dwarf, chimed cheerfully.

Charles's jaw dropped. "You mean to say you've come here all the way from Railla, in the short span of time since we arrived here?"

"Indeed," answered Bagor StoneHeart, "I myself am amazed at the miracle of this rail road. It is going to change our world!" A serious look came over the dwarf king's face. "It is my sincere hope that you will join us in this venture. Already I have committed my own personal fortune and the resources of my kingdom to this end. For it to succeed, it will be necessary to raise a fortune in gold."

Charles smiled. "The merchants of the Bright Kingdom have nothing to lose and everything to gain. I can count on their support. As for mine, you already have it."

Bagor's broad grin returned, and he offered up a toast to their success; Ninius, the elf king, eagerly joined. Servants arrived with the first course, and conversation all but ceased as everyone at the table busied themselves with doing justice to the feast. Later, Gaelwyth stood up and beat a small gong, commanding the attention of all present. He presented each of the three kings in turn to the crowd, and toasts were drunk to their health. Ninius gave a short speech about the prosperity the rail road would bring. Then Bagor stood and delivered a rousing, fist banging diatribe against orcs in general, and one orc in particular, an orc warlord named Gorathog, who was apparently responsible for the border raids against Rakhatz, Silvarre, and Glyth Gamel.

When it came Charles's turn to speak, he was at a loss for words, for he had no bombast prepared. Instead, he praised the elves and the dwarves, and what they had accomplished at RedCliffe. He concluded by saying, "The Bright Kingdom will stand with you, both in your war with the orcs, and in the construction of the great transcontinental rail road!" A wild, tumultuous cheer filled the hall, and hats of all sizes and not a few empty plates sailed into the air. The Grand Alliance had been declared at last.

CHAPTER THIRTEEN

Brooding

The chamber was dark, almost too dark to walk without holding a hand out in front of one's body to feel for unseen obstacles. But that did not seem to be a problem for the two speaking in low tones, huddled over the table in the corner. The smaller of the two passed his hand over a bowl hollowed out of stone; the water contained within, shivered and moved as though it had been stirred. It gave off a faint glow that illuminated the men's faces.

The second figure grew restive after long moments of silence. "What do you see?" he asked in a brusque voice that seemed unaccustomed to asking rather than commanding. He was silenced with a single, curt gesture. Long moments later, the second figure straightened and stared into the darkness. Finally he turned to his impatient companion.

"The Bowl of Night has shown me what to do. They have progressed further than we thought. Already, they are approaching the mountains south of Glyween. I had not expected them to have gotten so far with the hindrances we have thrown in their path."

"The mountains will suit our purposes well," the older of the two said. "The creatures of the night should be able to decimate their numbers and put an end to this project once and for all. I will give the orders and —"

"Threlgar, you do not understand. Even yet you do not comprehend what it is that we must do here. It is not my intent to destroy the project but only to slow it, to cause so much trouble that Tianna and my father will be required to take charge personally. Once they are on site, then, and only then will we unleash the hordes at our command and destroy them once and for all. If the 'unfortunate accident,' occurs far from the kingdom, no one will begin to suspect that their deaths are anything but what they appear: a tragic accident. I will become the sole heir of the Bright Kingdom and then, overcome by my grief, I will fall upon the Glyth Gamel, the cause of my father and sister's death, and eradicate the elves from the forest."

"A fine plan, sire," the older man quickly concurred. "But will the Glyth Gamel not prove to be a difficult and determined foe? The forest is their stronghold, they have lived there time out of mind. It is all but impregnable."

Kroner turned to him with burning eyes. "If I can summon the forces of nature to destroy my brother, and dispose of my sister and father do you honestly believe that a puny nation of wood dwelling elves will cause me any trouble?"

The older man averted his gaze, unable to stand up to the terrible light that smoldered within the young prince's eyes. He muttered a suitable reply, unwilling to anger the young man to whom his allegiance had long been pledged, although of late his misgivings over the young prince's actions had grown almost impossible to ignore.

He had been in BlueFeld since Kroner's fifth birthday and had watched over the prince from a distance as he grew. When he deemed it appropriate, he had apprised the young prince of his presence. Kroner had not been the least surprised, the boy had in fact been annoyed that his mentor had not presented himself sooner, even though he was, at the time, only eight years old. Threlgar was a senior mage who had been sent to the Bright Kingdom by Prince Kroner's grandfather.

In the Old World Threlgar had attended Kroner's mother. Even as she had departed the harsh world which she had detested and endured, she had given, or cursed, Threlgar had often thought, her newborn son with a special destructive ability. It was not until the boy had grown that he perceived this talent, but the evidence was clear.

It was an evil that was felt by all who had tended Kroner. The eyes that had stared out through his infant face were not the eyes of a newborn, but the eyes of an adult, smoldering with fury. No one, upon whom those awful eyes rested, was comfortable in the child's presence.

Throughout his childhood, the eyes condemned and the tongue cruelly lashed, those unfortunate enough to come into his circle. He was well-advanced of his years. No teachers could teach him; he devoured books, pamphlets, tomes on his own and bombarded his mentors with questions beyond their scope of knowledge which he then calmly answered himself. He stalked after generals and arms masters, seeking, prying, demanding that they teach him.

From the time he was four years old he wore a sword strapped to his side even though the tip of the scabbard dragged upon the ground whenever he walked. It was a comical sight, but no one dared to laugh. By the time he was six, he was fairly proficient with a short sword and often commanded soldiers to fence with him. At first, concerned about the consequences should they harm the young prince, they had treated him gently, but his fierce attacks proved time and bloody time again that it was they who were likely to be injured, not he. By the time Kroner was seven, he was as good at the forms as the best of them. Rather than earning their admiration and camaraderie, his proficiency merely won him their hatred, for they were shamed that a child of seven could best them at skills they had earned only after a lifetime of effort. Nor had it won the young prince his father's approval, for he barely noticed, and then thought the carefully planned exhibition to be nought but a clever bit of charade performed for his benefit. Charles had patted Kroner on the head, praised his efforts and gave him a new set of silver-plated bowling pins, "a more fitting occupation for one so young," and then cautioned his young son against hurting himself on the sharp blades.

Kroner had been devastated by his father's

reaction. For a time he had brooded in his room, then set about trying to win his father's love in a far more determined manner. He had done everything within his power to be the perfect son, he had even tried to make friends with Tyndal and Tianna, those adversaries who so enjoyed their father's affections without any extra efforts. All treated him in a pleasant, polite manner but always there was a distance between them, a holding back on their part as though they did not really trust him. It grated on his nerves, all the cloying niceness, the puppy dog fawning that he employed to earn their favor, but he fought back the sharp comments and biting barbs that he might have said and persevered in his campaign.

It was no one thing that happened that caused him to give up, but rather an intuition, a silent knowledge that he would always be the outsider.

Sea travel was the lifeline of the Bright Kingdom, the means whereby the nation carried out its international trade, supplying far-flung markets with both raw and finished goods. Tyndal had been in charge of this enterprise. Kroner had come to him with a new accounting system whereby the Bright Kingdom would benefit threefold over their current pricing structure. Tyndal had grown very angry and then calmed himself. Ripping Kroner's proposal in half, destroying the efforts of several months of intense work, he had carefully explained to Kroner that while enterprising, the system was also fraudulent and extortionary in nature and would earn them enemies, rather than friends.

In vain did Kroner try to explain that it did not matter what others thought, that the Bright Kingdom was the only source for those goods and that like it or not, they would have to pay the price. A look of disdain crossed Tyndal's features and without another word he took his leave of Kroner and from that moment on treated him with greatly exaggerated politeness such as one uses with strangers or those suffering a mental affliction.

Stung, Kroner, with the aid of his three mages, imaged up a great serpent which destroyed the next fleet that left the port. Kroner had not known until then the extent of his powers. So great was Tyndal's distress that Kroner allowed himself the amusement of summoning a terrible storm which also, quite sadly, engulfed the next fleet which dared to leave the kingdom. Nation-wide mourning followed and Tyndal cast troubled eyes on his younger sibling, which Kroner met with wide-eyed innocence. Sea dragons, water spouts, record storms and uncharted reefs confronted any ship which thereafter attempted to leave port. Nor were incoming ships any luckier. The Bright Kingdom was completely cut off from the rest of the world.

Kroner had been unable to stop himself, so great was his pleasure at bringing the proud Tyndal to his knees. Yet even he had not suspected the lengths to which his hatred would take him. He had known, of course, of Tyndal's plans to sail with the fleet. Trouble would dog his heels, of that there was no doubt, but even now Kroner was uncertain whether or not he had intended Tyndal's death. But once he had started the events in motion, he had been incapable of stopping.

In his innermost heart, at the darkest hour of night, sometimes he, too, grieved for his brother and wondered at the blackness of his own soul. But during the waking hours there was no doubt. He drew strength from the king's sorrow while avowing his own sadness. He had hoped, even then, that the loss of his oldest son would cause Charles to lean on his youngest. But that had not been the case. Instead he had all but ignored the younger man and withdrew inside himself, allowing only Tianna to comfort him.

Tianna seemed to recognize that Kroner should be included in what remained of the family, but even as she invited him to join them at meals or quiet moments following the funeral, he was like an afterthought with no appropriate place of his own. Charles seemed to have forgotten the fact of his existence.

Tianna seemed to pity him and he grew to hate her mollifying gestures. That she dared to pity him was like a nail in his heart.

Learning of Gaelwyth Grae's visit, and the gist of his mission, Kroner had forced his way into the king's chambers and, ignoring his own intuitive voice, asked and then demanded that Charles include him in the expedition. His pleas had been rejected without a moment's consideration.

"You are my father! I am your son!" Kroner had cried, baring his soul to his father, daring to beg for the recognition that was due him. "Do not refuse me! With Tyndal gone you need me more than ever. I can do things to make you proud of me. You'll never regret it, this I promise you. I am your rightful heir. You must recognize me as the heir apparent!"

There were other words, heated, and in the end, despairing. Charles had listened to all his young son had to say with eyes that had grown cold and hard. When Kroner's words came to a halt, leaving him empty and barren, Charles had spoken and the words fell like acid on the young man's heart.

"You are my son, Kroner, but you are not. You are of my flesh, but you are not. You are of my blood, but you are not. There is nothing of me in you. I have watched you from the day you were born and despaired. You are soulless and cruel. You are without heart or conscience. At first I hoped that I was wrong, that you could be swayed from your ways and taught all that the heir to a throne needs to know in order to one day rule with fairness and justice. But you have rejected all that I have sought to teach you, turned your heart from all that is good and embraced the ways of evil. I do not know how this came to be or why it is so, but that it is true, I do not doubt. You are my son in name and deed and you will always be cared for, but you will never take Tyndal's place and you will never be my heir. The Bright Kingdom will be Tianna's, upon my death. It will never be yours."

The words had echoed over and over in

Kroner's mind, replaying themselves endlessly until he felt them to be carved upon his soul. It was then, as he watched Charles and Tianna depart with the elves, that he had begun to plot their deaths.

CHAPTER FOURTEEN

The Assembly Line

The next morning was spent int a lengthy conference, as the three kings discussed plans and defined tasks that needed to be accomplished. Also present were Steffan, the IronFists, and several other important-looking dwarves to whom Tianna had not been introduced. Gaelwyth was in and out of the meeting, taking and delivering messages and papers. Tianna, at length, asked about all these messages coming and going and was impressed by the answer. The elves had set up an elaborate system of communication along the rail road line. At each stop along the tracks there was what they called a station master. Trained birds — crows, pigeons, and doves, mostly — carried messages tied to their legs, up and down the tracks.

Today, there was a good deal of message traffic between Railla, RedCliffe, and Glyween. As the talk turned to the sale of strange things called bonds to raise money, she became bored, even though she knew she ought to pay attention. These were important affairs of state and she was only a heartbeat away from being queen. Thankfully, a luncheon break relieved the monotony.

After the meal, urgent business called Ninius back to Glyth Gamel. Bagor, the dwarf king, suggested that the visitors from the Bright Kingdom might want to continue their tour of the facility that produced iron dragons. Charles and Tianna were eager, and soon Ragnor RockJaw appeared.

"Come along, and we can view young iron dragons in development," said the dwarf. "You only saw half the picture yesterday."

Charles, Tianna, and Steffan were led back through the chamber with the undercarriages, past the nesting pen, through yet another great hanging iron door, to a great dimly lit hall. Rails forming tracks of different widths seemed to roam all over the floor in meaningless patterns, and everywhere elf and dwarf workers were busy assembling still more undercarriages.

"Just how many iron dragons do you intend to make?" she asked.

Ragnor stopped and adjusted his glasses. "Well, let me see, I don't have the roster here with me, but we have ten working adults, not counting Fire King, who we can't really put in service." He began counting on his fingers. "Twenty in the second stage, um . . . thirty-two juveniles, and nearly forty just hatched."

"Why, that's a hundred iron dragons!" Charles exclaimed incredulously. Steffan whistled through his teeth in agreement.

"Sounds right," answered the dwarf. "And that won't nearly be enough. We expect to get close to ten thousand gold pieces for each one. If this trans-continental rail road gets built, we'll be hardpressed to keep up with the demand."

Charles shook his head. Thoughts of the costs he was about to incur began to loom dark in his mind.

The dwarf led them across the room to a clean work area where several elves were gathered around a medium-sized dragonling resting calmly on a flat cart. Four dwarves rolled a large shiny undercarriage up next to the creature, and, with the use of some ropes and pulleys suspended from the roof, managed to lift it onto the wheels. Watching as metal screws and pins fastened the polished machine to the dragon's flesh, Tianna thought it a cruel process, although she did not say so. But in all honesty, she had to admit that nothing they did seemed to cause the dragon any discomfort. If anything, it watched the process with great interest. The dragonling seemed as excited and as pleased as a child being fitted for new shoes.

Once the assembly was complete, one of the elves ran across the room and all work came to a stop. A minute later, a serious-looking dwarven mage dressed in black velvet robes carrying an odd shaped piece of twisted silver metal strode across the room with the elf following at a respectful distance.

"That's Preston, The Wise," whispered Ragnor in a soft voice. "The dragonling is about to be merged. Please keep silent."

An elf rang a bell three times, and in an instant all activity in the hall ceased and an eerie silence descended. Preston stopped and glared at the party of visitors. The warning was clearly

felt by Tianna, who was already tingling at the
power emanating from the mage. She hoped she
would have an opportunity to exchange notes
with him.

The mage turned to the dragonling and
walked slowly forward, holding the metal device
far out in front of him. The dragonling was
calmly waving its tendrils and seemingly took no
notice of the new arrival. Preston began a low
chant in a dwarvish sounding tongue and
touched the metal object to the side of the
dragonling. Immediately, the dragonling and its
undercarriage were enshrouded in a misty,
golden luminous haze. The creature's eyes
opened wide and its tendrils went still.

It was over as quickly as it had begun. The
glow faded from view and Preston marched back
across the room and disappeared from sight. The
clamor of work began once more as the hall
filled with noise. Tianna stared at the diminutive
iron dragon; it looked different. Where once the
lines separating beast and machine had been
obvious, the whole thing now appeared to be
fused as one. Iron chimneys blended into the
top of its head, and the flexible pipes that had
moments ago been bolted to its nose were now
part of its nose. The transformation was
astonishing.

Now a dwarf offered the creature some bits of
iron, and an elf poured water from a bucket into
a sort of opening near the dragon's mouth. Its
scales began to change color, and smoke started
to billow out of its twin chimneys. An elf climbed
into the small compartment that would someday

become a cabin as the dragon grew, and began to manipulate wheels and levers. The workers backed away as the new iron dragon began to huff and chuff. Steam sprayed out of its cylinders in rhythmic jets, and the dragon and its elf driver sped away down the rails laid upon the floor. It rounded a corner and came bustling back around, making a complete circle. As it passed the group of workers who had put it together, it let out an exuberant toot on its whistle. The scene reminded Tianna of a fine race horse being taken out for a trial run, anxious to be loosed, racing the wind for the joy of it.

After another rapid circle of the room, the elf in the back of the iron dragon yelled something indistinguishable. It was obvious the dwarves did not share the lighthearted enthusiasm of their charge and fretted and fumed as they unrolled a thick rope net and stretched it across the path of the oncoming dragonling. It plowed into the net, entangling and pulling the burly dwarves along behind, as they struggled to slow the newly created engine down. Eventually it was brought to a halt, and several dwarves jumped on top of it, endeavoring to hold a wriggling dragon leg in place long enough to adjust and tighten the fittings.

The dragon ignored them in a good-natured way and suddenly, playfully, butted heads with a cursing dwarf and sent him flying head over heels to land with a thump some distance away. At length the rambunctious iron dragon was brought under control and centered in the middle of the work area.

"Now they're going to fit it with a cabin, or cab as we call it," said Ragnor in explanation. "As you can see, it's a wee bit small for a dwarf right now, but when this fellow goes to his next stage, 'twill be roomy enough, even for me."

"Why do you need a cab?" Tianna asked the obvious question.

"It keeps the rain and snow off the drivers," he answered, smiling through his bushy beard. "It gets pretty cold in these mountains, you know."

The dwarves had fitted some kind of lever under the dragon's rear end, and each time they pulled on the handle, there was a clanking sound and the animal was visibly lifted up into the air. The dragon seemed bewildered and more than a little frightened about what was happening. The cab was no more than a light-weight, open framework of slender willow saplings, but as it was wedged gently under the dragonling's hind quarters, the frightened creature began to buck and twitch and fling itself back and forth. The elves circled around it on all sides attempting to calm the beast. Meanwhile, the dwarves continued installing the framework. For a moment, it seemed as though both had succeeded, but at the last instant, as the dragon settled on the wooden structure and the dwarves removed their lever, the creature flexed its back and gave a tremendous heave which sent the willow box and several dwarves tumbling backwards.

The dragon gave a terrified bleat, began chuffing again and started off down the tracks as fast as its wheels would carry it dragging several elves along by the ropes with which they had tried to control it.

"Sometimes it happens that way," the dwarf said with a sigh. "The design is not totally perfected as yet." Wisely, no one replied. "Come, let us go see an iron dragon ready for stage two; she'll be capable of running on our main lines, as she is nearly fully grown." They followed RockJaw the long distance across the great hall, passed through yet another sliding iron door, and into a chamber much like the one they had just left. Here, however, there was only one cluster of workers to be seen, and Tianna noticed the tracks on the floor were the same size as those on which she traveled to RedCliffe.

Again, dwarves were using their lever device to install a cab. The dragon being fitted was an adolescent verging on adulthood who stood quietly and proudly as her old cab was dismantled and the new one made ready to be fitted in place. "This girl is nearly full-sized, and all we need to do is install a new cabin," said Ragnor. He gestured toward the thing, which hung from a large derrick, that ran from floor to ceiling. Far from being a bare framework of willow, this cab was fully enclosed save for a number of windows and doors and was embellished with gold fretwork, handles, bells and shiny lanterns. A large number 12 was painted on the door in gold leaf. The body of the cab was painted a bright scarlet red.

"We asked her what color she preferred," said Ragnor, smiling proudly, "and this was her choice."

The cab was neatly swung round in place, and fixed onto the dragon. Dwarves and elves were all over number 12 with rags, polishing each brass fitting until it gleamed. At length, they stepped back and joined the iron dragon in admiring their handiwork. Tianna could see the gleam in the creature's eye.

A whistle sounded in the distance. "Time for a 'tea' break," commented Ragnor, with special emphasis on the word tea. "Hammner IronFist may call it tea time, for the elves around here, but we dwarves go in for a nice frothy beer."

They followed the group who had just put the finishing touches on number 12 off to a small lunch area. There were three long tables: elves sat at one with their tea and dwarves settled at another, laughing and joking, as beer steins were distributed among them. At the end of the third table sat the mage, Preston the Wise, and two older elves.

Tianna tugged at Ragnor's sleeve. "I'd like to meet Preston, if that's possible," she whispered.

"Of course, princess." RockJaw brought the royal party to the table and introductions were made. Now that he was free to address himself to pleasantries, Preston was both friendly and talkative. The elves who accompanied him were named Oakes and Ames, and were the accidental originators of the iron dragon project. Tianna begged them to tell the story.

Oakes, who was the larger of the two, did all the talking. He had silver gray hair, and deep blue eyes that met Tianna's in the same unnerving way that Steffan's always did. The elf leaned back in his chair and began.

"The dragons we raise here are unique in all the world; the result of a chance breeding between a red fire dragon and a silver dragon. You might even call them freaks of nature. There were only two eggs, one normal in appearance, the other four times larger than any we had ever seen before. The breeding was witnessed by a small band of hunters who watched from hiding as the male mounted the female. Silver dragons occasionally come here to the higher mountainous terrain for they feed upon the veins of pure silver found in these rocks. But fire dragons are seldom if ever seen this far south, for they favor the volcanic territory in the Northern Wastes. No one could explain its presence but no one could deny that he claimed the silver queen as his own. After they mated, which was a cataclysmic event you may be certain, the fire dragon departed and the queen immediately began to build her nest, which, as is the nature with all her kind, was made of stones and gravel and not a softer, kinder material.

"When the hunters deemed it safe to leave, they returned to Glyween and told of what they had observed. There was great excitement and speculation and a certain degree of fear as to what the result of this odd coupling would be. It was for that reason, the need to be aware of whatever new danger might present itself, that Ames and I were sent by Ninius and the Elven Council to keep watch over the nest. It was a tiresome wait, the eggs did not hatch for one very long year. We were fortunate that the site the dragons chose was above a dwarven iron mine, so there was companionship, food and shelter near at hand. We received full cooperation from the dwarves, as they had hopes of somehow using the silver dragon to locate veins of silver. Our vigil was not in vain — when the eggs hatched they surpassed our wildest dreams.

"The dragonlings were a dull gray, possessing neither the glossy silver sheen of their dam nor the brilliant scarlet scales of their sire. The smaller of the two dragonlings, a female, was of normal size; the other, a male, dwarfed it. It was huge, a great hulking thing unlike any we had ever seen before. Although larger than its sibling, it seemed to present no clear danger, for it was too large to even move in a coordinated manner.

"We continued to keep watch over the nestlings more from curiosity than from fear. When the dragonlings were some six weeks old, the larger male began to walk around the nest — or stumble really, for its little legs seemed almost too puny to support its great weight. But still, walk it did, months ahead of the time dragonlings normally learn to walk. It was precocious in the extreme."

It seemed to Tianna that he spoke of the dragon's accomplishments as proudly as if he himself were the parent of the creature.

"And then at eight weeks it did something even more amazing, it began to nibble on the gravel at the bottom of its nest! At first we were alarmed, for while infants will sometimes place the occasional foreign object in their mouth, the dragonling seemed to be systematically feeding on the rocks! Silver dragonlings will eat rock as well, but not until they are well over a year old and then only choice bits of silver fed to them by the queen. But this queen was not doing so; rather, she was replacing the gravel by the mouthful as it was consumed by the infant. Soon, the pattern of her days took on a wearying routine, nurse the infants, lick them clean, groom the nest of the infants' droppings and then fly away to replace the gravel. Nurse the dragonlings and then fly off to find yet more gravel to fill in what the male would consume in her absence. As the male grew, with rapid progressions, so did its appetite and the poor silver dragon was running to and fro in the attempt to keep her offspring's stomach filled. All the while attempting to feed herself as well and tend to her own needs.

"The effort to care for her young was draining and soon it became obvious that she was failing to meet the male's growing demands. It screeched and bleated constantly, wagging its head over the edge of the nest, screaming all the time she was gone, bullying and intimidating the smaller female who had just begun to take an interest in nibbling on the gravel, and feeding voraciously when the queen returned. And still it nursed, sucking the very life out of the poor queen until she was little more than skin and bones. Even her beautiful scales had lost their glossy sheen and appeared thin and brittle.

"Dragons are no friends to elves, but silver dragons offer little or no real danger as they feed

only on metal, and after keeping watch on the
queen for so long, it was hard to see her
deteriorating before our very eyes. Ragnor, here,
was one of the miners and he pointed out to us
that what we were calling gravel was actually low
grade iron ore. With his help we elves began to
assist the queen in the chore of keeping the
voracious child fed and cleaning the nest. At first
we kept our efforts to the times when she was
gone. The dragonling, who was already larger
than six elves put together, did not seem to care
who fed him so long as his appetite was satisfied.
The female was surprisingly sweet and affection-
ate and greeted our arrival with squeaks of
pleasure. We soon grew quite fond of her.

"It was for her sake as well as the queen's that
we dumped barrows full of crushed ore inside
the nest on a daily basis. The greedy male
learned quickly that our arrival meant food was
near and shoved the smaller female out of the
way as soon as he saw us coming. He was quick
to pick out the best bits of iron ore, gobbling
them down like a boar with acorns, leaving the
remains for his sister. Once we discovered this,
we distracted him with huge piles that he was
forced to scrabble through while we fed the
female choice nuggets from the far side of the
nest. So greedy was he to ferret out the tidbits in
his own pile that he never realized the deception.

"The quantities of ore needed to feed the
dragonlings became an onerous task. We soon
depleted all easily accessible surface ore and called
upon the dwarven miners for their assistance. This

began the partnership that has led to this whole complex at RedCliffe.

"When we asked Ragnor for assistance in the mining of iron ore to feed the dragonlings, he sent a crew to our aid. After viewing the situation for themselves, they brought silver for the poor queen who, despite all of our efforts to aid her, was looking more and more distressed. Indeed, one morning, we found her dead in the nest, her greedy child still attempting to suckle her poor dead body and bawling and complaining as though she had died to spite him!"

Tianna gave a little cry. Steffan reached out to clasp her hand while the elf continued his story.

"Upon that day, it was left for us to decide the fate of the infants. We had but to retreat to leave them to their fate, but so long had we fed them, and so great was our affection for the little female, it was unthinkable that we should allow them to perish. The selfish male spent not a moment grieving for his mother but worried only about his own stomach. The little female cried long and piteously and for a time refused to eat. It was then that we decided to separate the two for the male had grown so very large that we feared for the female's safety. The winter was nearly upon us and the dwarves were good enough to widen the entrance to the mine shaft and carve out a nursery wherein we might care for the two dragonlings. The dwarves fashioned separate pens of stone for them, using the wall of the mine as one side of the pen.

"The female, whom we named Ferria, recovered from her sadness and transferred all of her affection to us, receiving our ministrations with obvious appreciation. It was most gratifying. Never did she show us the least hint of violence and did as we bid her, even as she grew, following us around the cavern like a large dog and crying piteously when we left her. It was for her sake that we established a full time caretaker, and the two bonded as closely as mother and daughter.

"The male, now named Malus, was not so appreciative of our efforts on his behalf and scarcely cared whether or not we were present save to complain if we were late to feed him, which, so far as he was concerned, was all of the time. He soon took matters into his own hands by gnawing his way into the wall of the mountain, which as I have said, made up one side of his pen. At first we were aggravated, dwarves and elves alike, but soon we realized that he was aiding us, lessening our work loads, and in effect, helping to feed himself. All that was necessary was to shovel out the remains of his meals which, as his appetite and his efforts increased, soon required the full time services of round-the-clock shifts.

"Not even the dwarves could believe his enterprise, never had they seen such an avaricious tunneling machine. By some complex means the dwarves learned to communicate with the beast and after a time, they were able to control the direction of his progress, to a certain degree. Much of RedCliffe was not chiseled out by dwarven hammers, but through the controlled excavations of Malus. So, in spite of his vile temper, the dragon proved quite useful.

"We elves have no love for this beast but there is no denying the prodigious amounts of work that he has accomplished. Still, he is a dangerous and volatile beast; our control is minimal, if any, and we find ourselves in the unenviable position of having a dragon by the tail. We dare not let go for fear of what he might do, but neither can we continue to hold on."

"A remarkable story," said Charles, "but I still do not understand how it is that you have turned these creatures to your benefit. How is it that you first thought to create these machines?"

"It was not our thought at all, but that of the dwarves. It was apparent early on that the byproduct of their consumption of ore was heat. Their scales would turn bright scarlet and they would become burning hot, much as an iron bar placed on the forge will glow white hot with heat. Then, too, if they consumed water, as they always did upon completion of a meal, steam, scalding hot steam, issued from their nostrils for hours afterward and a dull glow like that of a banked fire could be seen glowing in their throats.

"Soon Orrik IronFist and many other dwarves arrived, and we learned of their rail road system. Workshops were built in the hollowed out chambers and track was laid to facilitate movement of ore and debris.

"When the young female entered her first estrus, the dwarves were anxiously waiting for the eggs, which by all accounts should have been unfertilized as she had not been with a male, and took them away to their workshop."

"Poor Ferria," cried Tianna. "How cruel to steal her eggs!"

"Do not fret, princess," replied Ragnor RockJaw. "We substituted an equal number of polished marble eggs which she happily nested upon."

Oakes continued. "Whatever Ragnor's intentions, they did not succeed, for Ferria's eggs did not hatch. Then, as the marble eggs did not hatch, Ferria soon cycled back into estrus. Once again the dwarves switched the eggs and this time they failed as well. The third time, the first of Ferria's eggs hatched, but lived only a single day. It was two full years before they succeeded and the first of our little iron dragons was born. By then the dwarves' plan was more fully thought out and now, twice a year, we are blessed with a clutch of little iron dragons. In fact, we are all but overrun with them and the last litter has been left with Ferria who is most content to suckle them for hours on end. No dragonling could ask for a more doting parent."

"And her nature?" queried Charles. "Is she not more dangerous in her motherhood, as is the nature of all shebeasts with young?"

"Far from it," answered the elf. "She regards us as her parents, her kin, and is most anxious still, for our approval. She shares her children with us willingly."

Tianna continued to look doubtful. "What do men, whether elves or dwarves, know of infants? I would not like to have my children taken away and experimented upon. And I certainly would not like having them turned into machines to serve some man's purpose!" she said hotly.

The elf did not seem the least distressed by her words. "Understandable," he said calmly. "But think upon this, princess, what man, or woman for that matter, whether human or dwarf, would have cared for two orphan dragonlings? Would have labored to feed them, clean them and their surroundings at a considerable cost of time and energy? None. You know that they would have been slain instantly or sold to wizards for potions. Nay, princess, although the end result has been that some of her offspring have indeed been used for our own purposes, none have suffered for it, certainly not Ferria, who loves us more strongly as the years go by."

Tianna, stung by his soft words, blushed deeply and busied herself with a loose thread that suddenly demanded her attention. Fortunately the whistle sounded, signaling the end of the "tea" break.

CHAPTER FIFTEEN

A Ride on the Beast

"Would you care to take a ride on number 12 and see firsthand how it all works?" asked Ragnor RockJaw. The group had returned to the great room and were making last minute adjustments to their creation. Tianna's heart raced at the thought of being aboard a real iron dragon. She was a little fearful but more excited than frightened. Her father considered the offer for a moment, glanced at Tianna and saw the excitement in her eyes before nodding his assent.

A ladder was brought forward, though the dwarves had not bothered to use one, merely scrambled up and down the creature's scaly flanks. The steps were more suited to the stride of a child or an elf, but they made do, and climbed up the dragon's gently heaving sides and stepped through small doors into the cabin. A thrill of excitement coursed through Tianna. Semi-tamed or not, a dragon was still a dragon. The cabin was crowded with the four of them, the driver, or, engineer as they called him, and his assistants.

Settling themselves along the perimeter of the cab, out of the way of the workers and the machinery, Charles, Steffan, Tianna and Ragnor clung to shiny brass handles conveniently placed on the woodwork along with a number of stout leather straps. The two dwarven assistants leaped to work at the elven engineer's command. Jumping down from the carriage they raced to the front of the dragon and began feeding it ingots of iron ore which the dragon swallowed eagerly.

"Those fellows are known as fire men," said their guide. "In the old style engines, they would stoke the fire with wood or coal. On an iron dragon, their job is somewhat different."

Slab after slab disappeared down the dragon's great gullet until the pile was completely gone. As she ate, an amazing transformation came over the creature. Her scales, which had been a dead dull black, began to change color as she consumed her meal, taking on a reddish brown hue which became brighter and brighter as the dragon fed. By the time the pile of ingots was entirely gone and the fire men were shoveling in the remaining crumbles of rust, the dragon's scales were a glossy, gleaming scarlet that all but matched the shiny carriage. It was a startling transformation. Next, the fire men pulled a long black pipe down from the roof of the cavern by means of ropes and pulleys and lowered it to the great head. Water began pouring out of the pipe and into the beast. Tianna leaned out the window for a better view. The dragon's tongue, a slender ribbon of glossy blue black, flickered out of her mouth as she set about taking in huge draughts of the crystal clear water. Instantly, the scales began to give off tiny wisps of steam which curled into the air creating a shimmering, vaporous curtain which veiled the creature in a rainbow of colors.

As the great creature took its fill of the water, it seemed to Tianna that she could feel a build-up of power beneath her feet. She clung ever more tightly to the handles and hand-straps. Ragnor RockJaw caught her eye and nodded in approval. "'Twould be best to hang on tightly now," he advised, shouting to be heard, for a curious chuffing sound had begun and the rows of metal fittings had begun to vibrate in a steady throbbing pattern.

The pipe was secured and the fire men scrambled aboard. The elven engineer, pulled on a lever and twisted a valve. He yanked on a cord and the whistle sounded. The great dragon-machine huffed and puffed and began to move, slowly backing across the cavern until it came to a stop on a curious circular wheel set flush with the floor. Tianna could see tracks emanating from this wheel in all directions. The fire men again hopped down, grabbed hold of a huge timber jutting from the wheel, and began to push. The iron dragon spun on its axis until it was pointed in the opposite direction. In the distance one of the huge iron doors squeaked open, and beyond that, Tianna could see a circle of daylight gleaming in the circular bore. The two dwarves were back in the cab now, and the engine had begun to move forward at a slightly faster pace.

"Right now," Ragnor RockJaw shouted,

gesturing with a stubby, callused finger, "the iron is being converted to energy within the beast's belly. As the water is taken in, the heat meets the water and the energy is immediately converted to steam which goes directly into internal pipes which then feed the pistons, or cylinders as we call them." He leaned out the window and pointed to pairs of gleaming silver pump heads that beat back and forth near the front of the engine at a steadily increasing pace. "The cylinders are connected directly to the large wheels and are controlled by the engineer who can bleed off steam by way of openings on either side of the carriage. The speed is thus regulated by the amount of steam allowed to reach the wheels."

"It would seem as though your engineer has complete control of the beast, then," Charles shouted, his face thoughtful. "I had wondered how you could handle such a large and inherently wild beast."

No sooner had he finished speaking than the engineer gave a shout of alarm and began to pull and push a number of levers and buttons on the control panel in front of his seat. The dragon's speed had gradually increased and now they were racing along at a goodly clip, the walls of the cavern rushing past in a blur. Faces of elves and dwarves were caught in expressions of astonishment as they sped past, their cries vanishing like windswept echoes as they were left in the wake of the speeding dragon. Tianna and the others clung to the handrails as the dragon shot through the cavern workshop like a bolt from a crossbow and then hurtled out into the cold clear air of the mountain peaks. Gangs of dwarves who were working on the rails with picks and sledgehammers leaped aside as the dragon came barreling out of the mouth of the cavern, their cries of alarm and shouts of anger whipped away by the wind of their passage. Up ahead an elf threw a switch and then waved at them as they steamed rapidly past him.

Then they were coursing down the mountain so swiftly that the frigid air brought tears to Tianna's eyes. Yet she dared not close them entirely; terrified as she was at what she could see, she was even more frightened of not seeing anything at all. Her stomach was doing flip flops and the speed at which they were traveling seemed to grow rather than diminish as they plummeted down the mountain, the trees and stony outcrops rushing by in a blur of colors.

They were being jolted violently from side to side as they careened downward, nothing like yesterday's sedate trip behind the Sardar. Tianna began to wonder if the wheels would hold their grip on the rails. What was to prevent them from flying off on one of the many sharp curves? Just then, she felt hands close over her own and Steffan stood beside her, wedging her into a corner and creating the semblance of safety with the very bulk of his muscular body. At that moment, the dragon flung back its massive head and trumpeted loud and long in its own voice, as well as with the whistle, into the frigid air, the primitive call exultant as well as challenging. Then and only then did it begin to slow, its wheels grabbing the rails, throwing up arcing cascades of sparks that flew past the windows like wind-driven showers. The engineer, and his dwarven assistants who moments before had been paralyzed with fear, went into action, tugging all manner of levers and pulleys. Either by their efforts or the dragon's own decision, their speed was soon reduced to scarcely faster than a horse could gallop.

Slowly, seemingly with great reluctance, Steffan separated himself from Tianna and she felt a great sadness as he left her, removing himself to a more appropriate distance. The air around her cooled, pointing up the loss of intimacy, and she found herself wishing that they were still plunging down the mountain out of control and Steffan beside her still.

The elven engineer apologized to his royal guests for the all too exciting ride.

They stopped at a small side track, pulled onto another circular device and iron dragon number 12 was turned around and pointed back in the direction from which it had come. The return trip was quite uneventful. The dragon having worked off her excess energy seemed content to wend her way back up the mountain at a leisurely pace.

Now, traveling without the fear of imminent death hanging over them, there was time to appreciate the splendors of the scenery which surrounded them, tall, fragrant trees perfumed the air with their crisp green scent, the mountain rose majestic and stark on their left, while broad vistas of the valleys and forests below were presented on the right. Beautiful as it appeared, it was still somewhat frightening to Tianna that the mountain fell away sharply on the right, sometimes with seemingly nothing between them and the sheer drop. Shivers ran up Tianna's spine as she realized how easily they could have plunged over the edge during the dragon's wild flight. Tianna gripped her father's arm tightly. He looked down at her and smiled reassuringly, no doubt aware of her thoughts. She returned his smile and it seemed to her that her father's face wore another look as well, a somewhat saddened and resigned expression. She cocked her head to one side and stared at him, wondering what could have given him cause for such sorrow.

All too soon, the new engine climbed to the summit of the pass and they were returning to the point of their departure. As they rounded the final bend, they were confronted by the sight of hundreds of dwarves and elves cascading out of the mouth of the cavern and running pell mell down the tracks, their faces masks of fear. The engineer pulled on a lever and brought his charge to a halt. Gaelwyth suddenly appeared at the side of the carriage, running alongside and panting out the words, "Stop! Go no further! Go back! The whole thing's going to blow up!"

The engineer seemed uncertain as to what to do, Gaelwyth was in no way one who could give an engineer orders. But the sight of another group of dwarves and elves, these carrying the precious hatchlings in their arms startled them all.

"Take her back!" exclaimed Ragnor. The

engineer pulled down on a lever which caused
the iron dragon to release a great cloud of steam.
He sounded the whistle and then the huge
wheels began to turn in reverse. Slowly, the
powerful dragon-machine backed away from the
opening until the bulk of the mountain separated it from the unknown danger.

The dwarves leaped forward as soon as the
iron dragon came to a complete halt and
inserted chocks in front of and behind the
wheels, driving them into the ground with long
metal spikes to prevent the dragon from leaving
should the desire take her. Tianna found it
difficult to believe that mere chocks could stop
the enormous monster, but it would, perhaps,
slow her down until other, more forceful steps
were taken. At present, however, the dragon
seemed quite content to remain as she was,
gently chuffing out little clouds of steam and
browsing on a pile of crushed ore which the fire
men had provided.

Gaelwyth caught up with them and steadied
himself against the carriage, leaning over and
heaving great breaths.

"What's the problem here?" Ragnor demanded,
as they piled out of the cab. All of them hung on
the elf's answer, save the engineer and his
assistants who had run off as soon as their charge
was seen to and were now gaining their own
answers from several excited dwarves.

"Big rogue male, a breeder . . . broke his
chains, devouring the stores of pure ore . . .
sucked a water barrel dry . . . turned bright
scarlet . . . going to blow! Too close," he said

looking about with a wild, terrified expression. "Got to get away! We're all too close. We're going to die!"

"Which one is it?" the dwarf demanded.

"Malus!" the ambassador blurted breathlessly.

Ragnor's lip curled with disdain and he did not bother to answer the elf who, having delivered his message, ran off down the tracks without bothering to see if any were following him. "Come on," Ragnor cried. "There may be hope yet, but I'll need help." The dragon master was sprinting up the tracks as fast as his stocky legs could carry him.

Tianna grabbed for Steffan's hand, disbelief and alarm written on her face. Steffan looked back at her and cried, "I must go! If he blows, he could destroy everything they've worked for! The rail road project would be ruined, and the hopes of the elven homelands with it!" His face was twisted with anguish. He squeezed Tianna's shoulder hard and then pelted off after the dwarf, his long strides quickly closing the distance between the two.

They forced their way against the mass of fleeing workers into the mouth of the tunnel, and soon they vanished amid the throng.

Charles grabbed Tianna and began to drag her away, back from the danger zone. The majority of those who had fled had taken shelter behind a spine of the mountain which would shield them from the worst of the blast. Others, perhaps fearing a fusillade of flying rock, continued down the mountain led by the cowardly Gaelwyth.

Charles and Tianna found themselves next to the engineer who had so ably mastered their own runaway dragon. Drawing Tianna firmly under his arm, Charles turned to the elf. "Tell us, good sir, what you know about all this. Is there truly danger of such great magnitude? Surely one dragon, no matter how large, cannot destroy the city and all that it contains."

"Would that it were so, sire, but such a thing is indeed possible." The elf's features were twisted with despair and ashy-white in color. This more than anything convinced Tianna that what he was saying was true, for he had acted coolly and without visible fear, even as their own iron dragon was hurtling down the mountain seemingly out of control. And Steffan had rushed back into the cavern, into the face of death without a second's thought for his own safety! Tianna's stomach twisted into a knot and fear clenched its icy fist around her heart. Steffan! She made a move as though to escape her father's grip, but even as he concentrated on the elf's words he tightened his hold on his daughter, as though reading her thoughts.

"Explain, good sir," she turned and pleaded with the elf, begging him with her eyes to tell her that it was not as he had said. "What is it that has caused him to run amok and will Ragnor be able to bring him safely under control?"

"Males of any species are often unpredictable, especially males in the heat of rutting. Malus is no exception and further, he is stubborn. He is always ravenous and demands to be fed constantly. But we cannot do so for there is no easy way to bleed off the excess energy. And now he's on the loose."

"But will they be able to stop him from blowing up?" Tianna asked again, terrified that Steffan would be killed. "Would he really blow up? Explode?"

"Indeed he would, mistress, if he manages to get himself to water. But Ragnor has some measure of control over the beast, just possibly . . ." His words dropped off and the engineer wiped his brow with his arm and raised up cautiously, peering over the edge of the rocks. Just then, a loud, frenzied howling sound filled the air, and the engineer dropped into a crouch. The throng nearby broke into rousing cheers and began slapping each other on the back.

"Well, that's over and we're all safe, for the time being, at least."

"Why, what's happened?" Tianna asked anxiously.

"That bellowing? That's him," the engineer said. "All that commotion means that they've stopped him, kept him away from the well and are herding him back to the pens. He's angry and while there's a certain amount of danger in that it's nothing compared to what might have happened had he succeeded in reaching water. Well," he said as he stood up and brushed off the seat of his pants, "I guess I'd best get myself back to number 12 and bring her in."

He turned to Charles. "Don't let this put you off iron dragons, your majesty, it really doesn't happen all that often."

CHAPTER SIXTEEN
Big Plans

The next day, Charles and Tianna were summoned by Hammner IronFist, mayor of RedCliffe. The conference of the three kings, concerning the rail road was to continue. Tianna and her father were led by a stout, red jacketed dwarf up a winding spiral stair that had been neatly carved into the heart of the mountain. She was beginning to wonder just how far it was to their destination as she struggled up the seemingly endless staircase. She could hear Charles breathing heavily behind her. They had passed numerous arched openings as they climbed, but their guide had not even given them a second glance. At last, just as Tianna thought she could go no further, the dwarf turned into one of the arched doorways and led them down a narrow corridor. He knocked on a door, and they were admitted.

Hammner's chambers were also hewn out of the mountain, but, like the staircase, the work had obviously been accomplished by dwarves and not Malus. The dragon was capable of removing great amounts of rock with a single bite, but there was no way that he could have

carved the beautiful, delicate embellishments
that adorned the room. A window had been
carved into the stone, allowing light to stream
into the interior. Leafy, sinuous vines framed the
window opening and had Tianna not known that
they were stone, she would have sworn that they
had been magically charmed. Several openings
had been carved into the ceiling as well and
sunlight streamed down, gilding the entire room
and all its contents with a rich, warm light. The
vine snaked around the room, which was not an
inconsiderable size, and curled around the pil-
lars and ornate columns that gave the
appearance of holding up the ceiling. Faceted
clumps of glistening crystals were showcased on
low tables and large stone orbs with windows
sliced into their sides invited viewers to pick
them up and view the wonders contained within;
carpets of infinitesimal crystals glittered in a
rainbow of colors, rich purples, sea green aqua-
marine and blood-red ruby. Richly colored
tapestries and brilliant carpets lent further
warmth to the room. They may have been
standing inside of a mountain, but the trappings
were as elegant and regal as any that graced
Charles's own chambers.

But there was little time for admiring the
room, for Bagor, Ninius, Gaelwyth, and all
others important to the project had already
arrived and were seated around a large stone
table, which, as with most of the furnishings, had
been hewn out of the stone and was still
attached to the floor. The surface had been
polished until Tianna could see her face in those

portions of it that weren't covered with documents. She was dismayed at the sun-burned condition of her skin and covertly tucked a wayward strand of hair behind her ear as she took her place at the table. The chairs had been constructed with dwarves in mind and she felt like a giant, towering with her father over the seated dwarves by more than a head.

Maps, such as those Gaelwyth had left in the Bright Kingdom, were spread over the tabletop and those present were so absorbed in their musings that the arrival of the Bright Kingdom contingent went all but unnoticed.

Ninius had returned from Glyth Gamel with dire news. There had been an elven uprising against advancing the rail road through the ancient forests of Elven Home. Anti-rail road elf activists had torn up strategic rails and a supply train had been waylaid and overturned. It had been ambushed on a narrow bridge that crossed a deep chasm. The iron dragon and its attendant cars had plummeted into the gorge and the bridge had been completely destroyed.

"Fortunately there was no loss of elven life," Ninius said in a somber voice. "The driver and his assistant saw the break in time, and leaped to safety. However, the iron dragon was of course killed and it was a life that many had come to care about. The engineer is taking the loss hard. Further, Carson, our field engineer, estimates the loss to have cost us over 35,000 gold pieces.

"The loss of the bridge will cost us in time as well as money. It was a difficult bit of engineering and those who tore out the rails saw to it that much of the buttressing rock face on which we built was destroyed as well. A new crossing will have to be sought and there is no assurance that it could not happen again. Guards will have to be posted." He sighed heavily. "We will have to sell another twenty bonds just to cover the loss."

"Sounds as if you had better add more guards all along the line," suggested Bagor StoneHeart. "We dwarves have been fortunate enough not to have had resistance from our own kind. The orc raids are bad enough."

"What about land sales along the route of the track?" asked Charles. The subject of land grants to the rail road companies had come up the previous day. "Could you not sell land to offset this loss?"

Ninius sighed. "Such a system might work well anywhere but in Elven Home. The Glyth Gamel consider the forest to be theirs already. We cannot sell to elves that which they already own. The only thing we would gain by selling land along the tracks is unwanted settlers from other lands . . . and that would just make things more difficult, raising the opposition to the grand scheme even more."

The discussion turned to the urgent need to raise more capital. Charles and Bagor had no problem deciding that Rakhatz and the Bright Kingdom would grant land along the track to the rail road company. Those who purchased the land could then sell, or otherwise use the land in whatever way they saw fit.

"All well and good for you," Ninius muttered, clearly disgruntled, "but having no land to grant, the cost of the Northern Division across Glyth Gamel must be borne entirely by me and the Council."

Hammner IronFist, the mayor of RedCliffe, was appointed head of the Iron Mountain Division, as the existing rail road had come to be called. It ran from Railla to the border of Glyth Gamel. An appropriate sum of gold was agreed on, and the elves would assume ownership of all track from the border into their kingdom when completed. As soon as was feasible, IronFist was to assemble a second work force in Railla and begin pushing rails south toward Risidan.

"By the time we get anywhere near Risidan, our southernmost city, we should have heard from the elves in Silvarre about the continuation of the line into their lands," Bagor remarked.

"Two of their emissaries are now with Carson and the construction site in Glyth Gamel," said Ninius. "I'm certain they'll bring back a favorable report."

At length, the discussion turned to who would manage the building of track across the Bright Kingdom. Charles turned to his daughter. "Tianna, I'd like you to take charge of the construction project; I need someone I can trust implicitly . . ."

Before he could continue, she interrupted. "As happy as I would be to do whatever you bid me, I have absolutely no knowledge of such matters and despite my good intentions, I fear that mistakes would be made." She lifted her eyes and looked at Sper Andros who sat opposite her and down two seats to her right. "Steffan, on

the other hand, is loyal, intelligent, brave, and
true, and he understands what must be done far
better than I." She almost thought she could see
him blush at her words of praise.

Steffan started to stand and respond to her
words, but Charles spoke first. "Yes, a wise
choice. I should have thought of it myself. So it
shall be." Steffan was given no choice in the
matter. "Study the maps and learn all that you
must know to lay the rail road," Charles instructed. "I shall send gold and help as soon as I
return to BlueFeld. We must build this rail road
as quickly as possible if the Bright Kingdom is to
be saved."

Steffan could do nought but nod in agreement. His eyes sought Tianna's and they stared
at each other solemnly.

"I have given the matter of funding much
thought," Charles said, rising and standing to
address the group. "It is my belief that this
project, in all its enormity, must be considered
one indivisible company, owned jointly and
equally by all stock and bond holders, despite
their various nationalities, and that we, the
builders, should be paid for our efforts with gold
and bond certificates, guaranteed by all three
governments." He smiled down at their
astonished faces, and then took his seat, believ-
ing that he had settled the prickly problem of
who owned what portion and the problems of
funding.

But no sooner had he settled himself than an
outpouring of objections rose from around the
table. Ninius and Bagor both leapt to their feet,

protesting loudly. The dwarf banged on the table with an immense fist. Even though it was solid granite and fixed to the floor, it shivered under the blow. " 'Twill not do!" he roared, his face suffused with dark blood and his temples throbbed. "We be all but finished with our rail and so be Ninius and his folk! Were we duncely enough to agree to your plan, why, we would be agreeing to pay for the honor of building your portion. NO thankee! We dwarves were na' born yesterday!" His words had taken on a thick slurring dwarven brogue with the heat of his anger, but the meaning of his words was clear to the humans. Having had his say, Bagor flung himself down in his chair and sat there fuming.

Ninius was less outspoken, but in essence, he agreed with everything his dwarven counterpart had said. "I appreciate your intention," he said diplomatically. "It is a fine idea that the three kingdoms share equally in the ownership and I am certain that Bagor agrees to this principle as well." His words were answered by a deep harrumph from the glowering dwarf. "But," he continued smoothly, "I believe that the costs of construction must fall upon the shoulders of the individual kingdoms." These words were embraced with a good deal of affirmative snorts and hearty "ayes," from Bagor and other dwarves.

"I had not thought to distress anyone with my suggestions," Charles began, clearly taken aback by the dwarf's reactions.

"Nay, Charles, you did not disturb anyone, my bearded colleague is both excitable and outspoken," Ninius said soothingly. "But surely you see the point, 'twould not be fair to structure the company thusly. The dwarves and the elves would be penalized for our forethought and industry, should we agree to your proposal as it stands. However, I do believe that the idea itself has great merit. I suggest amending it slightly. Following construction of our own rail roads, after we are all interconnected, the project will be merged upon completion into one entity. Until then, each kingdom will be responsible for the laying of the rail road and for its maintenance and safety, whatever that entails."

The amended proposal was put to the vote, and after a bit more haggling, everyone, including Bagor, put their hand to it until they formed a tall pile of hands, one placed upon the other, dwarf, elf, human, all around the table.

Details were ironed out long into the night and the final outcome committed to a length of parchment. The next morning it was signed jubilantly, by all three kings. It was further decided that each of the kings would send emissaries out to all other kingdoms in the New World in order to enlist cooperation and solicit stock and bond purchases.

The two elves from Silvarre who had been inspecting the construction site in the north had returned filled with enthusiasm and were anxious to return home to tell their tale. Over her objections, Tianna found herself dispatched to the southern elven land with Gaelwyth. Her mission was to assist the two emissaries in persuading the Southern Elven Council to join the alliance.

That afternoon, the princess stood beside her new companions and the guard who would guide and protect her once they reached the end of the tracks. As she took leave from her father, she thought back with astonishment at the speed with which everything had moved once an agreement was reached. Her mind had been set on returning to BlueFeld where she planned to contrive any number of reasons to bring herself into frequent contact with Steffan. Instead, she was being sent in the opposite direction and would not even be able to see Steffan for only the gods knew how long. Secretly, she fumed at being thwarted, but outwardly gave no hint at her inner turmoil. She listened dutifully to her father's last minute instructions, nodding agreeably to everything he said and at last he finished. They regarded each other somberly and then, surprisingly, Charles gathered Tianna to his bosom and hugged her tight. "Take care, my daughter. Never doubt that I love you."

Tianna's heart swelled and tears gathered hotly behind her eyes. It was unlike Charles to show emotion openly. He had not hugged her so since childhood. Her arms wrapped around his comforting bulk and she hugged him in return, thinking how very much she loved him. She was ashamed that she had cursed the charge he had laid upon her. She owed him so much, going to Silvarre as his representative should have been regarded as an honor, rather than a burden. She resolved to put all thought of Steffan out of her mind and do the very best she could on her father's mission.

Charles mounted the steps of the ornately decorated passenger carriage, specially built and luxuriously appointed to carry royalty, and stood holding the polished brass railing. Tianna in her sadness did not even notice the shiny blue paint that adorned the carriage, or the fancy gold inlaid trim, or the multitude of shiny brass fittings that surrounded Charles Edouard. All she could see was her father.

She waved, the whistle sounded, the carriage lurched gently forward and the train began to roll away from RedCliffe. Charles would return to BlueFeld to arrange the land grants and begin raising the necessary money, and she and her escort of elves would journey to Silvarre. A feeling of deep sadness fell upon her as her father diminished in the distance.

There had been many leave-takings in her lifetime. Why she should have been so disturbed about this parting was impossible to say, but she could not deny that she felt a feeling of heaviness gathering about her heart. She raised her hand, loathe to have Charles leave her sight, but then lowered it and watched as the train disappeared around a flank of the mountain and was gone. Her father would have thought her fears fanciful and capricious at best, foolish and silly at worst. She would not have prevented his departure, nor did she wish to be thought a fool. Still, her heart was troubled.

CHAPTER SEVENTEEN

Apprentice

Steffan stood high in a niche of the mountain face, a protective fold of rock screening him from the view of the leave-taking at the foot of the cliff. Thanks to the dwarves' clever skills, the stone had been pierced in a series of artful, natural-appearing cutouts, which allowed whomever stood in its shadows to see without being seen. He had been standing behind the screen, watching Tianna, for some time. His heart beat faster inside as she turned and scanned the face of the cliff. He took a step back before realizing that there was no way that she could see him. Nor could he have said why it was that he wished to remain invisible. He could just as easily have been down at the foot of the cliff saying farewell in person, rather than mooning about like some lovestruck adolescent.

As Tianna and her escort boarded the south-bound train and disappeared from sight, Steffan turned with a sigh and left the concealment of the aerie. As he entered the room that served as his quarters, it struck him that the problem was that he *was* behaving, and feeling, like a lovestruck adolescent. Which confused him

mightily. He had always felt a difference that
separated him from all others, no matter which
world he lived in. He was neither elf nor human,
but perhaps a combination of both, for with the
death of his real parents not even Steffan knew
the truth of his heritage. This apartness had
made it difficult for him to build relationships
with any of the women who had heretofore
attracted him. Humans were understandably
reluctant to consign their daughters to the gray
limbo that surrounded half-breeds. And while
elves had no such constraints, at least in regard
to Sper Andros who they regarded as one of
their own, all of their daughters had been
betrothed since birth and some even before
birth, as was their custom.

Elven marriages were complicated matters
involving alliances of clan, wealth and power, the
politics of far more concern than the individuals
themselves. Surprisingly, there were few failures
among such matches, matrimonial discord
among the elves of Glyth Gamel was all but
unknown.

So why was he feeling this way? Of late, every
time he caught sight of Tianna's graceful form,
he was stricken by a feeling of weakness that
seemed to invade every last corner of his body.
His tongue seemed to grow until it filled his
mouth so that words emerged in a stupid
stammer. But most of the time his tongue clove
to his palate like a dead fish, rendering him
speechless. When he was able to get words out,
they never seemed to be the words he had
intended and he was astonished that the princess

showed even the slightest interest in the doltish fool that he had become. Nor did her continued interest lessen his embarrassing behavior. He was certain that his face burned red each time she looked at him and he was ashamed that he had often arranged "chance" meetings just so that he might look upon her again.

He had memorized the graceful turn of her wrist, the sweet curve of her cheek and the way that sunlight turned her hair into a glorious reddish brown radiance that glowed with gold and bronze. He longed to run his fingers through that hair. He dreamed about her at night and, during the long tiresome talks of the past days, roused himself with great difficulty when spoken to. Tianna was all that he had really been thinking of.

He sighed and shook himself mentally. Now he must shut her out of his mind as best he could, at least temporarily. Thanks to her, he had been placed in charge of the Great Eastern Rail Road, that portion of the great transcontinental road that would cross the Bright Kingdom. He could not help but wonder whether it was a ploy to be rid of him. Perhaps that was her way of gently discouraging his interest, by tossing him the task that, at any other time in his life, he would have felt honored and grateful to receive. He sighed and wished that he understood women better.

His apprenticeship in rail roads began early the next morning. Shortly before dawn, he was awakened by a low throaty growl and a pressure gripping his foot. Steffan sat up with a start and reached instinctively for his sword, fear pounding in his chest. A deep, guttural laugh stayed his hand. A flint was struck and the lamp flooded the small stone room with a piercing light. At the foot of the bed stood a dwarf nearly as wide as he was tall with a beard that hung well below his belt — or would have, had it not been looped around the thick leather strap that encircled his considerable girth. The dwarf was beside himself, tears springing from the corners of his eyes as he congratulated himself on the fright he had given the half-elf.

Steffan, knowing something of the dwarven humor, did his best to give the dwarf as little pleasure as possible. As soon as he ascertained that he was not being attacked, he did his best to appear relaxed, rising and dressing as though being awakened in such a manner was an every day occurrence.

"Dingur Knorsen's my name," laughed the newcomer. "I wuz sent round by old king under the mountain himself, Bagor the Blowhard!" He plopped heavily down into a chair near Steffan's bed. "So you're going to build a rail road."

The half-elf dressed quickly then addressed his visitor, "Sper Andros," he said, extending his hand. "But that's my elven name. Please call me Steffan." The dwarf rose and shook his hand firmly.

"Ragnor has spoken highly of your courage." said Dingur, his eyes full of admiration. "It seems you saved RedCliffe the other day."

"It wasn't anything, really. All I did was help him get a chain around the dragon's head. Ragnor did the rest."

"All the same," the dwarf continued, "that Malus is a bad customer. What you did showed real courage."

"Or foolhardiness." Steffan grinned.

"Here, let's get off to breakfast, I'm starving. First ones down get the freshest bread and best of the tea." Dingur led the way down to the great dining hall. The dwarf, it turned out, had been assigned to Steffan, to teach him all there was to learn about the business of building rail roads.

They spent the day in the iron dragon assembly shops and Steffan's head was filled with facts and figures as the dwarf took him through the steps necessary for the creation of an iron dragon. By the end of a very long day, he could recite from beginning to end every step in the creature's transformation from dragon to machine.

That was but the first stage in his education. The next day was spent alongside an elven engineer who was to teach him how to drive and maintain the Sardar, that older class of engine that ran under its own power. At first, Steffan was given the duties of the fire man, and he spent his time at hard labor, chopping logs, feeding the fire, and on occasion, hopping down to throw a switch or uncouple carriages. His body ached, and his muscles were sore, by the time the day came that they put him in command as a driver. It was far more difficult than it appeared. Aside from the various valves, wheel, levers, and mechanisms that controlled everything from output of energy to expulsion of excess steam, he had to master the fine art of sounding the whistle and knowing when to do it.

When it was decided Steffan had become proficient with the Sardar, Dingur put him behind the driver's seat of an iron dragon with the beast's elven engineer hovering anxiously at his elbow. The wheels and levers and cranks here were more subtle, for some of them were not controls at all but devices to persuade the dragon to do the engineer's bidding. Pull on the long black lever in the Sardar and you knew it would stop. Pull the same lever in an iron dragon and you hoped it would stop. The difference was a little frightening. No matter that fully half of it was a dwarfmade machine, the remaining portion was still a living creature with personal quirks and vagaries that could not always be easily divined.

Although the engineer supposedly drove the great beast/machine it was not always clear who controlled whom . . . it was rather like having a dragon by the tail most of the time, with the engineer in charge only because the dragon allowed him the illusion. There was always a thrill of fear, a cold lurch in the belly, when one stood or sat in the cab behind the various levers and wheels that prodded the monster forward, backward and at different speeds. But in time, Steffan mastered those skills as well as anyone who had not bonded to the dragon could.

Finally, the day of his live-action test arrived. Steffan successfully coaxed an iron dragon, pulling one flatcar loaded with mail, out to the frontier outpost of Ritla. The mailbags were delivered, and the return trip was calm and uneventful.

His course in engine driving complete, Steffan packed his things and traveled with Dingur Knorsen by train to the new railhead that the dwarves were pushing south from Railla. They made the trip in a passenger carriage. It was a first for the half-elf. The ride was much more comfortable than those he had experienced earlier on the open flat car, or the wild dash down the mountain in the cab of the runaway iron dragon. The passenger carriage was filled with rows of comfortable padded leather seats. Panes of glass covered the windows, keeping out the smoke, yet allowing him to enjoy the beautiful mountain scenery.

Two hours later, after passing over incredible mountain terrain, crossing tall, spindly trestles, going through long dark tunnels and around steep, fearsome scarps, the track leveled out and they entered a broad valley, ringed by mountains on all sides and dotted here and there with low, treeless hills which were covered with a sprinkling of buildings.

"Railla, mother city of Rakhatz," said Dingur, staring wistfully out the window.

Steffan watched with disappointment as they passed through the dwarven capital. The hilly settlement seemed little more than a village, not the great city he had expected. "I thought this place was larger," he said as the stone houses rushed by.

"Aye, that it is," answered Dingur. "But tis all under ground. Full seven leagues in all directions run the hallways, chambers, and tunnels of Railla. And in some places, it goes that deep as well." His pride was obvious. "We dwarves are not overly fond of the winter snow here in the Iron Mountains, so we stay well away from it."

Their train rolled on, past the settlement and then came to a complete, wheezing stop. "Well, this is it," said the dwarf. "End of the line. Time we got to work."

This was a far more strenuous effort than the other lessons taught Steffan and the word "we," as used by the dwarf, was strictly euphymous. Steffan was the worker, Dingur was the "instructor," a role he thoroughly enjoyed. Dingur insisted that Steffan bunk in with the work crews and follow their routines, which involved sleeping in tents on the cold, hard earth, wrapped only in bearskin blankets, rising at dawn, eating a generous, if often unappetizing, breakfast and then expending more physical effort than Steffan had known was possible for one individual to endure. His back ached so terribly at the end of each twelve hour work day that he could not envision standing upright without pain ever again. His hands were soon swollen to twice their normal size and terrible blisters covered his palms and fingers which were broken and re-broken daily. His skin burned scarlet and peeled in long painful strips when exposed to the harsh, high-altitude sun. The only bright spot of the day was the fine evening meal, prepared by the cooks. A herd of cattle was kept nearby, and the work crews were served steaks, roasts, chops and stew on a regular basis. All this was washed down with either good wine from Silvarre, or a type of orcan beer that the dwarves seemed to enjoy immensely, for which Steffan had no taste at all. After supper, it was all the weary half-elf could do to struggle to his tent and topple into his sweat-stiffened bearskins to sleep the night through.

It was a rigorous routine and Dingur Knorsen seemed to derive great amusement from the discomfort of his pupil. The dwarf would join Steffan at his labors, and point out the numerous things Steffan was doing wrong.

At first Steffan was assigned to the track laying crew and the elf had to learn to shorten his strides when his gang would lift a steel rail from the handcar, carry it down the line and then drop it precisely in the right spot on the cross ties. Soon he was spiking rails, and Dingur criticized the way Steffan held his hammer as he drove the sharp bits of iron into the wood.

After a few days they moved forward to the grading crew, where hundreds of dwarves were busy carving a slice through several low hills and filling in the valleys between with the rubble. Steffan went to work with pick and shovel. Again the relentless Knorsen criticized him, this time about the manner in which his student pushed the wheelbarrow and the puny load of gravel it contained. He looked with a jaundiced eye as Steffan dumped that same gravel and then leveled it. It gave him great pleasure to remove a leather wrapped level from his pocket and, after much ceremony, place it upon the gravel and pronounce it not a level grade, urging Steffan to do better next time. Steffan learned to dread the sight of the leather wrapped packet and worked twice as hard, in order to make certain that the dwarf had no reason for complaint.

Then one afternoon, all work suddenly came to a halt, and the graders were ordered to clear away from the roadbed. Steffan and Dingur climbed up a slope and sat down between two spindly pines. "What's going on?" asked the half-elf, glad for the respite whatever the reason. Off in the distance they heard a familiar bellowing and a cloud of steam shot up from behind the next ridge.

"I heard last night," said Dingur calmly, as he took out a pipe and began to fill it with tobac, "that they're bringing old Malus up to the tunnel bore. The rock in there is hard, and the crew was only making one foot a day." He lit up and puffed a blue ball of smoke into the air.

Steffan leaned back against the tree and smiled. "Malus ought to make short work of that tunnel."

"Yep," the dwarf answered, "Provided he likes the taste o' that rock." A moment later two dwarves came round the cut pulling a bouncing cartload of iron ingots behind them on the grade. They wore worried looks as they hurried along. Soon, the ground began to shake and Steffan drew in a deep breath when he saw the familiar, malevolent face of Malus coming round the bend. The dragon was lumbering along in pursuit of the cartload of iron. Following alongside the great one came Ragnor and a crew of dwarves, holding carefully on to the chains which hung from the loop around the beast's neck. As the odd procession disappeared into the next cut, Dingur stood up in a leisurely manner.

"Well, Steffan, you have passed your trials with flying colors, and there is little more here for you to learn," he said as casually as if he was commenting on the weather. Steffan was speechless; he stared at the dwarf as Dingur began to amble down the slope. He rushed to rejoin him. Over! It had seemed that he would be consigned to the railhead forever, attempting to meet the dwarf's impossible demands!

When he caught up, Dingur continued. "As you will be building track through Glyth Gamel to reach the Bright Kingdom, you must learn some tricks I cannot teach you. So now you shall travel north and observe the elven way of building a rail road through the forests of your homeland. I will send word ahead to Carson, and tell him what you need to learn. Also, I have chosen a human field engineer named Groc, who is skilled in the building of bridges and embankments. I will send him out to get things ready. He will become part of your force when you begin work in earnest."

"Will you be coming along to Glyth Gamel?"

"Nay, I fear my services are required here. But let me just say that you have been a cooperative and ready learner. I'm confident you'll know what to do when you have to do it. As for me, I thank you for this pleasant rest away from my regular duties."

Now that Dingur Knorsen was actually making his farewells, Steffan felt a moment of deep sadness that it was over. At some point the agony of his labors had become an exhilaration of accomplishment, a feeling of pride at being part of something so important.

He looked into Dingur Knorsen's bright brown eyes, even now concealing a childlike gleam of humor, and shook the man's hand with his own, both were equally callused. Steffan allowed a hint of a smile to play across his lips as they exchanged far more than the touch of flesh.

Steffan realized that even as he had grown to dread the dwarf's every word, as he strived to surpass his expectations in order to avoid the stinging barbs or the need to tear down and redo the work from scratch, he had become a craftsman in his own right. Now, whenever he looked at a road bed, or the leveled gravel heaped upon it, or evenly spaced ties and spiked rails, he would assess the work with his own critical eye to see whether it met his exacting specifications.

No amount of reading could have given him that intimate understanding. Only the very hard, personal labor and a mentor such as Dingur Knorsen with his exasperating, annoying traits could have succeeded in turning a competent, half-elf into a superior field engineer, in record time. Steffan shook the dwarf's hand with warmth and gratitude.

Early the next morning, his bags filled with his gear, and some equipment the dwarf had given him, Steffan was able to catch a ride on a supply train running empty back to RedCliffe. Dingur Knorsen was there to see him off, and as the loud, huffy Sardar coughed and poured clouds of gray smoke into the air, the flatcar upon which he sat began to move. Steffan met the dwarf's eyes and the two smiled without speaking. Now that he had such an intimate understanding of just what went into the building of a rail road and the magic growth of an iron dragon, he could never take it for anything less than the miracle it was.

CHAPTER EIGHTEEN

The Long Thin Line

The trip to Glyth Gamel was pleasant, if cold. Steffan spent the first leg of the trip, the journey back to RedCliffe, bundled up in his cloak and bearskins to keep out the cold breezes and the light snow which began to fall soon after their departure. During the layover at RedCliffe, he was joined by Carson, the field engineer working at the northern end of the line. He was an average-sized, sunburned dwarf, with a short scraggly beard and a perpetual sad look to his face. By chance, Carson had come back on one of the supply trains, and was glad to meet his new associate.

The second leg of the excursion, the trip to the northern front, was much more comfortable than the first. Instead of riding bundled up on an open flatcar, he enjoyed the warmth and comfort of Carson's private carriage. It was richly decorated on the outside, and modified inside to be a rolling office and dining room. The two sat at a finely appointed table on padded seats, poring over the maps Carson had spread out.

"Care for some tea?" The dwarf knew the habits of elves.

"Don't mind if I do," replied Steffan. There had not been time for food or drink at RedCliffe, for the train north departed almost as soon as he had arrived. "Got any food?"

"Sure, help yourself, just round the partition there." Carson nodded his head to the front end of the car. Steffan found a perfectly outfitted, compact kitchen, complete with a cooking stove, storage shelves lined with food, cabinets filled with pots and pans, and, near the stove, a large tea urn, with a silver spigot for serving. Next to the tea urn was a huge cask of beer, strapped securely to the side of the car. Steffan smiled and filled a tin cup with warm aromatic tea, then grabbed a couple of cakes from the many that were set out on serving plates and made his way back to the table. He braced himself against the rocking motion of the carriage and while he ate, Carson spoke.

"Technically, the part of the rail road I am building will belong to the elves, so they are providing us with the money and as much labor as possible." He pointed with a stubby calloused finger to the chart. "The letter I received from Dingur informed me of the extent of your rail road education. What I intend to show you is how we go about choosing where the track will be laid and our procedures for mapping that route. So I am going to send you out with the survey party. Knorsen says he's assigned Groc to you. He'll teach you all about bridges, tunneling, and embankments." The dwarf talked on and the mountainous countryside sped by unnoticed. Almost before he knew it, the train had slowed and Carson peered out of the windows. "Ah, here we are." Steffan pulled on his cloak, grabbed his bags and followed the dwarf down the steps. As soon as they hit the ground a whistle blew and Steffan watched with interest as the train rolled onto a side track. As soon as the main line was clear, a second train, pulled by a mean looking iron dragon, roared to a start and chugged off down the line back to Railla.

"We run six trains a day," Carson said proudly. "Two of them are being pulled by iron dragons. Those trains are our lifeblood, as you well know, bringing us rails, food, and all the other supplies we need." He made a low whistle, the iron dragon let out a series of bellowing coughs, as though in reply, and the empty train picked up speed and clattered away. "I'm coming to like those beasts. They pull twice the load of a Sardar."

It was early afternoon, and though the sky was clear, the wind carried snowflakes. It swirled among the tall evergreens that surrounded the place, which was bustling with activity. There were strings of loaded cars on two side tracks, mountains of barrels and boxes in neat stacks all along the track, and behind every tree there seemed to be a tent. Carson introduced him, one by one, to the motley work force he had assembled. There were dwarves, elves, half-orcs, and even some Wee Folk from the southern land called Wislandor. Steffan had never met one before. They were shorter and thinner than dwarves, but very neat and polite. Most notably, even in the snowy wood, they wore no boots on their furry feet.

Carson led him up the track, proudly pointing out the string of special carriages that had been constructed for him.

"We move these up the line with each league of track that's laid. This is another of my personal cars," he said gesturing toward a compartment car which stood at the end of a string of carriages, all shunted onto a side rail, devoid of an engine. "I live in it when we're at the railhead and use it as my office. You can bunk in there with me tonight."

They walked on. "Here we have the bakery," Carson pointed to a boxlike car, painted green and pierced at the roof by several chimneys. The delicious aroma of fresh baked bread accosted him. "This is the kitchen car, the next one is food storage, and the next two back are dining rooms, where food is served to the gangs." Several humans and two half-orcs came tumbling out of the second dining room car, laughing and joking loudly. They caught sight of Carson, fell silent and hurried off in the opposite direction. The dwarf stopped on a low bank opposite the last four cars, which were much longer than the rest. They were long wheeled rectangles, with their sides pierced at regular intervals by small windows.

"These are the bunk cars," explained Carson. "Each can sleep over a hundred, but very few of the workers sleep there if the weather's good."

"Why not?"

"Filled with vermin," came the answer. "Damned near impossible to get rid of the bugs. But we'll try smoking 'em out before the big snows come."

They went back to the dining cars and climbed aboard. It was comfortably warm. Several potbellied stoves stood along one side, plank tables and wooden benches lined up along the other. The car was empty save for the two dwarf servers.

The furnishings might have been austere, but the meal of beef stew and fresh bread was far superior to any Steffan had partaken with the work crews south of Railla. The half-elf ate ravenously.

"You know," said Steffan, after his belly was satisfied. "If the crew south of Railla knew how great your food is, Hammner would lose all his workers to you."

Carson polished off his second tankard of beer, and wiped his beard with the back of his hand. "Aah! I've found good food keeps a crew happier than good pay. So I spend a little extra on provisions . . ." he winked at Steffan, "and pay a little less gold."

That night, before the half-elf crawled into his small bunk, he held the lamp over the bedding and inspected it carefully, but found no unwelcome visitors. The thought of the verminous bunk cars up ahead was still fresh in his mind. He slept fitfully, first awakened by the distant howls of wolves, and then intermittently by the roars of a mountain lion. Steffan had been brought up in the forests of Glyth Gamel, but such sounds were unfamiliar to him. He was glad to be safe and secure behind the stout wooden walls of the carriage. Finally, Carson's regular snores lulled the

half-elf to sleep in the wee hours of the
morning.

At breakfast, Steffan was introduced to a
pleasant dark-eyed elf named Persy Browne, the
scout who commanded the survey party. At
Browne's side sat two unusual creatures of a
most startling appearance, the likes of which
Steffan had never seen. They had the bodies of
men, yet they were covered with short, sleek
tawny fur, scantily clad with the lean, fierce
skulls of mountain lions. Their hands more
closely resembled great cat paws, and when they
spoke it was in whispery, breathy voices.

Steffan could hardly take his eyes off of them.
"Allow me to introduce my eyes and ears," said
Browne. "This is Cynarr," he nodded left, "and
Carras, catmen, as you may have guessed, from
the southern land known as Caicenden."

Steffan shook the furry hand/paws in turn. "I
have never met a catman before. Sper Andros is
how I am known in Glyth Gamel, but please call
me Steffan. I'm to join your party and learn what
I must from Persy."

"Ayuh," they replied, a coughing, grunted
exhalation. They had literally purred while Steffan shook their paws.

They inquired about his dual name, and
Steffan told them of his history. Their speech
was difficult to follow as the words were slurred
rather than distinctly articulated, but after a
time, it grew easier.

"Cynarr and Carras are our scouts," Browne
explained. "My elfen senses are nothing compared to these two. Our party will be safe

enough with them in the woods, you can be sure."

"Has there been trouble of late?" Steffan asked.

"Plenty. Even with regular patrols, bands of marauding orcs manage to slip through the forest and fall upon the isolated work crew, or the careless dwarf who wanders away from camp. Two weeks ago, a survey party was wiped out by orcs." The catmen growled menacingly.

Browne continued, "There's some kind of magic helping them get past us, I'll warrant."

Two elves looked in the door and called to Persy. "Time we were off. Got your gear, Steffan?"

The party assembled outside in the cold gray light of morning. Velvet deer, minus the tinkling bells, were brought up to carry the elves and their equipment. The catmen had a final word with Browne, then trotted off quietly. Carson was there to see him off and shook his hand, wishing him well. Several elves made up the rest of the survey party and, after they had mounted and ridden a short distance along the track, they were joined by a complement of twenty armed elven warriors, mounted, as usual, on snorting bears, who would plot the final route to Glyween.

They rode steadily past a familiar scene. Scores of humans and elves were marching forward in small groups, carrying rails. Ahead of them, humans lifted cross ties off carts and positioned them across the grade.

The deer were following a rough waggon

track, and often they were forced aside into the prickly underbrush to make way for empty oxcarts on their way back to the railhead where they would be loaded with additional supplies.

Ahead was a steep ravine, spanned by a neatly built stone bridge. No tracks, of course, had yet been laid and Browne led them across to the other side. Steffan noticed a pair of dwarves at the bottom of the draw, studying their handiwork and looking for flaws. The survey party was once again forced off the trackless grade by oxcarts headed for the rear. They passed through a tent city, where cooks were busy round a large kettle, chopping enormous piles of beef and vegetables, preparing the next meal. More beef stew, he thought. A small herd of cattle, grazing in a nearby clearing, confirmed the thought.

Now they were among the graders; a long row of dwarves swarmed down the grade, antlike, wheeling barrows full of rock which they dumped at just the right places. Having deposited their load, each dwarf would then turn around, and go back from whence he had come. Several gangs of half-orcs were busy shoveling, raking and spreading the gravely rock, and even as Steffan rode past, the level grade moved visibly forward. Watching this rail road being built was akin to watching a giant tree grow from a tiny sprout.

Once again they detoured around an oxcart and this time joined a silent path that threaded through the tall firs. Steffan could no longer see the great project, but the rumble of the carts and waggons, the clang of the picks, and the shouts of the workers resounded through the ever-greens.

He could easily understand the reason for the urgent pace. The builders were in a frantic race against the elements. At these high altitudes, the possibility of snow had been present for the past two months, and now the season was late. They had been fortunate so far, but their luck could not hold forever. Once the snows fell, and the blizzards began to rage, all work would come to a complete halt until after the spring thaw, five long, tiresome months.

Continuing on, climbing ever higher, most of the grading crews were left behind; now they passed only an occasional forest party, clearing away the trees, and the bridge builders, who laboriously brought their trestles out bit by bit on oxcarts to be assembled on site. They came to a particularly deep ravine, with a loud, roaring stream at the bottom, and the deer carefully picked their way down. As the survey party and its escort stretched and watered their mounts, Steffan watched in awe as a gang of elves erected a trestle across the frothy stream. He consulted his map; they had come nearly seven leagues from the end of the track, yet, here was a bridge under construction. Now he began to understand the job of the surveyors. After he refilled his canteens, his interest was caught by two members of the work gang.

"Giants!" Steffan exclaimed, half to himself.

"Hill giants, to be precise," said Browne who appeared beside him. "They charge old Carson an arm and a leg for their labors, but each one does the work of two steam derricks."

"I would imagine they come in handy during an orc raid, too," remarked Steffan

"I'll say. The orcs won't come anywhere near those fellows. This is a popular gang, it never gets attacked."

After the brief intermission, they forded the stream, and once again resumed their punishing pace.

Even though they had left most of the actual work crews behind, they were not alone on the trail. All along the route there passed a steady stream of waggons, mules and carts bringing up food and supplies and returning empty, or sometimes laden with firewood. Although steep, the path was wide, level, and beaten to a smooth finish by the thousands of hooves and footsteps that had gone before them. Entering a stretch of dense, towering pines, they soon encountered a team of forestry elves and dwarves, whose goal was to cut down as few trees as possible in order to preserve the forest. Browne explained that the foresters were accompanied by an elven mage, whom he was told, though he himself had never seen it happen, was sometimes able to persuade trees to move out of the way, or at least adjust themselves more conveniently, to allow the passage of the road.

They traveled deeper and deeper into the dark forest and, near dusk, reached the final frontier; beyond this point no further work had been done. This was where their job would commence. Steffan was more than anxious to begin. Between them and Glyween lay twenty to thirty uncharted leagues, as the crow flies. Unfortunately, they were not crows, and, although the rail road would eventually speed over that distance, the path it was to take would depend on the lay of the land, the depth of the valleys, the height of the ridges, and, this being elven country, serious consideration must be given to the ancient trees.

A clearing, close by a tiny stream, made an ideal camp. Heavy canvas tents were erected, and a cook-fire was welcomed as the group huddled around it for warmth. A gentle rustling of branches heralded the arrival of the catmen, who appeared suddenly out of the darkness. They reported to Browne, then walked over to the edge of the camp, curled up in a furry ball, and promptly went to sleep.

After supper and tea, the catmen wakened and partook of their own meal, large, bloody chunks of raw meat. Soon the first watch of elven soldiers was counted off and they silently entered the woods. Steffan went to sleep feeling much safer than he had in Carson's carriage, secure in the knowledge that the mountain lions he heard roaring in the darkness were on his side.

The next day, Persy Browne and his crew hurled themselves into their work. Steffan had noticed the surveyor making notes on his map all the previous day. Now the mapping was to begin in earnest. The scouts were sent ahead while a number of the soldiers marched out to form a line of protection around the work gang. Browne unfolded a small portable table, and promptly

covered it with papers. A small group of elves
marched off to the limit of vision and held tall
painted rods vertical to the ground, while still
others ran long lines of twine across the ground
between the painted sticks and what Browne
called a transit. It was a curious device mounted
atop three spindly wooden legs. Browne taught
Steffan how to sight through the device, and
note the markings painted around its metal base.
The elves with the twine reported precise
measurements of distance and soon a series of
triangles advanced across Browne's map.

It was now becoming clear what they were
doing. Steffan had learned geometry and had
been quite good at it. The sightings employed
the very basics of geometry. Browne showed his
pupil the minimum radius that the rails were
allowed to curve, and it became clear why the
most obvious route was not always the one
taken. In addition, there was another
requirement. The track could not have a grade
greater than twenty-one rods to the league, in
other words, it could neither rise nor descend.
Steffan acknowledged his understanding, and
whistled to himself. The great pass and the
rugged hills and valleys that loomed between his
own, future railhead, and the broad valleys of
the Bright Kingdom, suddenly seemed impossible to conquer. He said as much to Persy.

"Don't let it bother you. There's a way around
every mountain if you look for it long enough,"
came the reassuring answer.

Very quickly, Steffan was permitted to take his
place beside the elven surveyors as they charted

and mapped the route the rail way would take on its journey through the forest. He learned to sight through the transit with compass close to hand and direct, by means of elaborate hand signals, where the distant markers should be placed. He mastered the formulae necessary to convert their measurements into meaningful maps. By the third day out, the party had pushed two leagues into the forest, and that day, Browne had let Steffan do all the mapping.

That night, over the campfire, Browne congratulated his apt student. "Steffan, I think you're ready. If we're lucky, we may have a month before the blizzards come, and in that time you can accomplish much."

"Thank you for the patient way in which you led me through my instructions. I shall be forever in your debt." Steffan meant it, too. He had learned a lot in these few days in the forest. The rail road was an undertaking that boggled his imagination. It was more important than any one man, or dwarf, or elf. It represented the collective efforts of whole populations, all working together for a common cause. It was a concept he had never before experienced in his life.

A light snow fell that night, blanketing the camp in a silent layer of white. The catmen were unusually quiet as well. Steffan missed their voices. Some hours before dawn Steffan awoke to a tremendous clatter, and then a spine chilling howl. He knew that sound in his bones. Dire wolves! He sprang from his blankets and fumbled for his sword. The alarm sounded and the

camp roused quickly. One wolf had slunk into
their midst ahead of the others and turned over
the cooking kettle. That animal had been run off
easily enough, but others soon appeared around
the clearing and growled and howled menacingly. Someone had the sense to pile fresh wood
on the fire and the light drove the beasts back a
short distance.

Two elves had their bows at the ready and
were about to fire. "Not yet," cautioned Browne.
"Let them come at us a bit and build up their
confidence. When they're closer, make your
shots count." He also instructed others to fashion fire arrows.

The ravening wolves ran in busy circles,
looking for an undefended opening, and each
thrust was met by elven war cries and flashing
steel blades. At last the wolves rushed forward
on three sides at once and there were not
enough elves to throw them back. The archers
released their deadly missiles and there were
yelps of agony as three of the wolves fell dead
and several others fled with blazing flanks.
Three more times the cunning creatures tried to
rush the camp and each time they were driven
back with casualties. It was a tense time for
Steffan, who had no bow and could do no more
than brandish a sword at his most hated enemy.
But somehow, as the battle continued, hatred
overcame fear and he handled himself well. As
the sun slowly climbed high over the trees,
lighting up the somber ground, it was seen that
no more than a score of bodies littered on the
ground, but those animals that had not been

slain left the area looking considerably fatter than when they arrived. Dire wolves were so loathsome as to eat their own dead.

"Where are Cynarr and Carras?" Steffan wondered aloud.

"That worries me, too," came Browne's reply. And soon search parties filed out to look for the missing catmen. Steffan was bone-tired, chilled and hungry, when his little group returned to camp near dusk. They had found no sign of the catmen. Nor had those who had reported in before them. As each party returned to rest, eat, and warm themselves by the fire, the gloom grew deeper, and no one spoke.

A sudden familiar growl in the distance lifted all their spirits, instantly. Four elven soldiers burst into camp with smiles on their faces, followed closely by Cynarr and Carras. "Wolves had them treed up a big pine, down the next valley," came the welcome explanation. Somewhere, bottles of wine appeared, and a celebration was soon underway.

With the catmen safe, Steffan made his farewells the next day, and set out for the railhead. He had a job to do.

CHAPTER NINETEEN

The Great Eastern Begins

The last empty supply train left for RedCliffe near sunset, rolling south through the darkness along the track that led to the dwarven lands. As Steffan watched from the welcome warmth of the Sardar's cab, a bright lantern affixed to the front of the engine sent out a shaft of yellow light that illuminated the track hundreds of feet ahead of them. Snow had fallen during the day and the engine had been fitted with an iron plow that lay low to the rails in order to scrape away any drifts they might encounter. Every so often they would crash into one of these and a cloud of blue-white crystals swirled around them wildly.

It was a beautiful sight, but the half-elf was tired from the long ride, and the heat from the firebox soon coaxed him into a fitful sleep, only to be awakened by the thump and swirl of the plow as it powered through the next drift. They reached RedCliffe in the late hours of the night. Exhausted, and covered with the smoky grit from the stuffy cab, Steffan expected to be met by underlings, if any had yet been assigned to wait for his arrival. He stumbled down the ladder and followed the engine crew deeper into

the tunnel. No one appeared to meet him. Tired
as he was, this scenario met with his approval.
All he wanted was a large jug of water to wash
the smoke of the journey from his throat and a
bed to collapse in. However, his suppositions
were incorrect.

No sooner had the great iron door begun to
slide open, than a large party of dwarves
emerged from the gloom carrying torches. At
their lead was a massive, familiar dwarf, nearly as
tall as Steffan, who approached with outstretched hands. A cascade of reddish bronze
colored hair flowed to his shoulders and merged
with an immense beard that covered his entire
chest. The arms, hands and fingers that were
outthrust to greet him were covered with a
dense thatch of red hairs, there could be little
doubt that this was the Mayor of RedCliffe,
Hammner IronFist. Roaring his delight in having the Director of the Great Eastern Railway as
his guest, he led Steffan unwillingly away for a
night of feasting, drinking, and talk.

A heavy hammering on his door wakened the
half-elf the following morning. Certain that he
had only just laid his head down on the pillow,
Steffan groaned again and cracked his heavy lids
to gauge the time of day. It was, of course, still
dark, deep inside the mountain. *"Good, it's not
morning yet,"* he thought groggily. He rolled
over on his side covering his head with the pillow
hoping those outside would eventually go away.
It did no good. Receiving no answer to repeated
loud hallos, the door was thrust open and the

room filled with bright lamplight. A most ener-
getic, obscenely exuberant Dingur Knorsen
strode into the room. His feet, though clad in
soft leather boots, seemed to crash against the
stone floor, each step sending ripples of pain
through Steffan's head. Even the movement of
the air was an agony to his frazzled nerve
endings. The half-elf shut his eyes tightly and
pulled the pillow down more firmly atop his
throbbing skull.

No good. Booming laughter rattled inside
Steffan's skull as Knorsen stripped the covers
from his body and thumped him hard between
the shoulderblades in a manner reminiscent of
mornings in the construction camp. "Rise and
shine, my lad. No lollygagging abed when there's
work to be done!"

Steffan felt ridiculous, lying there exposed
with his head buried under a pillow. He felt a
childish surge of anger course through his body.
It did not help that his elven mother had
frequently used the same words on him when he
was a child. The feel of the dwarf's eyes on his
body burned in his imagination. Hating the
dwarf, hating himself, Steffan lowered the pillow
and sat up, the effort causing the blood to rush
from his head leaving only nausea in its place.
He barely made it to the wash basin before what
felt like every single thing in his body came
pouring out. Like rats deserting a sinking ship.
Dingur Knorsen watched in amusement as
Steffan tottered back to the bed feeling like a
mere husk with no bones, no flesh, and certainly
no brains.

"Methinks you have mistaken dwarven brew for that fairy piss the elves call liquor," Knorsen mused. "Well, you will not be the first to make that mistake. Nor the last. If we are to accomplish anything today you will have to take the cure." And without a word of explanation, the dwarf left the room with a chuckle, leaving Steffan to wonder at the ominous words.

He was not left in peace long, for just as he was falling back into his bed, two sturdy dwarves entered and gripping him firmly, dragged him tottering between them down a long curving corridor.

He heard the sound long before he identified it. A loud, almost deafening roar filled the entire corridor making speech impossible. The floor, walls, and ceiling seemed to quiver with the resounding rumble. It was only when the two dwarves stopped and put their shoulders to a door that Steffan identified the sound. Water. Rushing water. The door opened, he had a brief view of an enormous gout of water spewing under great force from the wall of the mountain itself and then, with his eye's huge with disbelief, found himself flung headlong into the mael-strom!

The force of the water struck him like a blow. It drove all the breath out of his body and pummeled him like a hundred orcs intent on murder. He tried to breath and swallowed water. Rising to the surface, he was met once again by the full impact of the torrent. As he sank yet again, his lungs screaming for air, his brain, shocked into functioning, helped him reason that he must not emerge directly under the stream. Struggling against his lung's instructions to surface anywhere, immediately, Steffan attempted to swim underwater, away from the water's source. Just as his lungs began to burn and red and black flashes strobed behind his eyelids, his fingers touched something. A stone ledge, slick with water and thick with mist, but clearly out of the main force of the water. He surfaced and found himself clinging to the edge of the watercourse that swirled around in lazy circles in the wet stone room. It took a while for his mind to work, but at last he realized that the water was warm and comforting, and a sense of well-being was beginning to throb through his complaining body. Finally he noticed four feet, carefully avoiding the water, standing directly in front of him. Fury began to build. They had done this on purpose! Trembling muscles at last began to obey his commands and he was able to heave himself up and slither onto the wet ledge.

He lay there gasping, feeling his heart pounding against his rib cage. He rose shakily and staggered toward the owners of those feet; arms outstretched, fingers reaching for their throats. They evaded him easily and had the nerve to laugh as though it were all a very amusing joke rather than an attempt to kill him. Steffan increased his pace and began to run, his anger demanding vengeance. As he rounded a bend in the corridor, he ran full force into Dingur Knorsen, all but bouncing off the vast, beard-covered chest. The dwarf threw an enormous soft blanket around him and led him back to his room like a chastised puppy.

"Ah, I see ye have taken the cure," intoned the dwarf as though it were commonplace to find one's guests running through the halls soaking wet. And perhaps in RedCliffe it was. "Maybe now we can get down to business."

"They tried to drown me," Steffan muttered, struggling to maintain his dignity. The dwarf grabbed his shoulders and propelled him forward, all the while roughly toweling him down.

"Let me go! You made them to do this to me. I could have drowned! I could have died! I could have been sucked into that little pipe over there and . . . and . . ."

"Aye, but ye were not. Besides, there's a grating over the pipe, ye would have just stuck to it." The dwarf looked at him with a critical eye. "Does yer head still ache?"

Suddenly, Steffan realized that he had not thought of his head for quite a while. In fact, aside from being soaking wet, every single part of his body felt alive and tingling. He looked into the dwarf's eyes, a rueful grin twitched at his mouth.

"The cure, eh?"

"Aye, the cure. It works every time — if they survive," Dingur replied with a straight face. "When ye've changed into some dry clothes, meet me in the dining hall, yer party has arrived. There's much work to be done and it's nearly noon, no more time to be foolin' about."

Steffan dressed in clean, dry clothes and felt the hour to be closer to eight than noon, but as he was coming to understand, dwarves had more than a passing acquaintance with exaggeration.

Arriving in the central dining hall, the scene of last night's welcome party, he found Hammner IronFist standing at one of the stone tables surrounded by a number of elves and dwarves and a few humans. All were studying a large sheet of parchment.

Steffan was glad to note a steaming carafe of acorn tea and poured himself a large stone tumbler full before joining the others at the table. They parted for him and he found himself seated between IronFist and Knorsen.

IronFist drew Steffan forward and introduced him to the others. There were representatives from all of the cities and townships committed thus far to the Great Eastern Rail Road. Of prime interest to Steffan was the human named Groc, whom Dingur had mentioned several days before. He was a tall, tanned, competent looking fellow with steady brown eyes. The sort of man one knew instantly could be depended upon and Steffan was glad to learn that the two of them would be working together. Soon they stood side by side, looking over the plans as Groc outlined his suggestions for the course across the Bright Kingdom. Steffan felt easy camaraderie flow between himself and Groc, as though they had known and worked alongside each other for many years.

Other than the meager party of surveyors who were all elves, most of those who would be working for him were a mixture of the three main races. He learned that BlueFeld had sent him a work crew of thirty strong men, as well as a large sum of money. Charles had acted swiftly.

"As some of you already know, we here at RedCliffe are responsible for building the southern division of the Iron Mountain Rail Road," IronFist intoned as he traced the proposed path with a thick finger. "We are, even now, building south from Railla, heading for Silvarre."

The big dwarf turned to Steffan. "I hope your princess can bring the southern elves in with us. It would be a great boost."

"It will happen. She is most capable," Steffan stated confidently.

There was much more talk, and then the division and assignation of work crews and bosses as well as those who would oversee larger portions of the whole. Steffan and Groc both knew that thirty humans and a smattering of elves, dwarves, and half-orcs was but a beginning. Hundreds more would have to follow. The crowd assembled here before them would likely all end up in charge of some important task, in command of the multitude to follow.

Steffan and Groc spent the next three days preparing the plans for the fledgling Great Eastern. With the funds thus far received, they were able to purchase two engines. Steffan chose iron dragon number 12 because he liked the look of intelligence in the creature's eyes and Ragnor personally recommended number 17, a gentle young male with two stages yet to grow. With a portion of the remaining gold, they bought some flat cars, rails, spikes, hand carts, tools, and food for the railhead.

Shipments were sent forward to their future railhead, attached to trains en route to Glyth Gamel. Groc went out twice to get things ready and put the first gangs to work.

Most of the rest of the gold remaining in the coffers of the Great Eastern were spent recruiting the local dwarves, somewhat of a problem, for the pay Groc had to offer was barely better than what the dwarves earned in RedCliffe. But they were hard workers and highly skilled when it came to stone. Even the least intelligent among them could grade and level to specification by mere instinct, what would have taken a human, or an elf, working with instruments, five times as long.

Messages were sent to Charles, requesting that he claim the roads that ran from BlueFeld to Bremmner, thence the coast road along the Bay of Boras, then south up the glacial valley and lastly, north to the elven encampment of Woodsong. The rest of their proposed route lay entirely within elven lands, and an arrangement was made with Ninius for permission to build, in exchange for a certain number of bonds in the company for each league of track constructed.

On the fourth day, everything possible had been accomplished, and men and supplies were loaded on the new flatcars of the Great Eastern Railway. As they set off, the iron dragon, on its own initiative, sounded the appropriate whistle before the engineer could pull the cord, and released a tall plume of white smoke. Several other iron dragons, chocked down on sidings in the great maze of tracks that surrounded

RedCliffe, took up the cry, bugling their own deep voices and tooting their own whistles into the cold air. Iron dragon number 12, pulling her first official train, bugled a sad farewell, and the forlorn sound trailed off into the hills as the last car disappeared from sight. The sound sent prickles up and down Steffan's spine as he stood watching from an observation platform. He hoped it was not an omen. The Great Eastern Rail Road was on its way.

Soon after that departure, another train pulled into RedCliffe from Railla. Its passengers caused an immediate stir. Tianna had returned with a signed treaty from the Council of Silvarre. The alliance was now ratified by all four countries (kingdom not being an appropriate term for Silvarre). Needless to say, there was much excitement. This extension of the Greater Rail Road was the cause of great jubilation! Soon, bottles of wine and kegs of beer were being passed around among the crowd that surrounded the newly arrived train. All thoughts of imminent departure by the second of the Great Eastern's trains, vanished. Especially in Steffan's mind.

His heart began to beat faster as he glimpsed a bit of blue skirt and a fall of red curls. Tianna! He leaped down from his observation post and ran along the tracks, arriving just in time to assist her from the royal passenger carriage. There were streaks of soot on her forehead and cheek and her clothes were rumpled and creased from hard days of travel, but it did not matter, in his eyes she was the most beautiful woman in the world.

Groc tried to stem the flow of his work crews as they leaped off number 17's flatcars, but with all the excitement and liquor being passed around, it proved an impossible task. Groc shook his head in bemusement. And his new boss mooning about with his head in the stars. Women. Oh, well, they would make up the time by working longer hours, if necessary. The princess was, indeed, a woman of beauty. He only hoped she was at least half as smart as his boss. There was a schedule to meet and by the gods, females or no females, he intended to keep it. A nice bonus, in stock, bonds, and gold, had been promised if that deadline were met.

Another banquet was laid on for Tianna's arrival and to celebrate the good news that Silvarre had eagerly embraced the notion of the rail way and had pledged financial as well as physical assistance. Multiple courses weighed down the granite tables as whole roasted deer, sheep and boars were placed on them in vast oval steel platters. Bowls of boiled potatoes, onions, turnips, mountain sorrel and mushrooms, filled in the spaces between the roasted meats and mounds of hot whole grained breads, which were juggled up and down the lines of feasters. And of course, there was the beer, a deceptively mild-tasting brew that went well with the meal.

It was no problem for Steffan to pace himself, knowing what he did about its true potency. He cautioned Tianna against the brew and attempted to do the same with Groc, but the man waved him to silence, assuring him with a laugh that he had been weaned on orc beer and the stuff that would put him under the table had yet to be brewed.

The evening continued with much feasting, laughter and revelry, but for Tianna and Steffan, it was as though they were alone, everyone else had ceased to exist and they were lost in each other. Without Charles's presence to inhibit them, they found themselves leaving the table, walking and talking beneath the waning moon. They spoke of their life plans, which, before the evening was over, had been tacitly expanded to include the possibility of one another.

Their rather chilly, early morning departure was a silent affair, as all, except the dwarven members of their crew, nursed massive hangovers. Not a few of the men, including Groc, boarded, still slightly damp around the edges, recent victims . . . or recipients of "the cure." Steffan could not resist a grin and prodding Groc in the ribs said, "The cure, eh?" In reply, Groc wandered in a wobbly path back along the tracks to a place on a flat car, as far as possible from Steffan, flopped down on a pile of grain sacks and promptly fell asleep.

A whistle sounded, a bright, piercing shriek and, accompanied by the assorted groans and moans of the crew, train number 12 of the Bright Kingdom pulled out of RedCliffe after a considerable, but enjoyable, delay.

It was hard to stifle the rush of excitement and Tianna and Steffan soon gave up all pretense of sophistication. It was a grand adventure. Never had its like been seen in the world and they were

fortunate indeed to be a part of it. They were
seated in the cab behind the engineer aboard
iron dragon number 17, which was, in all
respects, like the one in which they had both
previously ridden. In no time, they passed
through Ritla on the border.

Now the tracks led downhill, and the train
picked up speed. A little too much speed,
thought Tianna, and she grabbed the engineer
by the shoulder.

The elf turned to her. "Don't fret," he yelled
above the roar of the engine, "this fellow's just
enjoying himself." He twisted two valves, and
although the rapid pace did not slacken, there
was no further increase in speed. The train
rounded a long curve and passed into a deep
rock cut. Suddenly, there were shouts and cries
from all aboard the train, as it hurtled past an
armed party of orcs, far from the Wastes, deep
inside elf and dwarf territory. One of the elves
got off a single arrow, which missed its mark,
and then the scattered group of orcs disappeared behind them. The dwarves clamored for
the train to stop, blood lust in their eyes. But
the fired-up iron dragon traveled several
leagues further before it could be brought to a
halt.

By the time they backed the train, arms at the
ready, to the spot where the orcs had been
sighted, they had vanished. Steffan had no
difficulty raising a party of elves and dwarves to
track the enemy down. A light dusting of snow
had fallen during the night and the trail was
clear. With any luck at all, they would be able to

catch up with the raiders and slay them before
they could do any damage.

"Send me a report of your success by carrier
crow," Steffan instructed the leader of the
expedition. "And don't be gone more than two
days. You are all needed at the construction site."
Several caged birds were passed down off the
loaded flat cars and given to the battle party. The
elves soon sorted out the trail and the trackers
moved off swiftly.

Groc shook his head. "This worries me, losing
them even for two days. And what if there are
casualties? We're badly understaffed as it is.
Now twenty of our best elves and dwarves are
gone . . ."

"We had no choice," Steffan answered, nodding in agreement with Groc's appraisal of the
situation. "We must catch them and kill them
before they can do us any harm. This is
dangerously close to where we'll be grading. We
don't want them to come crashing into our camp
some night while we're asleep."

Groc agreed reluctantly, still obviously troubled by the loss of manpower. They climbed
back aboard and the train headed down the
grade into the broad valley that lay ahead.
Thanks to the delay, it was nearly noon when
they arrived at the point from which the Great
Eastern would set out for the Bright Kingdom.
It was a station called Junction. It was the place
Steffan had seen his first rail road. Startled
sheep stared in disbelief, and then leapt out of
the path of the train, as it was switched off the
main line and came to a stop on a side track.

A town of sorts had sprung up at what had until recently been nothing more than a few livestock pens. There was a tent city, filled with an assortment of half-orcs, clanless dwarves and the sorts of men who are always drawn to such rough and tumble frontiers. Tianna's presence drew a number of rude calls, wet kissing sounds and crude laughter, to which Steffan replied with a drawn sword. Mocking laughter and squeaking sounds of pretend fear greeted this action and red-faced, he realized that such behavior could only be met with polite indifference, anything else would only make matters worse.

Steffan turned to Groc. "Is this the best we can do?"

"Labor is in great demand," the engineer said with a shrug. "What with the gangs at work up in the north and south, we're lucky to have this lot." Tianna was escorted to a tent which had been hastily erected, and Steffan posted two guards despite her protests. "The sooner they were out of this place, the better," he thought grimly.

Tianna changed out of her skirts and donned a pair of buckskin breeches and tall boots, proclaiming them much more practical than petticoats. As they did nothing but enhance her already lissome figure, Steffan was disinclined to argue.

They toured the bustling settlement, viewing with interest the extensive pens which contained elven bears and velvet deer, as well as cattle and sheep. There were numerous tents and crude shacks providing services such as food, laundry and supplies. But the majority of the establishments, if they could be called that, were in existence, solely for the purpose of providing liquor, gambling and temporary female companionship. It was from these places that the worst of the comments came. Steffan was of a mind to run the proprietors and their customers off.

Groc smiled, "I was hoping to hear you say that, but I must warn you, the only way we're gonna run them off is to bust some heads."

"Then that's what we'll do," came Steffan's reply. "Gather up your most trusted bosses, and the toughest crew. Have them spread the word. The gambling houses and pleasure pits must pack up and be gone by morning, or . . ."

"I'll provide the rest of the words, boss," beamed Groc, obviously happy to do what should have been done long before.

There was a good deal of furor in the camp that evening, and several delegations demanded to see Steffan. To each irate proprietor, the half-elf delivered the same ultimatum, pack up and go, or suffer the consequences. Groc had armed dwarves on patrol all night, and by morning a lot of gambling equipment had been turned to splinters and the undesirables were gone. Not a single head, however, had been busted.

Two sections of track branched off of the mainline forming a wye that pointed in the direction of the Bright Kingdom. Steffan was glad to see that some progress had been made while he was away learning his job. Already, a

small crew was building a gentle grade that
sloped up toward the pass. Steffan remembered
the ride down from the cave at the top of that
pass. Remembering the abrupt manner in which
the pack trail dived down the slope with no
concern for the requisite gradient of so many
rods per league or the minimum radius allowed
for a curve, Steffan began to worry.

Groc showed him the maps that had been
drawn so far. There was enough work to keep
his small crew of graders and track layers busy
for several days. But decisions had to be made
about how to surmount the pass. Leaving a
competent dwarf in charge at Junction, Steffan
gathered Tianna, Groc, the few elves qualified
to work as surveyors, some dwarven graders,
armed body elves, and twenty humans who had
come up from the Bright Kingdom to work.
This motley assemblage, plus two supply waggons pulled by ox teams, rode and walked out to
the end of the existing survey where they established an advance camp three leagues from
Junction in the heart of the forest. While the
humans cleared the campsite and set up tents,
Groc and Steffan and their crew immediately
began sighting the course of the road bed. Two
of the best elves and a small escort scouted up
the valley for likely routes with instructions to
report any findings as quickly as possible. By
early afternoon, the dwarves had begun to cut,
grade and level a small portion of the newly
mapped route. A message was sent back to
Junction and soon waggons came slogging up
the path to the camp where a crew of half-orc

teamsters began to unload piles of ties and rails.

The first day's work went well, ending only when dusk fell, making further progress impossible. A hot meal had been prepared by a half-orc named Kruk who had a surprisingly deft hand when it came to biscuits and had created a hearty, yet delicious, venison stew. A single cup of beer was all that was allowed. But even without a flowing jug, the talk around the campfires was exuberant and enthusiastic, the work crew eager to advance speedily. It was soon learned that the workers had established a wager, and a sizable one at that, as to how far the track would be advanced before the snows of winter closed around them. The contest lent an edge of excitement to their work, but it worried Steffan. How willingly would a dwarf be to lay track beyond the point of his wager? No matter, he would deal with that problem when, and if, it arose. All present were exhausted from the day's labors, and soon the camp resounded to a symphony of sawing, trilling, blatting and rasping snores.

By mutual agreement, neither Tianna nor Steffan were of a mind to retire. Hand in hand they walked out away from the fire and wandered in the woods until they came to a huge moss-covered boulder alongside a small, crystalline waterfall. Here they stopped in silent accord. Steffan brushed the snow off the top of the boulder, and threw a bearskin down. They sat atop the rock, sheltered warmly under his cloak, and looked up into the night sky.

CHAPTER TWENTY

Madness

Kroner sat resolutely before the Bowl of Night, rarely leaving it. Food and drink were brought to him several times a day but he scarcely did more than pick at it before returning to the pool of dark water with its constantly changing scenes. Scenes that were not giving any sign that his plans were meeting with success. Everywhere, there was failure. The ravening horde of dire wolves, so painstakingly gathered up from the vast forest, had failed to slay the troublesome half-elf, falling upon one another when they met with unexpected resistance. The rock fall in the mountain pass had fallen after, rather than upon, the passage of the iron dragon carrying his sister. And the winter storms had refused to come, despite his mage's most powerful spells. It was almost as though something or someone powerful knew of his intent, and was purposely foiling him. The thought drove him insane with fury. Kroner hated being thwarted. "Why are my commands for sabotage failing?" he demanded of his mages, but none could answer the question. Kroner kicked the leg of a chair upon which the most elderly of their

number, Threlgar the Unwise, sat. An insult
under any circumstances, the sorcerer's eyes
flared bright with anger and then dimmed.
Kroner was the grandson and sole heir of his
king, to whom he had pledged absolute obei-
sance. He and the others had been instructed to
guide the boy and assist him in whatever was
needed. The mentors had scarcely thought to
find themselves embroiled in this kind of evil
doing, nor had they thought to assist in the
slaying of a royal personage, but now that they
had bowed to his demands, they were completely in his power. Nor had they expected their
charge to become a hate-filled, twisted young
man, obsessed by bitterness and a litany of self
pitying grievances. But there was little they
could do now, other than obey their mandate.

During the days and nights that followed,
being persuaded by his mentors to attempt little
acts, more likely to meet with success than major
attempts to sway nature, he did succeed in
bringing about numerous small incidents. Picks
broke, shovels disappeared, rocks crumbled to
dust, and termites devoured the surveyor's rods.
Food supplies were contaminated by weevils
and bedrolls swarmed with lice and biting mites
too small for the eye to see. Any man who slept
in the bunk cars was soon covered with red,
itching welts and painful angry boils that refused
to be eased by medication. Iron dragon number
17 developed a nasty case of rust and sickened
and for a time his keepers feared for his life, but
it was taken back to RedCliffe and so placed out
of reach of Kroner. Soon, constant tending and

loving care pulled it through. All of these incidents, and more, succeeded in doing what Kroner's grander schemes had not: they interrupted the work on the rail road, insuring that progress was only achieved only on an erratic basis and then only occasionally. Kroner watched in delight as Steffan and the other gang bosses strode about in helpless dismay, unable to put an end to the string of bad luck.

Unfortunately, Kroner had failed to take into account the carrier crows. By means of messages, Steffan was able to communicate with the other camps, and found that he was not alone in his misfortunes. It soon became obvious that there was a definite evil loose among them that was responsible for the mischief. Tianna met with Preston, and several elven mages were immediately summoned and ways to combat the onslaught were devised. Special blessings were placed upon all engines that left RedCliffe. The mages began walking the perimeters of the camps and drawing protective rings about the workers and their tools. The perimeter was advanced daily, as the crews once again began to move forward, and the mages stayed close at hand to detect, and ward off, any future spells.

Kroner, through the eyes of his far-seeing hawks, soon discovered what had occurred and attempted to have the bird service plucked out of the sky and devoured by eagles. But it was too little, too late. Preston and Tianna were actively campaigning against his magic, and other magic-users were already in place, busily protecting the construction camps.

Kroner raged and stormed, heaping insults and slander on the stoic Threlgar, Brogalf, and Agrippa who had been unable to help him. The boy soon retreated into a brooding, black silence, contemplating some new bit of evil.

Unaware that the cause for all the trouble could be found in his own household, Charles fretted at the steady stream of worrisome news. Having raised the necessary funds, and having dispatched a hundred more good men to Junction, there was little that could be accomplished in BlueFeld. Anxious to be of some use, and feeling that he was out of touch with the project, he wanted to get back to Tianna and Steffan, and meet with Bagor and Ninius to discuss the stalled construction. He could just as easily have gone south to Bulatz and Brevandes, the two other major cities in the Bright Kingdom, talking up the rail road in an effort to raise funds. No, the problems at hand must be dealt with first, then would come the business of selling the rail road to the rest of his kingdom.

Once his decision was reached, plans were swiftly set in motion. Servants packed, and the royal coach made ready . . . this trip would be a bit more comfortable than his last. He also sent word ahead to Bremmner for a pack train loaded with sturdy tools, spikes, and other needed supplies which he would bring along to the Great Eastern to undo some of the damage by the mysterious mischief.

The night before his leave-taking, Charles met Kroner in the corridor. The king told his dark

son of his plans and bade him a cool, perfunctory
farewell.

"I must be allowed to accompany you, father,"
Kroner said in a polite, respectful tone. He had
known for some time what was afoot.

Charles looked down at his son, noting with
distaste that the boy seemed incapable of meeting his eyes. At each glance, Kroner would look
off in a different direction. His mere presence
filled Charles with an intense distrust, which he
had ceased to try to overcome. Blood or no
blood, the fact was that the boy was flawed in
some grievous manner. If he had been a bit of
livestock or a plant, Charles would have had him
eradicated. Fortunately, or unfortunately, as the
case might be, such things were not possible
with people . . . at least not to a person with
Charles Edouard's code of honor. There was no
real reason why Kroner could not have accompanied him, it was a harmless enough request, and
maybe he and the boy could somehow come to
know each other better.

He began to change his mind, to allow his son
to . . . Then his eyes met Kroner's again, and the
king's heart hardened. Even the thought was like
a bad taste in his mouth. No, it would not do.
More harshly than necessary, he told Kroner that
he was too young. Such a thing would not be
convenient and, stepping around him, he hurried off down the corridor.

Kroner turned and watched his father's swiftly
retreating figure, hurrying away as though even
the mere contact was distasteful. "Well, my
father, perchance you will have something even

more bitter to swallow than my presence. The decision was yours to make and you have decided. So be it," he whispered malevolently after the father who had rejected him.

The castle fell silent as the night advanced and the candles in their sconces dimmed. There was a sense of alert watchfulness in the darkness. A venturing mouse felt the tension on its quivering whiskers and skittered into hiding as fast as its tiny feet could carry it. Toward morning there was a flurry of furtive activity and a single sharp cry, then silence once again. This time, had the mouse been bold or foolish enough to be out, it would have felt a self-satisfied gloating carried on the air, which, in its way, was even more frightening.

Charles left at daybreak with a mounted troop of the Royal Guard. Four servants accompanied him, one of whom had been substituted at the last moment when his old, trusted page, Seymour, inexplicably came up missing.

Kroner waved ostentatiously to his father from the ramparts. Charles nodded curtly in his general direction and called up to the coachman to be off. At a crack of the whip, they lurched off and passed rapidly through the city gate. This caught his guard by surprise, causing them to scramble for their horses, bidding those left behind a hasty farewell.

They traveled uneventfully to Bremmner, where the king once again enjoyed the city's hospitality. The local businessmen and the dwarves who ran the foundries were beside themselves with joy over the prospect of the rail road and the contracts for rail building. In the morning the pack train was ready, and followed along behind the royal procession at such a slow pace that the king finally ordered the rest of the expedition to move on and the pack train to follow, proceeding at its own best speed.

The king's party was once again met at the edge of the forest by a large contingent of armed elves. He, his servants, and his baggage were loaded on velvet deer, and the carriage sent back to BlueFeld. Charles was escorted through Glyth Gamel and on to the railhead just outside of Junction. Throughout their journey, the elves had been watchful and silent, binding their mount's muzzles with strips of soft cloth to keep them silent as well. Following suit, the royal guard had muffled their horses' hooves with cloth bags. The elves were none too pleased to have the human cavalry along at all, but Charles had insisted. They passed through the tiny settlement of Woodsong without stopping, and few elves came out to greet them. No fires were lit and meals were eaten cold and on the move.

"There have been numerous sightings of orcs and rabid packs of dire wolves running amok in the forest," whispered the captain of the elven guard, one Sylvan Shade, his silver eyes constantly scanning their surroundings, never at rest. "Far more than is the norm. Also, mysterious fires that occur where there is no reason, no lightning or travelers careless with their torches. A number of elves have been slain as they went about their business. Something is afoot in the woods and we like it not. Our king has instructed

us that we are to guard your life as though it
were as precious as our own. No harm is to come
to you inside of Glyth Gamel lest suspicion of
wrongdoing fall upon the elven nation."

*"And too bad for me if harm arrives one step
over the border,"* Charles thought grimly. But he
could see the wisdom of the elven king's concern, and he himself grew more watchful. All
were relieved on the evening of the fourth day
when the king's party rode down from the pass
and into Steffan's camp.

The half-elf showed the king the progress that
had been made, and Charles was pleased. There
was a shout and Tianna rushed into Charles's
arms.

"They didn't tell me you had arrived," she
complained. He held her in a tight embrace, yet
he could not help but notice that a strong bond
seemed to have developed between his daughter
and the half-elf. Charles felt a moment of
intense, irrational jealousy and then it receded,
leaving only calm in its wake. He looked into the
half-elf's eyes and nodded. No word had passed
between them but words had not been necessary. Steffan's worth had been weighed and not
found lacking.

A long evening of eating, drinking and talk
took place around the campfire, and the campsite itself was ringed by armed elves secreted in
the woods. Tianna, Steffan, and Groc listed the
numerous incidents that had occurred and various explanations were put forth, but none was
satisfactory. It was clear to all that magic was the
root from which all the evil had sprung. Yet the

who, or the why of it, escaped them. All likely candidates were named and discussed, but it seemed that none of their various enemies fit the profile of what was happening. Destruction of the railway, itself, appeared to be the motive, and none of their enemies had any reason to destroy it. If anything, it would give them greater opportunities for plunder. Furthermore, all the incidents had one thing in common, a sense of malevolence. Whomever was responsible did not appear satisfied by merely halting progress, they wanted it to hurt, as well.

The hour grew late and one of the king's men, the new page, a fellow who seemed to be walking in his sleep most of the time, mentioned the hour to Charles and suggested that the morning would come all too soon. Charles thanked the servant graciously. Goodnights were said all around and Tianna was enfolded in her father's embrace before all turned to the comforts of their beds.

Sometime during the night, a thin, strangled cry echoed through the camp, and Tianna, alert even in her sleep to the sounds of the night, her unconscious mind noting anything other than ordinary in the way of women everywhere, answered the cry before it had trailed away. Leaping from her cot, she threw aside the flap of her tent and raced across the campsite barefoot and entered her father's sleeping quarters.

Charles was lying with fully half of his body off of his bed, his mouth twisted in a terrible rictus of pain, his fingers clenched into tight fists, blood ran down his sides and dripped into the earth, gouged out of his flesh by his own fingernails.

"Father!" Tianna rushed to Charles and tried to right him, for the blood had flowed to his head turning his face an ominous dark color. But he was immovable, his body frozen in a solid wall of unrelenting agony. Tianna screamed as loud as she could, calling out Steffan's name over and over.

As worried voices cried out and footsteps began to pound toward the tent, a glitter of glass caught her eye and reaching down she plucked up a tiny broken vial with a dusting of blue powder in its rounded bottom. She was staring at it without understanding when Steffan appeared at her side. Two of the king's servants also arrived and the captain of the guard came in and shouted with dismay for his men. Steffan and the others gently lifted their king and laid his rigid form flat on his cot, but nothing they did eased the awful spasms.

The elven mage, whose name was Othvarr, arrived soon after Steffan, and did his best to alleviate the man's suffering without success. Tianna, without thinking, was fumbling with the tiny glass capsule she had found, and suddenly let out a yelp as it pricked her palm. She stared at it in wonderment and sudden suspicion.

"I found this on the ground," she explained. Slowly, she extended her hand to the mage who cautiously took it and examined it with great interest. He sniffed it carefully and from a distance of a foot or more. Sudden realization filled his eyes and he threw the capsule into the brazier that had been brought to warm the tent.

"Let me see your hand!" he cried with alarm. Tianna held it out for his inspection. It had begun to tingle soon after she pricked it and the tingling had spread down to her fingertips and up as far as her elbow. Further, the tingling was turning to pain and with every pulse of her heart it increased. She had been telling herself that it was nothing but her overwrought imagination, but now, with a sinking heart, she intuited the worst. If but a single prick of an all but empty container could hurt this much, what would the whole dose feel like? Her eyes were drawn to the now comatose figure of her father, and it became all too obvious what the answer was.

Mercifully, Tianna was spared the agony of her father's final hours, for she herself was made insensible by the pain that swiftly grew too intense to bear. Othvarr mixed up a heavy potion of sleeping powders, as well as an antidote for the poison that was spreading through her system and had her bedded down on a second cot opposite her father so that he could keep constant watch on both.

Charles died in the hour before dawn without ever regaining consciousness, which was a blessing, for his pain was almost too much for the strongest of those present to endure merely watching. As Charles breathed his last, agonized breath, the mage sagged with exhaustion as well as the knowledge of his failure.

"I did everything I knew how to do," he said to Steffan, clearly distraught. "The poison was of such virulence, and in such strength, that he was

as good as dead when it was first administered.
Furthermore, an additional ingredient was
added that prevented him from dying, kept him
alive, rather than slaying him outright."

"Why would such a thing be done?" Steffan
asked, aghast.

"There was no reason other than to prolong
the agony," the mage said. "Whoever caused this
death went to great lengths to insure that it
would be long, slow, and exceedingly painful."

"Do you have any notion what it was, or how it
was administered?" Steffan asked grimly. "In his
food?"

"Perhaps," the mage answered after a
moment of thought. "But I think not. The
presence of the vial the princess found on the
floor, suggests that it was broken on the spot,
and more than likely, held under the sleeping
man's nostrils to be inhaled by his own breathing." He paused a moment longer.

"I think I know this poison. It is an obscure
mixture not often seen on this continent. But I
once took advanced studies under the great
wizard, Sosarian in the Doldavian Mountains of
the Old World. He showed me a type of
mushroom that was gathered in those parts that
was said to create symptoms such as we have
seen. It was but rarely available, for even the
touch of the living organism could cause death,
and to inhale even its spores, so tiny as to be
invisible without a magnifying lens, was decid-
edly toxic. These mushrooms were a bright and
vile shade of blue. As I remember, they were
dried in the light of the moon and then ground

to powder. So lethal were they, that even a pinprick's dose can cause death. Even one so great as my master was wary of their power. They were said to be favored by assassins."

"But Tianna . . . !" Steffan's eyes grew large at the thought of Tianna's injury by the same poison that had killed her father.

"Do not fear," the mage said quickly. "Whomever concocted this abomination cheated themselves of another victim. To prolong the travail, they added something like firebrand, or stinging nettle, which are irritants and have the side effect of increasing the heartbeat and stimulating the senses. Thus, she did not die at the first touch, which gave me time to administer an antidote taught me by Sosarian. Fortunately the poison, virulent as it is, is easily counteracted if recognized, and treated in time."

Othvarr pulled a sheet over the king's twisted features. "I could not save you, oh king, but your princess is blessed that it was I who tended her, rather than one of my brethren who have never journeyed to the Old World."

Steffan could not thank the mage enough for what he had done and despite the elf's self-deprecating manner, Steffan determined to find a way to reward Othvarr for saving Tianna's life. Not until that very moment, did he realize how very much she meant to him. He knelt by her side, took her limp hand in his, and prayed for her speedy recovery.

All work had ceased; one and all were stunned by the death of the king and the precarious position of the princess whom they had come to love and admire. A deep gloom had settled on the camp, which was silent, and watchful, throughout the long day. At dusk, came the first bit of good news. Tianna's fever broke, her breathing eased, and she fell into a deep, but natural slumber. The crisis had passed.

It was only after breakfast the following morning when work crews once again set out for the railhead, that loud hallo's brought everyone on the run. There was a great crashing in the underbrush, as man, dwarf and elf ran as fast as they could in answer to the urgent cry, their tools raised against whatever menace they might find.

But the supposed menace had long since ceased being a problem to itself, or anything else. One by one, the workers filed up and stared at the body of a man clad in the king's own livery. It was the page, the new man, substituted at the very last for the king's missing servant. He too, lay contorted in a posture of extreme agony, and it appeared that he had been dead for some time.

"The assassin," stated Othvarr when he came forward and examined the body.

Steffan saw to the burial of the two men. Charles was laid to rest with much sorrow and weeping, for he had been much loved as a benevolent and caring sovereign, with pomp and as much ceremony as the rough camp could muster. He was buried in the center of a clearing and his grave covered with stones and then a great mound of earth. Flowers would be planted in the spring and tended forever more by the elves who took his death as a personal blow.

Evermore, trains of the Great Eastern would sound their whistles as they passed, in honor of Charles Edouard, the founder and father of the Bright Kingdom's rail road.

The false page was tumbled into a deep hole and buried without any thought other than a curse and a spit of tobac juice. Great care was taken so that neither corpse came into contact with the living, lest they cause even more deaths.

Tianna did not waken for several days and when she opened her eyes and looked up at Steffan, his sorrowful gaze told her everything. So overwrought was she that it became necessary to give her another sleeping potion to ease her grief.

Word of Charles's death spread like wildfire throughout the land, creating shock, dismay, and not a little fear. If a king could be dispatched while surrounded by trusted servants, and his own armed guard, could it not happen to any one, at any time?

When the news reached the Bright Kingdom, Kroner was ready. Outfitted in black velvet and black leather, he immediately proclaimed himself the new King of the Bright Kingdom. He promptly issued a series of royal decrees, and had them distributed throughout the land.

The first decree contained the text of a document, evidently written in Charles's own hand, whereby the kingdom and all he possessed on earth, were bequeathed with love, and devoted affection, to his beloved son, Kroner. Of Tianna, there was no mention.

The second decree was a charge of murder leveled against Tianna, holding her personally responsible for the death of *his* father and offering an enormous reward for her head.

In a mocking ceremony, attended by only himself, his three mages, and a reluctant cleric, Kroner placed his father's crown on his own head and took up the gold and bejeweled scepter that was the symbol of the king's power.

He headed off whatever criticism might be leveled at him for the hasty and unusual ascendancy to the throne, by stating that the kingdom was in deep grieving, and it would not have been seemly for the pomp and circumstance that the occasion would normally warrant. The truth of the matter was that he was afraid that the members of the king's council and the chamber of deputies sent from the cities of the land, might have defied his orders. Therefore, his third decree was to dissolve the council, dismiss the chamber of deputies, and in general, rid the kingdom of whomever else he thought might oppose him.

The Bright Kingdom was a hotpot of conflicting rumors. The populace was worried and confused, and the army grew nervous and restive as more and more of Kroner's accusations were made known. Supposedly, Tianna had been seen riding toward BlueFeld at the head of an army of elves. Also, Tianna and Sper Andros had allegedly sent winged messengers to dwarf, elf and half-orc alike, offering vast sums for Kroner's life. A trio of would be assassins robed all in black had been discovered in the small agricultural town of Bomen and beaten to death with cudgels, before it was discovered that they were clerics, deaf and dumb and unable to protest their innocence. Assassins and enemies were seen all around the kingdom and the citizens were stirred to a boil by the simmering rumors and innuendo.

Kroner had planted the first few seeds, but the harvest he reaped was a bumper crop, beyond his wildest expectations. Perhaps the people were not so pleased as Charles Edouard had thought about the rail road and the new taxes levied to pay for it. No doubt, if he had lived, Charles would have been able to calm his people's fears. But his untimely death, and Kroner's decrees, had thrown the kingdom into utter distress. Kroner's success gave him the incentive he needed to progress to the next stage of his plan.

Announcements were posted that King Kroner would address the good people of BlueFeld from the ramparts of the castle, in two days time. Irate citizens flocked to the city in droves.

When the fateful day arrived, Kroner carefully dressed himself all in white, and rubbed a potion on his face and hands to make himself appear even more pale and wan, if such a thing were possible. Dark circles of sorrow were artfully applied beneath his lower lids to simulate grief. He combed his hair down around his face, page boy fashion, to appear even younger, and more innocent. He waited until the enormous crowd that filled the park and courtyard below the castle became restless, before making his appearance.

Stories of Kroner's unpleasant personality and difficult ways were familiar tales to the common-folk, but few had ever seen the young man in person. Therefore, there was much interest in viewing him, and deciding for themselves. What they saw tugged at their hearts, and took much of the malice out of their whispers.

"Why look, he be nothing but a little lad. Could use some fattening up," said one good country mother.

"Don't look at all what I pictured him lookin' like after all them stories when he was growin' up," another said with a contemptuous sniff. "No doubt them city nanny's an' wet nurses just don't have the knack of it. What he needed was a good dose of country fixin'."

Throughout the crowd, similar comments were expressed, and watchers took careful note of those few who dared to utter doubts.

Kroner judged his moment nicely, and only when the crowd hushed, did he begin to speak. His words floated out on the cool air, fragile and pitched somewhat uncertainly, with the occasional quaver of emotion. With grief riding on every word, and weighing on his thin shoulders, he spoke to the crowd, softly at first and then stronger as he went on. He told them in painful detail of the manner in which his father died, bringing to their attention the fact that Charles's death was deep within Glyth Gamel, elven territory. Next, he reminded them that it was elves who had come here with the scheme that had led to his father's death . . . in elven lands. Nor was it an accident that the elves' emissary was Sper Andros, one of unknown heritage, who dared to pass himself off as a human, although suspected from new information, only recently gained, to be in truth, of pure elf blood. Nor was it coincidence that his sister, the princess Tianna, was seldom separated from this treacherous elf.

Even more damning was the fact that Tianna had been present at the death of both his father and his older brother. Here, his voice clearly broke, and he passed a hand over his eyes as though to shield the scene of his un-kinglike tears, from the crowd. In truth, he was merely taking measure of his performance.

Had Kroner been anything other than the role his birth had cast him in, he might have achieved greatness as an orator, a politician, an actor or even a master criminal, such was his genius even at such a tender age. But none of those, and all of them, were now his calling. Satisfied with his roleplaying, and the response of the crowd, confident he had them in his hand with the last bit of tears, he continued.

He wept, allowing the tears to pour down his cheeks (fortunately he had taken the possibility into account and made certain the dark shadows were waterproof), and exhorted the crowd to follow him, to give him their allegiance, despite his young age.

He ached, no, he burned, in every fiber of his body, to avenge the untimely deaths of his brother and beloved father. He could do so, only with their support. He flung his young, earnest, tear-stained persona at them, and placed his future in their hands.

Unseen, in a dark room, deep beneath the castle, Threlgar sat before the pool of darkness, watching the young prince and the crowd. At his side were Brogalf and Agrippa, and the trio were busily insuring that young Kroner's performance would be a success. The threads of a mass charm were channeled through the being of the prince and wound into and around the minds of the people.

It was a bravura performance. It brought down the house. Every man, woman and child present clamored for the right to enlist in the army to be created on the spot by volunteers. He would press no man into service against his will, in order to hunt down the traitoress Tianna and the vile elf known as Sper Andros, and he had no need to.

Furthermore, once the Glyth Gamel were driven out of the forests forever, every man, or boy who proved his loyalty by joining the army, could lay claim to 160 acres of prime forest land. The rush to sign included nearly all who were present, and of those who declined, their names were also noted.

CHAPTER TWENTY-ONE

Battle

A great bat fluttered through the darkness and glided into the damp cave that was the headquarters of Gorathog. The pig-nosed flying creature landed clumsily on a roost and a little bell sounded its arrival. Moments later an old orc carrying a smoking lantern hobbled out of a side passage and inspected the newcomer.

"Ah, word from Him!" The orc hung his lamp on a hook and removed an object that had been fastened to the bat's leg with a bit of twine. That done, the orc pulled a bit of raw meat out of his pouch and offered it to the bat. "Here y'are, me beauty." The creature took the reward and began greedily gnawing. The orc took up his lantern and hobbled off, plunging the cave into darkness once again.

Several large orcs, all dressed in black leather, sat round a wooden table, ripping hunks of meat off a mutton roast. They were arguing with one another, grunting and growling, and smacking their lips as they ate. Torches set in cressets dimly illuminated the foul place. The stone walls surrounding the scene were wet, and the floor was naught but damp, blackish mud. At the head

of the table sat Gorathog, the Mighty, as he
called himself. And around him were the captains of his army. The noisy feast continued a
while longer, then beer was brought and they
drank their fill, belching loudly, and making
other rude sounds that set most of them to
laughing. The festivities were interrupted by a
stooped old orc who hobbled into the room,
made his way to the head of the table, and
handed a small object to his master.

"Enough!" shouted Gorathog. The others fell
silent. "Good. Now I have yer attention. The
gold and jewels have arrived, as promised."
There was a general growl of approval. "The
raids are over. The time for the attack is come!"
More growls of assent and cups were banged on
the table. Gorathog, by far the largest of those
present, suddenly jammed a dagger into the
table, startling the others.

"That!" he said with great emphasis, "is
Railla." There was another loud thwack and a
second blade rose from the wood. "That is the
new road to Glyween. They haven't finished it
yet . . ."

"And they never will!" snarled one of the
others. Gorathog glared across the table then
continued. "Oksokh, Osbin, are your tribes in
place?"

"Yes, great one!" came two swift replies.

"You will begin the attack . . . here." Gorathog
pointed a gnarled black finger at the knife that
represented Railla. "At dawn, two days hence.
Make a great show of your orcs. Set the fires and
then pour oil, but do not press the dwarves.

When foes come at you, you are to fall back into the mountains."

A distressed look crossed the twisted dark features of his chieftains. One of them dared to speak, "But . . ."

"Silence, fool! Have you not seen their rail road? Before you could get near the city, every dwarf in Rakhatz would be brought there to destroy you. You must follow my plan. You are there to make a disturbance and draw them to you, but not to fight." He glared at the two for a moment. "Am I clear?"

They nodded sheepishly. "Then begone! Ride to your standards and do as your lord commands!"

Oksokh and Osbin did as they were told and vanished quickly so as not to anger Gorathog further.

"The rest of you will attack at noon that day. When you hear the trumpets sound, we all advance as one. I, myself, will lead you to our glorious victory." There was a satisfied growl from the rest. "Onthal, you must direct the wolves up the river valley and set them upon the elves the night before, to cover our approach."

"To hear is to obey," grinned the orc.

The first thing that alarmed Dingur Knorsen, when he awoke that dawn, was the strange burning smell that drifted across the camp. The others noticed it too, and one of the more industrious dwarves climbed to the top of the bluff above the construction camp.

"It's Railla!" the dwarven scout shouted

excitedly, as the others sat down to breakfast. "It's on fire!"

Knorsen stood up at the table and addressed the others, "C'mon, boys, let's go!" A whistle blew and bells rang all around the various camps. The track-laying crew was the closest, and therefore the first aboard, the waiting train. Soon an army of graders, carrying picks and shovels, came running down the grade and climbed aboard.

"That's enough for this one," shouted Knorsen and waved the engineer off. The iron dragon sensed the urgency and blew off a cloud of steam, spun its wheels, and in a trice, the train jerked and rolled rapidly down the track.

Dingur was not sure exactly what was wrong, but somehow sensed his men were needed. He was not about to wait for a message to call for help. A second work train was backed up to the railhead, and it, too, was soon filled with even more graders and a gang from the tunnel crew. Just as he was about to wave the train off, a messenger from the bird service arrived. It merely confirmed his suspicions.

It read:

"Large force of orcs attacking city from the west. Send all possible help," and was signed Borgrund.

"It's orcs!" Dingur yelled up to the dwarves already aboard the train. "Axes and shields!" The crews swarmed down off the flat cars, armed themselves from one of the many weapons caches stacked by the track for just such emergencies, and were soon ready to go. Dingur armed himself too, and, at the last moment, hopped aboard the moving train as it began to gather speed.

Persy Browne was perplexed. Cynarr and Carras had reported unusual smells and sounds coming from the west. They felt the movement of many feet on the ground and smelled orcs and wolves. But this was not unusual. Orc raids had been occurring on and off since they had entered these woods, and his little band of surveyors had beaten off an attack by dire wolves only a week previous. The catmen had recommended pulling back to the relative safety of the grading camp, but that meant losing a day's work, if no trouble materialized. It was no use asking the rest of his crew what they felt. As one, they agreed to follow his lead. If he stayed, he might be leading them all to their deaths.

It was evening, and Cynarr and Carras would soon be going out for the night unless he decided to break camp. By then it would be too late to change his mind.

"Curse it all!" Browne shouted to himself. He pulled out a coin and flipped it in the air. His hand missed it in the firelight and it fell into the snow. As he stooped to pick it up, Cynarr's fur-lined feet planted themselves in front of him.

Cynarr stepped on the coin, burying it in the snow. "We go — now," he rumbled and Browne did not disagree. Soon the fire was out, the gear packed, and the survey party stumbled back toward safety in the dark of night.

❖   ❖   ❖

Carson was awakened by a banging at his door. He'd had a hard day and was in no mood for solving another petty dispute between humans and dwarves. He pulled open the door and beheld a breathless elf, holding a lantern.

"Hate to bother you, boss, but we just got a message from Browne." The elf paused.

"Go on, son, what is it?"

"Says he's bringing his crew in. Trouble brewing."

"And . . ." demanded Carson.

"That's it, that's all it says." The elf held a slip of parchment up to the light.

"What in blazes? Why doesn't anybody tell me anything? What trouble? A forest fire? Orcs? Wild dogs?" The dwarf cursed out loud. He was about to give the messenger what for, when he realized the poor elf was only doing his job.

"Well, better go roust the crews up the line. Wake every other one. The rest can sleep till something happens." He shut the door and hurriedly began to dress.

All along the narrow path that would someday be a rail road, the word was passed, and soon half of the crews were up and armed. Those who were to be allowed to sleep were taunted noisily by the others, and the net effect was a sleepless night for all. Of course, with trouble imminent, none of the designated sleepers were particularly keen on being killed while they rested.

Fires were lit at each major campsite and armed workers stood alongside the soldiers to form great circles, peering out into the night awaiting the unknown. Other catmen scouts streamed into their various camps and, suddenly, the threat seemed very real. The word was out. Dire wolves were coming.

The first attacks hit in the north, and Browne was glad he had taken the precaution of falling back. Secure amid a ring of sturdy armed dwarves, the furtive attack was easily beaten off. Almost too easily, he thought at the time. Then, all down the line, each camp in turn was tested, and each time, the menacing beasts were driven off into the night.

Well before dawn, the wolves disappeared into the forest, no more to be seen. When reports came in that all were safe and there had been no casualties, Carson congratulated himself. But soon his joy turned to worry. He wondered how much work he'd get out of his crews after they'd been up all night beating off wolves.

Shortly after dawn, he decided to chuck the day's work and let them rest. The crews had earned it. He was about to give the order when the urgent message came from RedCliffe. Railla was under attack, send help.

In no time, a scene similar to the one supervised by Dingur Knorsen in the south began to unfold. One by one, trains were backed up to the railhead, heavily armed crews climbed aboard, and the trains sped off to the aid of the dwarven capital.

Bagor StoneHeart peered at the map of Railla etched in stone on the great table before him. As reports came down the speaking tubes, dwarves moved the colored stones that represented the various forces as they moved about on the battlefield above. At first, StoneHeart had been worried, and considered going to the surface to direct the battle, rather than remain safe in his underground headquarters. Now the battle was nearly over, and the last black stone representing invaders was removed. He smiled. Things were under control.

When the orcs had come up during the night, overwhelming the outposts as they marched, it appeared as though a major assault was in the making. At dawn, when the fires were lit in the outlying villages, the smoke obscured the reality of the situation. The number of orcs appeared to be greater than they actually were. The situation looked dangerous enough to summon help, and he was very pleased at the response he received. Within the space of three hours, nearly four thousand armed dwarves, elves, and humans had been rushed to the battle by rail.

The orcs had been overwhelmed, beaten soundly. Unaware of the interconnecting network of underground passages around the dwarven capital, the black creatures had advanced a little too far. Secure in the knowledge that help was on its way, Bagor had ordered the local garrison out, through the mountain to surface through secret tunnels behind the black invaders. Surrounded, and without hope of escape, the orcs fought bravely to the last, but it had been in vain. Bagor's armies had destroyed all save a few, who escaped the trap by dropping their arms and fleeing south. Now, there was nothing to do but clean up the mess, burn the enemy dead, and bury his own.

It was past the lunch hour and he had missed breakfast. The dwarf king had just ordered his meal when the disturbing news arrived.

"Damn!" exclaimed Bagor. "Get my commanders down here at once!" he yelled to the dwarf who had been moving rocks on the table. "And find Dingur Knorsen!"

The dwarf king fumed at his own stupidity. He should have seen through the ruse, but he had been so smug in his confidence in the rail road to solve all his problems. Now, his enemies had used that very weapon against him.

The station at Railla was a complete and utter mess as thousands of armed dwarves descended upon it in a desperate attempt to board a train, any train, heading north. And the tracks were clogged with trainloads of soldiers still arriving from as far north as Glyth Gamel. It would be some time before traffic was sorted out and the reverse procedure could begin.

Ovaak and his small band of orcs had traveled under cover of darkness for two nights, cowering by day under rocks and dead trees to avoid detection. His men had grumbled at the conditions of their march, slogging up cold mountain streams until they where crusted over with ice, then shivering, unable to build a fire to warm themselves, during the day. Poor Gezzner had broken his leg slipping on a rock and they had to leave him behind, hopefully to pick him up and carry him back to safety, if they themselves survived their mission.

Now Ovaak and his men were hiding behind bushes at the bottom of the gorge with their goal in sight. It was a tall, spindly wooden bridge that held up a portion of the dwarves' devilish rail road. The orc had marveled at the great iron machines that had come rumbling over the bridge all morning in a headlong rush to the south. He had no idea what it all meant, but he had certainly noticed the thousands of armed dwarves that had passed by and was glad that none had stopped here.

There were four guards at the bridge and Ovaak had noted their patterns. Each hour, one of the dwarves would walk out onto the bridge, and carefully inspect the timbers beneath him. Another would scramble down a stone stair and scout a short distance along the stream bed on either side of the structure. But they had not seen him or his band. The next time the guards came out, they would die.

Ovaak had orders to destroy the bridge, but not until five hours after the sunrise. Harakn, who crouched next to him, kept the hourglass. He had turned it four times already and it was almost time for action. Two of his orcs were the best archers in Gorathog's army. They had been specially chosen for this mission.

Ovaak checked his supplies: the oilskins were intact, and he had both flint and steel in his pocket.

Steffan had called Groc when the message arrived, and they debated whether to send part of their small construction gang to aid the dwarves. Then there was Princess Tianna to be considered. With her father dead, she *was* the Bright Kingdom and it fell upon him to see to her safety. At last he and Groc rode down to Junction on a handcar, assembled a small group of armed dwarves, and sent them off on some flatcars behind number 12. At least the Bright Kingdom could make a token gesture of support.

As train after train came roaring through Junction, Steffan began to worry. He had received no further messages concerning the state of the battle and began to wonder if all was lost.

"Take number 17 down to RedCliffe," suggested Groc, aware of his boss' worry. "You can find out the latest news, and if things are all right, bring back a load of rails while you're at it."

So it was done. Groc was admonished to keep his forces on full alert . . . no rail work today. When Steffan arrived in RedCliffe, the place seemed deserted. Gone were the miners, and the dwarves that manned the furnaces. Gone too were all the engines and cars that usually filled the maze of tracks that surrounded the place. Number 17 and the few flat cars it pulled were the only pieces of rolling stock to be seen. He made his way inside the tunnel complex and sought out the bird service office. There he found Hammner and two of his aides.

"What news, IronFist?" Steffan asked. "Every dwarf north of Junction seems to have gone off to Railla."

"So they have, so they have," Hammner

replied absently, reading handfuls of messages as they were given to him. "Bagor has crushed the orcs at Railla . . . Damn! Now there's something wrong up north. Carson's under heavy attack . . . thousands of orcs . . . and most of his crews are down in Railla." He handed the messages to Steffan who read the bad news for himself. The dwarf was reading the next message and suddenly made a spluttering sound.

The normally red-cheeked dwarf had gone pale. "The bridge over Beaver Creek has been partially burned by orcs! It will take a day to repair!"

Steffan was not quite sure what that meant. He turned to the map of the system painted on the wall. Suddenly the significance was all too clear. Practically every engine and car on the entire rail road was south of that bridge, and for that matter, so was the whole dwarven army.

"What men do you have left at your camp outside Junction?" asked the dwarf anxiously.

"Only a small force," Steffan answered worriedly. "Not enough to be of any help against thousands of orcs."

"Carson will be crushed and the camp destroyed."

"Glyth Gamel may be destroyed!" Steffan's fears went a bit farther than those of IronFist. He paced back and forth, nervously searching for a solution. Othvarr and Preston might be able to do something with magic. The princess was too weak to help. They needed something, and they needed it fast. Something that would stop the orcs. . . . a memory flashed before his eyes, of dwarves and elves streaming in fear out of RedCliffe.

"Hammner, is Malus still down south, mining that tunnel?"

The dwarf looked at him quizzically, as if this could have no bearing on their predicament.

"Well, is he?" demanded Steffan.

"Um . . . no. He wouldn't touch the rock down there, not enough iron content, so they brought him back."

It only took a little persuasion, for even the dwarf could think of no alternative. Ragnor RockJaw was harder to convince, but finally he resolved the war between his dedication to the rail road, and his loyalty to a certain cantankerous old dragon, saving one and dooming another.

Steffan's plan had been to load Malus aboard the one remaining train north of Beaver Creek, overfeed him on the way north, give him all the water he could hold and let him explode amidst the orcan army. Ragnor's proposal made even more sense. Malus was at least useful as a tunneling dragon. Fire King, on the other hand, was already mounted and joined to an undercarriage. He had grown more disagreeable by the day, and they had been trying to find a way to dispose of the monster. Here was a chance to let the evil beast do his masters a service.

With great difficulty the massive Fire King, for he was truly the largest of the iron dragons ever assembled, was persuaded out of the tunnels and hooked up, face first, to a flatcar loaded with steel rails. A water tank car was connected behind the engine and a leather hose coiled up for use when the time was right. Two volunteer elves climbed aboard, along with Steffan and Ragnor, who took the controls. Fire King was so busy greedily consuming the steel rails, that he paid no mind to what was going on in the cab.

"Well, here's hopin'," Ragnor said stoically. He wiped his glasses on his sleeve and ordered the elves to run the hose up to the dragon's intake pipe. This was done. A moment later the dwarf turned a valve and fed a bit of extra water to Fire King. The monster instantly let out a cloud of steam and began to huff and puff and roll along the rails, pushing his food before him and pulling his deadly drink behind.

Already, the creature was glowing bright red, but Ragnor carefully fed the iron dragon only enough water to keep up a steady pace down the track. They began to pick up speed as the strange train rolled down towards Junction. There was much consternation and worry in the camp when it roared past at high speed. Groc yelled something at them as they passed but the words were lost to Fire King's roar.

Now they were out of the broad valley and back into the hills and woods, fast approaching the railhead. Steffan was amazed how well-behaved Fire King had been, and was having second thoughts about his decision to destroy the monster/machine. Well, it was too late now. Steam was hissing in great jets from beneath the dragon's shimmering scales and Steffan was certain the beast had grown several feet in circumference, for it was becoming difficult to see around the monster's midsection, to the track ahead.

What if Carson and his men still held the railhead? Would he and Ragnor be able to hold Fire King back until the orcs came? Would there be time to tell the work crews to fall back and give up this prize to the orcs? Maybe his plan was not as well thought out as it should have been.

Ragnor suddenly pulled down on a long handled lever and great clouds of steam billowed out in puffy clouds from the cylinders. The engine slowed significantly.

"I can slow the train!" yelled the dwarf, "but I can't slow the dragon. Get ready to jump." Ragnor turned the water valve all the way open allowing Fire King to drink his fill.

"Jump?" Steffan exclaimed in horror. That wasn't the plan. "We have to warn Carson!" he screamed. Ragnor looked him in the eyes for a moment then snapped his fingers. The dwarf reached up, pulled on the whistle cord and tooted out the signal for a runaway train. Needless to say, there was plenty of steam to spare for such doings. Another tense minute passed and Steffan saw a pile of ties beside the track go by. They were near the camp now, traveling behind a hot, glowing cloud of roaring steam. It was almost impossible to see anything. The elves suddenly leaped from the cab. Ragnor pushed Steffan to the door, and together they jumped, landing with a crash, high in the branches of a pine tree. They tumbled and rolled over one another and then bounced down onto the needles at the base of the tree.

Fire King rolled away noisily on his deadly mission, invisible inside a giant screaming cloud of white-hot steam. Ragnor came to his senses first and pointed at a low culvert that ran under the track. The two of them crawled down under it and there found their elven volunteers already in hiding.

Soon there came a horrifying, high-pitched scream, followed by what felt like every clap of thunder Steffan had ever heard in his entire life. The earth shook violently. Moments later a violent blast of steam rolled over them through the forest, knocking over trees for miles in all directions.

Kroner rode at the head of the long column. He was mounted on a great black horse, sword and buckler at his side. He wore the crown of the king and a long black cape hung loosely from his shoulders. Behind him came the regular soldiers of BlueFeld, marching in neat rows, with their shields brightly polished. Next came the pikemen, black flags fluttering from their polearms. Bringing up the rear was the ragtag army that Kroner had signed up to go conquer Glyth Gamel.

When they first learned of his plan to go to war, his generals were outraged.

"We cannot wage a campaign against the elves in those forests," complained one.

"We would need an army a hundred times as large," stated another. Two swift executions brought the remainder of his commanders

around to their new king's point of view, no
matter how impossible they believed it to be. So
now, five thousand citizens of the Bright Kingdom were marching through the snow to do
battle with a nation of elves in the forests of
Glyth Gamel.

The great march passed Bremmner, where
Kroner, with the aid of his magicians, managed
to persuade more to join his ranks. They
marched along the coast road, then up the broad
valley of the grain belt. The disciplined soldiers
of the Bright Kingdom stayed steady and
marched dutifully, if uneasily, behind their mad
young king. The citizen army, however, began to
shrink under the relentless pace Kroner insisted
on keeping. Only the regular army had supply
waggons and food, the others were left to forage
off the land, laying waste to much of the
beautiful valley.

By the time the border with Glyth Gamel was
reached, Kroner's army numbered only half its
starting force. The elves of the wood knew long
in advance of his coming, and of his intent, for
relations with the humans on the border had
long been friendly and the elves were fore-
warned. Therefore, Kroner met no opposition as
his forces crashed wearily into the woods and up
into the foothills of the Iron Mountains. They
passed through the village of Woodsong, without
even knowing it had been there, so well did its
inhabitants conceal it.

CHAPTER TWENTY-TWO

Treachery

It took a day or more for the stragglers to come in, the heads to be counted and the dead buried, but all in all, the last wild ride of Fire King had been a success of unprecedented magnitude. Steffan's fears that he had destroyed Carson and most of his work gang were relieved when the dwarf, his clothes ragged and torn, came staggering into the new, temporary railhead at the front of what was left of his crew. When Carson had seen how heavily outnumbered he had been, he ordered a slow but methodical retreat. To give his gangs time to escape into the forests, he had had all the supplies in the main camp broken open. Barrels of salt beef, kegs of beer and wine were left everywhere, along with the bags of gold and silver used to make the payrolls.

As the orcs descended on the camp, wild looting ensued, and Gorathog lost control of his army. The orcs were in the process of tearing apart the boarding train when Fire King screamed into their midst and exploded. Where once there had been an orc army many thousands strong, there was now a great barren crater, hundreds of rods deep and fully four leagues in diameter.

For years after, the tracks circling the edge of the crater became a popular landmark and tourist attraction. At the moment, however, word had reached Steffan of a new menace, marching through the woods of his homeland, heading for the pass near Junction. Ninius and Bagor assembled a sizable army and it was entrained and sent to Junction.

The combined elf/dwarf army left Junction in the middle of a howling blizzard and slogged laboriously up the mountainside through the entire night. It was nearly daylight when they arrived, all but frozen to the bone, their feet and legs sodden and painfully numb, staggering with exhaustion. The royalty and a few lucky aides took shelter in the cave. The others slept where they fell, huddled beneath bushes and stacked against one another with only their bearskin bedrolls to protect them from the elements.

Dawn crept in on drifts of icy fog and hesitant trickles of opaque grey light. The combined armies of Rakhatz and Glyth Gamel rose stiff and aching from beneath their frosted, ice encrusted bearskins, shivering in the bitter cold. The storm had blown itself out while they slept and branches gathered to build fires did little to warm their freezing bodies.

Soon, a pack train came up from Junction, bringing food. Cauldrons of double-strength acorn tea were brewed in record time and distributed among the elves and dwarves. The chatter and clinking of teeth on stone cups sounded like the tinkling of icicles breaking. Fresh loaves of bread baked in the rail road camp were distributed, and each was given a solid bar composed of high bush cranberries, mountain blueberries, whole grains, honey and bear fat; nourishing and wonderful when meals and fires were an impossibility.

The kings and Tianna gathered together in the cave with their commanders and listened to the scouts as they reported what they knew of Kroner and the massed army of the Bright Kingdom which faced them across the saddle of the pass. It was an awesome sight, Kroner's men were aligned under crisp standards, drawn up into neat formations, spears, pikes and swords glinting in the thin, cold sunlight.

To the rank and file of the elf/dwarf army it appeared that they were heavily outnumbered and, fearless fighters though they were, their hearts weighed heavy with despair. Then, one of the elves with his keen eyesight was able to discern that many of the enemy appeared to be town-folk and farm boys, old grandfathers, and even young children. They were armed, but waving their weapons in an awkward fashion, if indeed they were able to raise them off the ground at all.

"Hah! Look at 'em, scared sheep!" chortled a dwarven dwarf general, as he examined the opposing forces through a magnifying glass. "I'll bet this is their first battle. What did Kroner do, kidnap anything that moved? I'd be willing to bet real gold that most of 'em 'll cut an run, after we make for them. If'n they don't kill themselves first on their own blades, the poor, dumb stupid clucks. I'd feel sorry for 'em if they weren't the enemy."

"I'd take that wager if I didn't happen to agree with you," the elven commander said, shaking his head at the senseless battle that would doubtless transpire. These humans had no understanding of what war was, and if they were not killed outright, they would likely spend the rest of their lives maimed and in pain.

"But look there," pointed out Steffan, who stood nearby with the two kings and Tianna. "Those are the regular soldiers of BlueFeld. They are well trained and will give as good as they take."

The dwarven general trained his glass on the soldiers with the polished shields and ready weapons and grunted. "Right you are, lad. Sure this'll be no picnic today."

Throughout the day, liaisons crossed back and forth across the no man's land of the small valley carrying messages to and fro from Kroner and the elf/dwarf command. The waist-deep snow was trodden into mush beneath their frozen feet.

Each side demanded that the other surrender immediately, to their superior forces. Each side declined the other's offer. It was with great relief that the elves and dwarves realized that the day would likely be filled with posturing and planning. While the commanders of the opposing forces and the unfortunate liaisons continued the farce, the fighting men, dwarves and elves and humans alike, stepped down from battle readiness, all except a forward line who positioned themselves just above the skyline so that it could not be seen that the majority of their comrades were taking the opportunity to establish better bivouacs, set up a mess area and latrines, then grab as much sleep as would be allowed them.

Kroner's forces, however, were further down the slope and were unable to execute such a charade. By nightfall, it could be seen that many of their numbers had succumbed to the cold and exhaustion. Already their numbers were dwindling. However, it seemed certain that neither side would capitulate and that morning would see the first bloodshed.

In Kroner's camp, the would-be king had lapsed into a manic frenzy. Repeatedly, he ordered his generals to charge the enemy, which they wisely refused, death threats or not. Kroner turned his rage on his three mentors ordering them to do everything from controlling the weather, "make it colder for the dwarves and elves, yet warmer and more endurable for our side. . . ." to turning the enemy army into stone statues. As it became more and more obvious that his army was paralyzed by the cold and exhaustion and as good as useless, Kroner's behavior became more and more atrocious.

Finally, raging at the three wizards who were clearly on the verge of outright rebellion, Kroner marched haughtily down the lines of his army and began berating those who had fallen where they stood, victims of insufficient apparel and the unaccustomed hardships. He ordered men physically dragged to their feet and had them pushed and shoved back into line. Finally, he came to one youth, no more than thirteen and wearing only a tattered summer jacket and pants stuffed with straw. The boy's fingers had frozen to his pikestaff, which was two heads taller than he, and heavy enough for a full-grown adult. His hands were without gloves and his feet without shoes. Already his extremities were a blotchy dead-looking, blue-white. If he survived the battle, he would most certainly live the remainder of his life without fingers and toes. No matter to Kroner who became totally enraged when he could not waken the lad. To no avail did those around him try to tell the young king that the boy was unconscious.

Kroner kicked the unresponsive form hard, and then screamed at those who made tentative moves to stop him. "If he will not take up his position, then he is no better than a stinking deserter," and before the crowd realized what he intended, he drew his sword and with a single slice lopped off the boy's head. A great silence fell upon those who had been close enough the see and hear what was taking place.

A moment of sanity returned to Kroner's eyes as he looked into hundreds of eyes, glazed with shock and more than a little animosity and perhaps even a hint of knowledge of who and what they were dealing with, and he quickly sheathed his sword and retreated to the safety of his tent.

Threlgar the Unwise, had watched the child's murder with sadness in his eyes. Years before, he had been expressly chosen by the boy's grandfather to guide Kroner's education, to school him in the magic arts. In vain had he attempted to direct and shape the lad to fulfill the role, to achieve a binding alliance between his native land and the Bright Kingdom. In the early days of Kroner's childhood Threlgar had tried to persuade himself that Kroner was merely strong-willed rather than stubborn, intelligent and seeking, rather than clever and devious. He had also sought desperately to convince himself that Kroner was interested in the physical make-up of creatures, and perhaps in time would become a great healer. But at length he was forced to admit that Kroner had none of those positive qualities, and all of the negative. Further, his interest in the physical sciences only went so far as discovering how to inflict the most pain without actually killing. The numbers of dead creatures — rabbits, cat, dogs and even a horse — mounted steadily, until the day that Threlgar had issued an ultimatum, telling Kroner that he would return to his grandfather and tell him everything, taking the other two mages with him, if Kroner did not cease the torture.

It had not been a pleasant moment, but the killings ceased, or at least became more surreptitious. From that point on, there had been a truce of sorts, between Threlgar and his young charge. Kroner made certain that Threlgar knew nothing of what he was doing, and Threlgar pretended that nothing was amiss. But now the boy had gone too far.

The murder of Charles had been Agrippa's

doing. Terrified of being sent back in disgrace, the lesser mage had allowed himself to be used by the young man who would soon be his king. He had also assisted Kroner in dispatching Tyndal and destroying the fleet. All of which, Threlgar had learned, after the fact.

But with the murder of the poor, frozen child, something snapped inside of Threlgar. He looked at Kroner with cold eyes and admitted to himself that something had gone terribly wrong either in birth or in breeding. This cruel young man could not be taught. Further, his soul was black and twisted, and whatever he touched withered and died. Threlgar's course was clear, Kroner had to be stopped.

Late that night, while his exhausted army slept as best they could in makeshift shelters, Kroner himself was tucked away deep inside a multitude of down quilts, thoroughly insulated against the cold and sleeping soundly, thanks to a sleeping potion that Threlgar had mixed into his hot cider. The thought had crossed his mind to increase the dose, but even loathing the boy as he did, he could not bring himself to kill the one he had served all his life.

Instead, Threlgar crept from the tent after Kroner had fallen into a deep and dreamless sleep, and made his way through the darkness to Tianna's camp. He was captured by sentries and brought to the cave. The kings were awakened and Threlgar was given a seat and warm tea. Upon questioning, the mage readily admitted everything the boy had done from the first tortured insect, to the murder of his father.

Tianna was stunned by Threlgar's revelations, not only by the depth of Kroner's duplicity, but by the degree of hatred that had to exist for such actions to have occurred. Had he really hated them that much? Could she have done anything different, and had she done so, would her brother and father still be alive. She buried her head in her arms and sobbed deeply and bitterly.

Steffan's eyes met those of the wizard who seemed somehow diminished, shrunken with the catalog of his charge's black deeds. Steffan took Tianna into his arms and stroked her hair softly, comforting her in the only way that he knew how. Her generals silently removed themselves from the tent, and the sight of their mistress' grief.

"Do not blame yourself, my child," Threlgar said, sinking to his knees beside her. "I tormented myself for years, thinking that his actions were somehow a reflection of my teaching. I told myself that I should have been able to stop him, to turn him in other directions, but I realize now that I was wrong. He contaminated even me. He is evil, like a blighted tree that grows twisted and diseased, despite the very best husbandry. Such a tree must be destroyed, torn out by the very roots so that no sliver of it remains to poison that which grows around it. And so it must be with your brother. You must slay him. It is the only way."

Tianna raised tear bright eyes and stared at him in horror.

Threlgar arose anxiously. "I must return to his tent," he said sadly, grasping Tianna's hands gently. "I have betrayed him, but he is still my charge, my king and I will remain at his side as I have been bid. Adieu, princess . . . nay, Queen. Although I have no right to such a request, I pray that you do not hate this old man." The guards stepped aside and Steffan followed the mage outside.

"Give this man safe passage back to the enemy lines."

Tianna knew that she should hate Threlgar, but her heart refused to obey. As young as she was, she suddenly realized how very easy it might be to allow wrong to occur, simply by doing nothing at all.

At first light, Tianna sent a runner into Kroner's camp with a parchment listing his numerous wrongs against crown and state, including the death of his father and brother by use of black magic. She ordered him to surrender himself immediately, to answer the charges of high treason. Ten minutes after he had received the missive, she ordered the entire document read aloud through a trumpet horn, so that his troops might know what kind of master they were serving. "You are hereby, formally released from your services, and ordered to return to your homes and families. Those who obey immediately will be granted clemency, any who defy the Queen's orders will be regarded as the enemy, and treated accordingly."

For a moment, there was stunned silence from Kroner's camp, then mass confusion as his army began to mill about, talking excitedly. The majority of them had had their fill of war. What had seemed a jolly, patriotic lark in the valleys of the Bright Kingdom now appeared quite different, in the cold and snow of the high mountains. Many did not even need to think twice, but cast down their weapons and without further ado, turned and began the long trek home.

No sooner had the reader begun reciting Tianna's demands, than Kroner rushed out of his glorious blue tent, gently billowing in the cold wind and commanded his archers to shoot the reader. "Kill him, shoot him! Stop his lying tongue," he raged, fairly dancing up and down in demented fury. The archer laid down his bow and refused to do as he was commanded.

"The distance is too great, my lord," the man said deferentially. But his manner did not assuage Kroner, and he drew his sword and raised it high to cleave the man in two. But Threlgar stopped his blow, seizing his wrist high above his head in a steely grip. Kroner glared at his mentor.

"You," Kroner hissed. "You told her, you caviling worm. She could not have known had you not told her. There was no way . . ." Threlgar met his eyes and did not reply, which in itself was an admission of the charge. Kroner struggled, increasing the pressure against the elderly wizard, forcing him to give way slightly. Threlgar braced himself and then used both hands to prevent Kroner from using the blade on him. He did not think for a minute that their long association would prevent the boy from killing him. Kroner struggled and increased the pressure on Threlgar's grip so that the mage would bring up the second arm, leaving his midsection totally unprotected. In one swift motion of his left hand, Kroner drew a small dagger from his belt and drove the point into Threlgar's chest, directly below the sternum, and then thrust it up into his mentor's heart.

Only then, did Kroner realize that the entire army had stopped whatever they were doing to stare at him in disbelief. He looked around him with wild eyes, stained with blood from head to toe, the body of his most trusted friend and mentor lying in the snow at his feet.

"Why are you looking at me! Stop looking at me like that!" he screamed. "I command you to stop looking at me! Pick up your swords and fight! Look! They're coming! You have to fight or we'll all be killed. Do you want that? Do you want to be dead? Cowards! I'm king! You have to obey me! I'm king!" It was terrible to watch, the dissolution of the young man who had killed his father and brother, plotted his sister's death and proclaimed himself king. The troops, ragged farmers, tattered, chilblained townsmen, and hardened army men, advanced on the miserable figure, blades at their sides, advancing, until he was penned inside a circle fifty men deep, all staring at him with condemning eyes.

Kroner was handed over to Tianna's army without protest. And, after swearing allegiance to Tianna, and laying down their weapons, what remained of the army of the Bright Kingdom, availed themselves of the dwarf and elven fires.

Tianna and Steffan had conferred the entire

night long on what to do with Kroner, now securely wrapped in chains and watched over by the guard who had accompanied Charles into the mountains.

"You must put him to death, beloved," Steffan urged. "If you allow him to live, he will cause unending mischief no matter where on earth he is."

"I cannot," Tianna said, distraught, pulling at her hair and pacing back and forth. "I cannot slay my own brother, despite what he has done. Perhaps if I . . ."

"But, princess, you heard what Threlgar said," Steffan argued. "There was no way you could have prevented this. Nothing you could have done would have changed things."

"You don't know that!" Tianna shrieked, hair wild and eyes drowned in tears. "If I had been nicer . . . No, I cannot do it, Steffan. I will send him away, far, far away, to the very ends of the earth, banish him forever. But I cannot kill him."

And despite everything Steffan said to convince her otherwise, that is what she decreed on the following morning. Kroner was banished to the dungeons of Nordkassel, a lonely castle lost in the vastness of the Northern Wastes. To ensure that he did not escape, she sent him in the custody of the same royal guard who were with her now, still grieving the loss of their king. She admonished the men not to slay her brother, merely see that he remained imprisoned for life. Kroner was led away screaming.

Kroner's remaining two mentors, Brogalf and Agrippa, were taken under guard to the coast and there to be placed on the first ship bound for the Old World, from whence they had come, never to show their faces in the Bright Kingdom again. If a serpent or a storm took their lives . . . so be it.

Groc and his crews were given an opportunity to hire workers from the army of the Bright Kingdom. The construction gang was swelled by several hundred men in this manner.

Tianna would march home with the rest. She was mounted astride a velvet deer, and Steffan stood at her side. Ninius and Bagor had already made their farewells, and their armies were trudging back down the slope to Junction.

"I must go home to BlueFeld. I have a kingdom to put in order." Tianna looked into Steffan's eyes and for once, he avoided her stare. He kissed her hand.

"And I have a rail road to build."

In the months that followed, little, if any, progress was made in the pass. Steffan and Groc, however brought their work force over into the Bright Kingdom and in its low, warm valleys, much was accomplished. The survey was completed. Two new railheads were formed in Bremmner, and although they had no engines, wheels and rail were forged. Hand and horse cars were built, and rails and supplies conveyed to the track-layers. Quickly, the route of the Great Eastern snaked its tracks eastward and westward across the Bright Kingdom.

Summer saw a flurry of activity of unprecedented scale. Tianna had done a good job selling the rail road to the people of the Bright Kingdom and money and men were made available. At the peak of summer, Steffan had ten thousand men working in the mountains. There was one troublesome spot on the route and the Great Eastern was forced to dig a short tunnel. Steffan was glad that his plan to explode Malus had been turned aside by Ragnor. The irascible dragon was brought up from RedCliffe and put to work. The beast liked the rock so well, they found themselves in possession of a double-track tunnel before Ragnor could restrain him.

Once the tunnel and the grades were completed, the rails were pushed over the pass and hurried down to the border, there to connect with the track that had been constructed out from Bremmner, earlier in the year .

It was a proud moment for Steffan, as he sat next to Dingur Knorsen in the cab of iron dragon number 12. In time for the harvest of wheat, the first train rolled into BlueFeld, amid the cheering crowds and stopped neatly at the new stone station built just across from the castle. Steffan stepped out the door and looked up at the rampart.

There was Tianna, smiling at him.

THE END

If you enjoyed this adventure set in the world of the game *Iron Dragons*, you should try *The Bard's Tale*™ novels, also from Baen. Here is an excerpt from *Castle of Deception* by Mercedes Lackey and Josepha Sherman.

0-671-72125-9 * 288 pages * $5.99

As the minstrel troop rode and rattled along the wide dirt road, the day was as bright and cheery as something out of a story, full of bird song and pleasant little breezes.

Kevin hardly noticed. He was too busy struggling with his mule to keep it from lagging lazily behind.

"Here, boy." One of the musicians, a red-clad fiddler with instrument case strapped to his back like Kevin, handed the bardling a switch broken from a bush. "Wave this at him. He'll keep moving."

The fiddler's eyes were kind enough, but it seemed to Kevin that his voice practically dripped with condescension. *Thinks I've never ridden before*, Kevin thought, but he managed a tight smile and a "Thanks." It didn't help that the man was right; as long as the mule could see the switch out of the corner of an eye, it kept up a nice, brisk pace.

The North Road cut through brushland for a time, then through stands of saplings, then at last through true forest, green and lush in the springtime. This was royal land, not ceded to any of the nobles, and the road was kept clear, Kevin knew, by the spells of royal magicians. But those nice, neat spells hardly applied to the wildness on either side. The bardling, trying to pretend he'd travelled this way a hundred times, couldn't help wondering if bandits or even dark creatures, orcs or worse, were hiding in there.

Oh, nonsense! He was letting his Master's fussing get to him. It was forest, only forest. No one could see anything sinister in that tranquil greenery.

He'd let the switch drop and the mule was lagging again. Kevin waved it at the beast yet again. When that didn't seem to do any good, he gave it a good whack on the rump. The mule grunted in surprise and broke into a bone-jarring trot, overtaking the wagons and most of the riders. The equally surprised bardling jounced painfully in the saddle, lute banging against his back. For a moment Kevin wished he'd kept it in its case rather than out for quick playing. Struggling to keep his stirrups and his balance, he was sure he heard snickers from the troop.

Then, just as suddenly, the mule dropped back into its easygoing walk. Kevin nearly slammed his face into the animal's neck. This time, as he straightened himself in the saddle, he *knew* he'd heard muffled laughter. Without a word, he pulled the mule back into the troop.

Although the minstrels kept up a steady patter of cheerful conversation and song all around him, Kevin clamped his lips resolutely together after that. He had given them enough entertainment already!

It wasn't helping his increasingly sour mood that every time someone looked his way, he could practically hear that someone thinking, *Poor little boy, out on his own!*

"I'm *not* a baby!" he muttered under his breath.

"What's that?" A plump, motherly woman, bright yellow robes making her look like a buttercup, brought her mare up next to his mule. "Is something wrong, child?"

"I am not a child." Kevin said the words very carefully. "I am not a full Bard yet, I admit it, but I am the apprentice to — "

"Oh, well, bardling, then!" Her smile was so amused that Kevin wanted to shout at her, Leave me alone! Instead, he asked, as levelly as he could:

"Just how far away is Count Volmar's castle?"

"Oh, two days' ride or so, weather permitting, not more."

"And we're going to stay on this road?"

"Well, of course! We can hardly go cross-country through the woods with the wagon! Besides, that would be a silly thing to do: the North Road leads right to the castle. Very convenient."

"Very," Kevin agreed, mind busy. He hadn't dared hope that the castle would be so easy to find, even for someone who'd never been there before. Even for someone who just might happen to be travelling alone.

That night, the minstrels made camp in a circle of song and firelight that forced back the forest's shadow. Dinner had been cheese and only slightly stale bread from the inn, water from a nearby stream, and rabbits the older children had brought down with their slings. Now Kevin, sitting on a dead log to one side, nearly in darkness, watched the happy, noisy circle with a touch of envy. What must it be like to be part of a group like that? They were probably all related, one big, wild, merry family.

But then the bardling reminded himself that these were only minstrels, wandering folk whose musical talents just weren't good enough to let them ever be Bards. He should be pitying them, not envying them. Maybe they even envied him . . . ?

No. Two of the women were gossiping about him, he was sure of it, glancing his way every now and then, hiding giggles behind their hands. Kevin straightened, trying to turn his face into a regal mask. Unfortunately, the log on which he sat picked that moment to fall apart, dumping him on the ground in a cloud of moldy dust.

Predictably, every one of the troop was looking his way just then. Predictably, they all burst into laughter. Kevin scrambled to his feet, face burning. He'd had it with being babied and laughed at and made to feel a fool!

"Hey, bardling!" Berak called. "Where are you going?"

"To sleep," Kevin said shortly.

"Out there in the dark? You'll be warmer — and safer — here with us."

Kevin pretended he hadn't heard. Wrapping himself in his cloak, he settled down as best he could. The ground was harder and far colder than he'd expected. He really would have been more comfortable with the minstrels.

But then, he didn't really intend to sleep . . . not really. . . . It was just that he was weary from the day's riding. . . .

❖ ❖ ❖

Kevin woke with a start, almost too cold and stiff to move. What — where — All around him was forest, still dark with night, but overhead he could see patches of pale, blue-gray sky through the canopy of leaves and realized it wasn't too far from morning. He struggled to his feet, jogging in place to warm himself up, wincing as his body complained, then picked up his lute. Safe and dry in its case, it hadn't suffered any harm.

Stop stalling! he told himself.

Any moment now, one of the minstrels was bound to wake up, and then it would be too late. Kevin ducked behind a tree to answer his chilly body's demands, then tiptoed over to where the horses and his mule were tied. One horse whuffled at him, but to his relief, none of them whinnied. Although his hands were still stiff with cold, the bardling managed to get his mule bridled and saddled. He hesitated an uncertain moment, looking back at the sleeping camp, wondering if he really was doing the right thing.

Of course I am! I don't want the count to think I'm a baby who can't take care of himself.

Kevin led the mule as silently as he could down the road till the camp was out of sight, then swung up into the saddle.

"Come on, mule," he whispered. "We have a lot of ground to cover."

The minstrels would be discovering his absence any moment now. But, encumbered with their wagons and children as they were, they would never be able to overtake him. Kevin kicked the mule; frisky from the still chilly air, it actually broke into a prance. The bardling straightened proudly in the saddle.

At last! He finally felt like a hero riding off into adventure.

By nightfall, Kevin wasn't so sure of that. He was tired and sore from being in the saddle all day, and hungry as well. If only he had thought to take some food with him! The mule wasn't too happy with its snatches of grass and leaves, but at least it could manage, but the few mouthfuls of whatever berries Kevin had been able to recognize hadn't done much to fill his stomach.

Overhead, the sky was still clear blue, but the forest on either side was already nearly black, and a chill was starting up from the cooling earth. Kevin shivered, listening to the twitter of birds settling down for the night and the faint, mysterious rustlings and stirrings that could have been made by small animals or . . . other things. He shivered again, and told himself not to be stupid. He was probably already on Count Volmar's lands, and there wasn't going to be anything dangerous this close to a castle.

He hoped.

"We're not going to be able to go much further today," he told the mule reluctantly. "We'd better find a place to camp for the night."

At least he had flint and steel in his pouch. After stumbling about in the dim light for a time, Kevin managed to find enough dead branches to build himself a decent little fire in the middle of a small, rocky clearing. The firelight danced off the surrounding trees as the bardling sat huddling before the flames, feeling the welcome warmth steal through him.

The fire took off the edge of his chill. But it couldn't help the fact that he was still tired and so hungry his stomach ached. The bardling tried to ignore his discomfort by taking out his lute and working his way through a series of practice scales.

As soon as he stopped, the night flowed in around him, his small fire not enough to hold back the darkness, the little forest chirpings and rustlings not enough to break the heavy silence. Kevin struck out bravely into the bouncy strains of "The Miller's Boy." But the melody that had sounded so bright and sprightly with the inn around it seemed thin and lonely here. Kevin's fingers faltered, then stopped. He sat listening to the night for a moment, feeling the weight of the forest's indifference pressing down on him. He roused himself with an effort and put his lute back in its case, safe from the night's gathering mist. Those nice, dull, safe days back at the inn didn't seem quite so unattractive right now. . . .

Oh, nonsense! What sort of hero are you, afraid of a little loneliness?

He'd never, Kevin realized, been alone before, really alone, in his life. Battling with homesickness, the bardling banked the fire and curled up once more in his cloak.

After what seemed an age, weariness overcame misery, and he slipped into uneasy sleep.

Scornful laughter woke him. Kevin sat bolt upright, staring up into eyes that glowed an eerie green in the darkness. Demons!

No, no, whatever these beings were, they weren't demonic. After that first terrified moment, he could make out the faces that belonged with those eyes, and gasped in wonder. The folk surrounding him were tall and graceful, a touch too graceful, too slender, to be human. Pale golden hair framed fair, fine-boned, coldly beautiful faces set with those glowing, slanted eyes, and Kevin whispered in wonder:

"Elves . . . "

He had heard about them of course, everyone had. They were even supposed to share some of King Amber's lands with humans — though every now and then bitter feelings surfaced between the two races. But Kevin had never seen any of the elf-folk, White or Dark, good or evil, never even dreamed he might.

"Why, how clever the child is!" The elvish voice was clear as crystal, cold with mockery.

"Clever in one way, at least!" said another.

"So stupid in all other ways!" a third mocked. "Look at the way he sleeps on the ground, like a poor little animal."

"Look at the trail he left, so that anyone, anything could track him."

"Look at the way he sleeps like a babe, without a care in the world."

"A human child."

"A careless child!"

The elf man who'd first spoken laughed softly. "A foolish child that anyone can trick!"

So alien a light glinted in the slanted eyes that Kevin's breath caught in his throat. Everyone knew elvish whims were unpredictable; it was one of the reasons there could never be total ease between elf and human. If these folk decided to loose their magic on him, he wouldn't have a chance of defending himself. "My lords," he began, very, very carefully, "if I have somehow offended you, pray forgive me."

"Offended!" the elf echoed coldly. "As if anything a child such as you could do would be strong enough to offend us!"

That stung. "My lord, I — I know I may not look like much to someone like you." To his intense mortification, his empty stomach chose that moment to complain with a loud gurgle. Kevin bit his lip, sure that those keen, pointed elf ears had picked up the sound. All he could do was continue as best he could, "But — but that doesn't give you the right to insult me."

"Oh, how brave it is!" The elf man rested one foot lightly on a rock and leaned forward, fierce green gaze flicking over Kevin head to foot. "Bah, look at yourself! Sleeping on bare ground when there are soft pine boughs to make you a bed. Aching with hunger when the forest holds more than enough to feed one scrawny human. Leaving a trail anyone could follow and carrying no useful weapon at all. How could we *not* insult such ignorance?"

The elf straightened, murmuring a short phrase in the elvish tongue to the others. They laughed and faded soundlessly into the night, but not before one of them had tossed a small sack at Kevin's feet.

"Our gift, human," the elf man said. "Inside is food enough to keep you alive. And no, it is not bespelled. We would not waste magic on you."

With that, the elf turned to leave, then paused, looking back over his shoulder at the bardling. With inhuman bluntness, he said, "I hope, child, for your sake that you are simply naive and not stupid. In time, either flaw will get you killed, but at least the first can be corrected."

The alien eyes blazed into Kevin's own for a moment longer. Then the elf was gone, and the bardling was left alone in the night, more frightened than he would ever have admitted.

He's wrong! Kevin told himself defiantly once his heart had stopped racing. *Just because I'm a bardling, not a — a woodsman who's never known anything but the forest doesn't make me naive or stupid!*

Deciding that didn't stop him from rummaging in the little sack. The elvish idea of food that would keep him alive seemed to be nothing more exciting than flat wafers of bread. But when he managed to choke one of the dry things down, it calmed his complaining stomach so nicely that the bardling sighed with relief and actually slipped back into sleep.

Kevin stood with head craned back, sunlight warm on his face, feeling the last of last night's fears melting away. How could he possibly hold onto fear when it was bright, clear morning and all around him the air was filled with bird song?

Maybe the whole thing had been only a dream?

No. The sack of wafers was quite real. Kevin gnawed thoughtfully on one, then gave another to his mule, which lipped it up with apparent delight. He saddled and bridled the animal, then climbed aboard, still trying to figure out what the purpose of that midnight meeting had been.

At last he shook his head in dismissal. All the stories said the elf folk, being the nonhuman race they were, had truly bizarre senses of humor, sometimes outright cruel by human standards. What had happened last night must surely have been just another nasty elvish idea of a joke.

"Come on, mule. Let's get going." At least he wasn't hungry.

The road sloped up, first gently then more steeply, much to the mule's distaste. When it grew too steep, Kevin dismounted now and again to give the animal a rest, climbing beside it.

But at last, after a quiet day of riding and walking, they reached the crest. Kevin stared out in awe at a wild mountain range of tall gray crags, some of them high enough to be snowcapped even in spring. They towered over rolling green fields neatly sectioned into farms. On the nearest crag, surrounded by open space stood:

"Count Volmar's castle!" Kevin cried triumphantly. "It has to be!"

The castle hadn't been built for beauty. Heavy and squat, it seemed to crouch possessively on its crag like some ancient grey beast of war staring down at the count's lands. But Kevin didn't care. It was the first castle he had ever seen, and he thought it was wonderful, a true war castle dating from the days when heroes held back the forces of Darkness. Bright banners flew from the many towers, softening some of the harshness, and the bardling could see from here that the castle's gates were open. By squinting he could make out the devices on those banners: the count's black boar on an azure field.

"We've done it," he told the mule. "That is definitely the castle of Count Volmar."

He forgot about elves and hunger, loneliness and mocking minstrels. Excitement shivering through him, the bardling kicked his mule forward. Soon, soon, the real adventure was going to begin!

INTERLUDE THE FIRST

Count Volmar, tall, lean and graying of brown hair and beard, sat seemingly at ease in his private solar before a blazing fireplace, a wine-filled goblet of precious glass in his hand. He looked across the small room at the woman who sat there, and raised the goblet in appreciation. She nodded at the courtesy, her dark green eyes flickering with cold amusement in the firelight.

Carlotta, princess, half-sister to King Amber himself, could not, Volmar knew, be much younger than his own mid-forties, and yet she could easily have passed for a far younger woman. Not the slightest trace of age marred the pale, flawless skin or the glorious masses of deep red hair turned to bright flame by the firelight.

Sorcery, he thought, and then snickered at his own vapid musings so that he nearly choked on his own wine. Of course it was sorcery! Carlotta was an accomplished sorceress, and about as safe, for all her beauty, as a snake.

About as honorable, too.

Not that he was one to worry overmuch about honor.

"The boy is safely ensconced, I take it?" Carlotta's smile was as chill as her lovely eyes.

"Yes. He has a place among the squires. Who, I might add, have been given to understand that he's so far beneath them they needn't bother even to acknowledge his presence — that to do so, in fact, would demean their own status. By now, the boy is surely thoroughly disillusioned about nobility and questioning his own worth."

"He suspects nothing, then? Good. We don't want him showing any awkward sparks of initiative." Carlotta sipped delicately from her goblet. "We don't want him copying his Master."

Volmar's mouth tightened. Oh, yes, the Bard, that cursed Bard. He could remember so clearly, even though it was over thirty years ago, how it had been, himself just barely an adult and Carlotta only . . . how old? Only thirteen? Maybe so, but she had already been as ambitious as he. More so. Already mistress of the Dark Arts despite her youth, the princess had attempted to seize the throne from her half-brother.

And almost made it, Volmar thought, then corrected that to: We *almost made it.*

Amber had been only a prince back then, on the verge of the succession. His father had been old, and there hadn't been any other legal heir; Carlotta, as the court had been so eager to gossip, was only Amber's half-sister, her mother quite unknown.

But there were always ways around such awkward little facts. Once Amber had been declared dead — or so it was believed — in heroic battle (when actually, Volmar thought wryly, Carlotta's magics had turned him to stone), the poor old king would surely have . . . pined away. Volmar grinned sharply. Why, the shock alone would have finished him; Carlotta wouldn't have needed to waste a spell. The people, even if they had, by some bizarre chance, come to suspect her of wrong-doing, would have had no choice but to accept Carlotta, with her half-share of the Blood Royal, as queen.

Ambitious little girl . . . Volmar thought with approval. *What a pity she didn't succeed. Sorceress or no, she would have been too wise to try ruling alone. She would have taken a consort.*

And who better than one of her loyal supporters? Even one whose role in the attempted usurpation had never become public.

Volmar suddenly realized he was grimacing, and forced himself to relax. His late father had been an avid supporter of the old king, and if he had ever found out his own son was a traitor . . .

But he hadn't. And of course if only Carlotta had safely become queen, it wouldn't have mattered. The only traitors then would have been those who failed to acknowledge her!

If only . . . Bah!

Carlotta *would* have become queen if it hadn't been for the boy's Master, that accursed Bard and his allies. . . .

"Forget the past, Volmar."

The count started, thrown abruptly back into the present. "You . . . have learned to read minds . . . ?" If the sorceress suspected he planned to use her to place a crown on his own head, he was dead. Worse than dead.

"You must learn to guard your expressions, my lord. Your thoughts were there for anyone with half an eye to read."

Not all my thoughts, the count thought, giddy with relief.

Carlotta got restlessly to her feet, dark green gown swirling about her elegant form. Volmar, since she was, after all, a princess and he only a count, stood as well: politic courtesy.

She never noticed. "Enough of the past," the sorceress repeated, staring into the flames. "We must think of what can be done *now*."

Volmar moved warily to stand beside her, and caught a flicker of alien movement in the flames. Faces . . . ah. Carlotta was absently creating images of the boy, the bardling. "Why do you suppose he sent the boy here?" the princess murmured. "And why just now? What purpose could the old man possibly have? You've convinced me the manuscript is merely a treatise on lute music." She glanced sharply at Volmar. "It *is*, isn't it?"

"Of course," Volmar said easily, hiding the fact that he wasn't really sure which of the many manuscripts stored in the library it might be; his father had been the scholar, not he. "My father collected such things."

"Yes, yes, but why send the boy *now*? Why is it suddenly so urgent that the thing be copied?"

"Ah . . . it could be merely coincidence."

"No, it couldn't!" The flames roared up as Carlotta whirled, eyes blazing. Volmar shrank back from her unexpected surge of rage, half expecting a sorcerous attack, but the princess ignored him, returning to her chair and dropping into it with an angry flounce. "You're the only one who knows how I've been in hiding all these years, lulling suspicions, making everyone think I was dead."

"Of course." Though Volmar never had puzzled out why Carlotta had hidden for quite so many years. Oh, granted, she had been totally drained after the breaking of her stone-spell on Amber, but even so . . .

"Maybe that's it." Carlotta's musings broke into Volmar's wonderings. "Maybe now that I've come out of hiding, begun moving again, the Bard has somehow sensed I'm still around. He *is* a Master of that ridiculous Bardic Magic, after all."

Volmar was too wise to remind her it was the Bardic Magic she so despised that had blocked her path so far. "Eh, well, the bardling is safe among the squires," he soothed. "I've been debating simply telling him the manuscript isn't here and sending him away."

"Don't be a fool!" Sorcery crackled in the air around Carlotta, her hair stirring where there was no breeze. "The boy was sent here for a purpose, and we will both be better off when we find out just what that purpose might be!"

"But how can we learn the truth? If the boy becomes suspicious, he'll never say a thing. And I can hardly order the imprisonment or torment of an innocent bardling. My people," Volmar added with a touch of contempt, "wouldn't stand for it."

"Don't be so dramatic. The boy is already quite miserable, you say. No one will talk to him, no one will treat him kindly, and he's faced with a long, boring, lonely task." Carlotta smiled slowly. "Just think how delighted he would be if someone was *nice* to him! How eager he would be to confide in that someone!"

"I don't understand. An adult — "

"No, you idiot! Don't you remember what it's like being that young? The boy is only going to confide in someone his own age."

As usual, Volmar forced down his rage at her casual insults. *Ah, Carlotta, you superior little witch, if ever I gain the throne beside you, you had better guard your back!* As innocuously as he could, he asked, "Who are you suggesting? One of the squires?"

"Oh, hardly that."

Her shape blurred, altered . . . Volmar rubbed a hand over his eyes. He'd known from the start that Carlotta was as much a master of shape-shifting as any fairy, but watching her in action always made him dizzy.

"You can look now, poor Volmar." Her voice was an octave higher than before, and so filled with sugar he dropped his hand to stare.

Where the adult Carlotta had sat was now a cloyingly sweet little blonde girl of, Volmar guessed, the bardling's own age, though it was difficult to tell age amid all the golden ringlets and alabaster skin and large, shining blue eyes.

"How do I look?" she cooed.

Honest words came to his lips before he could stop them. "Sweet enough to rot my teeth."

She merely threw back her head and laughed. *Her* teeth, of course, were flawless. "I *am* a bit sickening, aren't I? Let me try a more plausible form."

The sickening coyness faded. The girl remained the same age, but the blonde hair was now less perfectly golden, the big blue eyes a bit less glowing, the pale skin just a touch less smooth. As Volmar grit his teeth, determinedly watching despite a new surge of dizziness, he saw the perfect oval of her face broaden ever so slightly at the forehead, narrow at the chin, until she looked just like . . .

"Charina!" the count gasped.

"Charina," the princess agreed. "Your darling little niece."

Too amazed to remember propriety, Volmar got to his feet and slowly circled her. "Marvelous!" he breathed at last. "Simply marvelous! I would never know you weren't the real — But what do we do with the real Charina?"

Her voice was deceptively light. "I'm sure you'll think of something."

"Ah, yes." Volmar smiled thinly. "Poor Charina. She always *has* been a bit of a nuisance, wandering about the castle like a lonely wraith. How unfortunate that my sister and her fool of a husband had the bad taste to die. Poor little creature: too far from the main line of descent to be of any use as a marriage pawn. No political value at all. Just another useless girl."

"Not so useless now." Carlotta/Charina dimpled prettily.

"Poor Charina," Volmar repeated without any warmth at all. "So easily disposed of. She never *will* be missed."

GRAND ADVENTURE
IN GAME-BASED UNIVERSES

With these exciting novels set
in bestselling game universes,
Baen brings you synchronicity at its
best. We believe that familiarity with
either the novel or the game will
intensify enjoyment of the other.
All novels are the only authorized
fiction based on these games and
are published by permission.

THE BARD'S TALE™

Join the Dark Elf Naitachal and his apprentices in
bardic magic as they explore the mysteries of the
world of The Bard's Tale.

Castle of Deception
by Mercedes Lackey & Josepha Sherman
72125-9 * 320 pages * $5.99   _____

Fortress of Frost and Fire
by Mercedes Lackey & Ru Emerson
72162-3 * 304 pages * $5.99   _____

Prison of Souls
by Mercedes Lackey & Mark Shepherd
72193-3 * 352 pages * $5.99   _____

And watch for **Gates of Chaos** by Josepha Sherman
coming in May 1994!

PRAISE FOR
LOIS MCMASTER BUJOLD

What the critics say:

The Warrior's Apprentice: "Now here's a fun romp through the spaceways—not so much a space opera as space ballet.... it has all the 'right stuff.' A lot of thought and thoughtfulness stand behind the all-too-human characters. Enjoy this one, and look forward to the next." —Dean Lambe, *SF Reviews*

"The pace is breathless, the characterization thoughtful and emotionally powerful, and the author's narrative technique and command of language compelling. Highly recommended." —*Booklist*

Brothers in Arms: "... she gives it a geniune depth of character, while reveling in the wild turnings of her tale.... Bujold is as audacious as her favorite hero, and as brilliantly (if sneakily) successful." —*Locus*

"Miles Vorkosigan is such a great character that I'll read anything Lois wants to write about him.... a book to re-read on cold rainy days." —Robert Coulson, *Comics Buyer's Guide*

Borders of Infinity: "Bujold's series hero Miles Vorkosigan may be a lord by birth and an admiral by rank, but a bone disease that has left him hobbled and in frequent pain has sensitized him to the suffering of outcasts in his very hierarchical era.... Playing off Miles's reserve and cleverness, Bujold draws outrageous and outlandish foils to color her high-minded adventures." —*Publishers Weekly*

Falling Free: "In *Falling Free* Lois McMaster Bujold has written her fourth straight superb novel.... How to break down a talent like Bujold's into analyzable components? Best not to try. Best to say 'Read, or you will be missing something extraordinary.'" —Roland Green, *Chicago Sun-Times*

The Vor Game: "The chronicles of Miles Vorkosigan are far too witty to be literary junk food, but they rouse the kind of craving that makes popcorn magically vanish during a double feature." —Faren Miller, *Locus*

MORE PRAISE FOR
LOIS MCMASTER BUJOLD

What the readers say:

"My copy of *Shards of Honor* is falling apart I've reread it so often.... I'll read whatever you write. You've certainly proved yourself a grand storyteller."
—Liesl Kolbe, Colorado Springs, CO

"I experience the stories of Miles Vorkosigan as almost viscerally uplifting.... But certainly, even the weightiest theme would have less impact than a cinder on snow were it not for a rousing good story, and good story-telling with it. This is the second thing I want to thank you for.... I suppose if you boiled down all I've said to its simplest expression, it would be that I immensely enjoy and admire your work. I submit that, as literature, your work raises the overall level of the science fiction genre, and spiritually, your work cannot avoid positively influencing all who read it."
—Glen Stonebraker, Gaithersburg, MD

" 'The Mountains of Mourning' [in *Borders of Infinity*] was one of the best-crafted, and simply best, works I'd ever read. When I finished it, I immediately turned back to the beginning and read it again, and I can't remember the last time I did that."   —Betsy Bizot, Lisle, IL

"I can only hope that you will continue to write, so that I can continue to read (and of course buy) your books, for they make me laugh and cry and think ... rare indeed."   —Steven Knott, Major, USAF

What do you say?

Send me these books!

Shards of Honor • 72087-2 • $4.99 _____
The Warrior's Apprentice • 72066-X • $4.50 _____
Ethan of Athos • 65604-X • $4.99 _____
Falling Free • 65398-9 • $4.99 _____
Brothers in Arms • 69799-4 • $4.99 _____
Borders of Infinity • 69841-9 • $4.99 _____
The Vor Game • 72014-7 • $4.99 _____
Barrayar • 72083-X • $4.99 _____

Lois McMaster Bujold:
Only from Baen Books

If these books are not available at your local bookstore, just check your choices above, fill out this coupon and send a check or money order for the cover price to Baen Books, Dept. BA, P.O. Box 1403, Riverdale, NY 10471.

NAME: _____

ADDRESS: _____

_____

I have enclosed a check or money order in the amount of $ _____.

MERCEDES LACKEY

The Hottest Fantasy Writer Today!

URBAN FANTASY

Knight of Ghosts and Shadows with Ellen Guon

Elves in L.A.? It would explain a lot, wouldn't it? Eric
Banyon is a musician with a lot of talent but very little
ambition—and his lady just left him lovelorn in a deserted corner of the Renaissance Fairegrounds, singing
the blues and playing his flute. He couldn't have known
the desperate sadness of his music would free Korendil,
a young elven noble, from the magical prison he has
been languishing in for centuries. Eric really needed a
good cause to get his life in gear—now he's got one. With
Korendil he must raise an army to fight against the evil
lord who seeks to conquer all of California. And Eric's
music will show the way....

Summoned to Tourney with Ellen Guon

Elves in San Francisco? Where else would an elf go
when L.A. got too hot? All is well there with our elf-lord,
his human companion and the mage who brought them
all together—until it turns out that San Francisco is
doomed to fall off the face of the continent. Doomed that
is, unless our mage can summon the Nightflyers, the
soul-devouring shadow creatures from the dreaming world—
creatures no one on Earth could possibly control....

Born to Run with Larry Dixon

There are elves out there. And more are coming. But
even elves need money to survive in the "real" world.
The good elves in South Carolina, intrigued by the thrills
of stock car racing, are manufacturing new, light-weight
engines (with, incidentally, very little "cold" iron); the bad
elves run a kiddie-porn and snuff-film ring, with occasional forays into drugs. *Children in Peril—Elves to the
Rescue.* (Part of the SERRAted Edge series.)

HIGH FANTASY

Bardic Voices: The Lark & The Wren

Rune could be one of the greatest bards of her world,
but the daughter of a tavern wench can't get much in the

way of formal training. So one night she goes up to play for the Ghost of Skull Hill. She'll either fiddle till dawn to prove her skill as a bard—or die trying....

Also by Mercedes Lackey:

Reap the Whirlwind with C.J. Cherryh
Part of the Sword of Knowledge series.

Castle of Deception with Josepha Sherman
Based on the bestselling computer game, *The Bard's Tale*.™

The Ship Who Searched with Anne McCaffrey
The Ship Who Sang is not alone!

Wheels of Fire with Mark Shepherd
Book II of the SERRAted Edge series.

When the Bough Breaks with Holly Lisle
Book III of the SERRAted Edge series.

Wing Commander: Freedom Flight with Ellen Guon
Based on the bestselling computer game, *Wing Commander*.™